PROOF
of HEAVEN

By Mary Curran Hackett

Proof of Heaven

PROOF *of* HEAVEN

MARY CURRAN HACKETT

WILLIAM MORROW
An Imprint of HarperCollins*Publishers*

This book is a work of fiction. The characters, incidents, and dialogue are drawn from the author's imagination and are not to be construed as real. Any resemblance to actual events or persons, living or dead, is entirely coincidental.

Designed by Diahann Sturge

ISBN 978-0-06-207998-5

For my proof,
Brigid Claire
and
Colm Francis

Pace e bene

To love another person is to see the face of God.
—*Les Misérables*

Le cœur a ses raisons que la raison ne connaît pas.
The heart has reasons that Reason does not know.
—Blaise Pascal

Faith is the recognition of what is hoped for
and evidence of things not seen.
—Hebrews 11:1

❧ Part I

When we are green, still half-created, we believe that our dreams are rights, that the world
is disposed to act in our best interests, and
that falling and dying are for quitters. We live
on the innocent and monstrous assurance that
we alone, of all the people ever born, have a
special arrangement whereby we will be allowed to stay green forever.

—Tobias Wolff, *This Boy's Life: A Memoir*

❧ Chapter 1

COLM FRANCIS MAGEE HAD DIED SEVEN TIMES BEFORE his seventh birthday. Cardiac arrest. Not to be mistaken for a heart attack in which clogged arteries prevent blood from reaching the heart and then the muscle withers. There was nothing wrong with Colm's strength of heart. No, Colm Francis Magee's heart simply and inexplicably stopped beating at the most inopportune moments.

The first time it had happened he was an infant. He was sitting up in the bathtub while his young mother gripped his arms as he kicked and splashed water into her smiling face. His auburn hair was wet and formed a crown around his head as he gazed at his adoring mama. His green eyes gleamed, wide with pride and wonder at what he could do with his tiny feet.

"That's a boy. That's my good boy. You're gonna swim the Hudson. Swim for your mama."

When Cathleen cooed at him, she used her Irish mother's nonsense-sounding baby-speak, a mixture of brogue and Brooklyn. She scooped the warm, cloudy water in her hand and poured it gently over the boy's head, careful to keep soap from running in his eyes. His body relaxed and slowed with each pour, and so did her own.

When she first arrived home from work to feed, bathe, and put Colm to bed, she still carried the stress and anxiety of her day. She could feel it rise through her shoulders and neck, where it settled with an excruciating pressure in her temples. But as each moment passed while bathing the boy, her eyes brightened and her limbs loosened as a smile spread across her entire face.

Every morning had been the same for the past six months. She woke up tired at five A.M. a moment before Colm did and, out of lifelong habit, she said a quiet Hail Mary to herself before getting out of bed. Though her body needed sleep, it seemed to defy its own biology for the sake of another's. Their bodies seemed to be in perfect tune; even his hunger brought her pain. Rising out of the bed slowly, she wondered about the odd evolutionary design of mother and child. *It's one thing to feel my own pain, but to physically feel it for my own child?* She was at once grateful for and confounded by this phenomenon. And as she thought this she said her own version of a made-up prayer, *From the beginning of time it has been the same. Every mother knows exactly what her child needs. And every child is dependent on that knowledge. May I always know what to do.*

She concluded her silent prayer and, with an audible *Amen,* walked over to Colm's crib and found him looking at her as if he had been waiting all night for her to come and get him. She lifted him before he even had a chance to let out his first sound and carried him over to her mother's rocking chair from the old country, which she had set facing the window. The dawn always lightened the room just enough so that as Cathleen looked at Colm, he seemed to her to glow from within. As he drank from her, she rubbed his head softly and felt the folds of his fat thighs rippling around the edges of his diaper. Every day he seemed longer, larger, more ungainly.

Then, after taking more than his small stomach could handle, he'd pull himself away from her. He would do it so quickly that the release of the suction sent a surge of pain throughout her entire body. Before she had a second to shout out in pain, she would curse herself for lingering too long. She always gave him more than he needed, and she always paid the price. *So much for knowing what to do.*

Every day the same routine played out. Running late, she set Colm down in his bouncy chair and got ready for work before lugging the boy and his gear out onto the busy street. From the time they left the apartment, she was on a mission. She worked up such a sweat pushing the stroller that by the time she reached his day care, her freshly pressed blouse revealed sweat rings under her arms and down the center of her back. Once there, she set Colm down again and only had a couple of minutes to chat with his caretaker and kiss him good-bye before she dashed out the door and hustled to catch the subway to Midtown, where she began her daily duties as an office assistant.

While waiting at Starbucks to place her coworkers' usual orders, she watched through the window as her bosses and peers arrived with designer handbags and expensive haircuts. She would never know what it would be like to be one of them—to live a single life without a child, let alone to build a career of her own making. Somewhere deep inside she also knew that married life and all that came with it was just another pipe dream for her. Dreams were like prayers, she thought. They brought comfort and moments of serenity, but in the end one couldn't expect much of them. So Cathleen, like her mother before her, who had spent her life in the service of God and her children, did whatever she could to get by. Still, she never escaped the nagging feeling that in another time, in another place, in another world, she might have been able to realize her hopes for herself and her son.

Contrary to Cathleen's constant state of concern, Colm was thriving. When Cathleen picked him up every evening, he always greeted her with an openmouthed smile. She often asked his teachers if he did OK without her. Did he cry or seem to miss her? They always responded the same way: "Nope. Not once. He's a happy little guy."

He seems to do just fine without you.

She knew she should be relieved he was doing so well, but it always hurt to hear. *I'm so desperate and needy,* she reprimanded herself. And then she would force herself to be grateful that Colm seemed no worse for wear.

Colm was a special sort of child. She even knew it from the night he was born, when she had asked the nurse to put him in bed with her so she could cut the loneliness in the room with no husband. She knew right then and there she would do anything for him. And then it happened. The moment everything changed. She thought it was an aberration at first, some sort of trick of her own eye or that she must be hearing things, but it was no such thing. Colm laughed. He laughed a small, almost silent laugh in his sleep. She stayed up all night—waiting for it—and he rewarded her for her vigilance again and again. There she sat in wonder, watching his slanted eyes, his two pronounced dimples, and his round toothless grin as he chuckled to himself in his sleep.

She had hoped to turn around and to share the miracle with someone. *Did you see that? Did you see him smile?* But there was no one there to hear her and no one to see him smile then or thereafter. His father was long gone by then. She had thought of reaching for the phone, pulling out the number scribbled on a piece of paper, and begging him to come back. But she knew he wouldn't come, so she never made the call. Instead she lay in the quiet hospital room alone with her son.

There was no one in the bathroom with Cathleen either the day six-month-old Colm finished his imaginary swim down the Hudson and looked at his mother before his eyes rolled back into his head as he blacked out, slamming his head on the porcelain tub.

"Colm Francis."

Cathleen ran with him to her bed where she felt for his pulse. Nothing. Panic filled her neck and face with a hot searing burn. She dialed 911 and yelled her address into it.

"Hurry, my baby isn't breathing."

Colm lay on the bed. She watched as his lips and nose and fingers turned blue, and his cheeks went from pink to gray. He made no sound. She could, for the first time since before she gave birth to him, hear only her own breathing in the room. She howled a deep guttural moan, the same sound she had heard once before as she pushed Colm out of her and into the world.

Without another thought, she grabbed Colm from the bed and held him close, pushing him to her breast as if forcing him back into her own body, as if she could start it all over, redo the past six months, minute by minute, hour by hour, day by day, and rewind all the way to the beginning to start over. And stop it.

She held him tightly as she rushed down the hall and down the stairs, where she heard the first faint sound of the ambulance on its way. When the paramedics arrived, she was already waiting for them on the sidewalk. Her gray work slacks and white shirt were drenched with bathwater, and she stood alone holding Colm, still naked in her arms.

Colm Francis Magee died his first godless death at seven in the evening on a Tuesday in June. His mother would find it hard to ever forgive him.

🌿 Chapter 2

BY THE TIME HE WAS FIVE AND A HALF, COLM HAD experienced various versions of this first encounter with death. There was the time on the subway platform, when his mother, carrying their groceries in a large burlap bag, was making polite conversation with a stranger. Colm began to notice the all-too-familiar sensation—the *prodrome,* he heard his doctors call it. "It's when you know it's about to happen, Colm. A prodrome is your warning sign to get down to the ground as soon as you can." But there was little time for thinking, noticing, let alone getting down. When he felt this way, he would forget what the doctors told him to do, because his mind would go blank.

The first thing to go was his hearing. He could see his mother's soft lips moving and the chalkiness of her fading lipstick, but he could not hear what she was saying. He squeezed the robot he held in his hand and held it up to get his mother's attention. But then his vision went, and he knew by the small tightening feeling in his chest, the rapid fire of his heart, and the empty feeling in his brain that it would all be over soon. And then, without further warning, Colm entered a state of black nothing.

Cathleen dropped her groceries and called out for someone for help. Even though this was the fourth time he had died on her, she was not any more composed than the first time. Each time Colm collapsed, all the fear that someday he would not awaken returned and pierced her heart.

On the subway platform, Colm lay absolutely still. Everyone on the platform (witnesses for whom Cathleen secretly thanked God) watched as Cathleen felt for his pulse and asked the stranger with whom she had been speaking to begin chest compressions while she breathed into Colm's mouth. Meanwhile, without oxygen, Colm's brain slowly began to shut down. As each minute passed, images of his mother's face, his yellow Tonka trunk on the floor of his bedroom, the sandcastle he had built at Coney Island in June with his uncle, and nonsense dreams of cities built out of layered cakes and Legos slowly began to disappear. With his heart no longer beating on its own, he entered a realm of complete and utter darkness. And then he was gone.

By the time the medics arrived, Cathleen had lost her initial composure and was out of her mind. Screaming and crying and yelling for all the world to hear for Colm to wake up.

"Dammit. Dammit. Dammit," she shouted.

She wanted to shake him. One of the police officers who had arrived with the medics wrapped his arms around her from behind and pulled her off Colm. She fought with him to let her go to her son's side. Two medics worked to squeeze air into Colm's lungs, while another pulled out portable shock paddles and injected atropine into Colm's bloodstream. After two shocks, Colm's heart started beating again on its own. His eyes opened wide and he slowly turned his head, found his mama's eyes, and began his all too familiar empty, soulless stare.

Cathleen knew she had lost a little bit more of him that day on the platform. But it didn't matter. She would take whatever part of him was left.

By this, the fourth time Colm had died, Cathleen had built up a steel reserve—not in the face of Colm's collapses, but in the face of the doctors who failed to provide a logical medical explanation for Colm's condition, and who quickly considered the possibility that she was harming her own son. She could see it in their eyes, but before they openly accused her of any wrongdoing, they sent Colm to hospitals all over, some out of state, for tests. EEGs for seizures. Scans for tumors. CT scans and MRIs for malformations, ECGs for coronary heart defects. EKGs, EP, and heart studies for abnormal rhythm patterns. Every test came back with no clear indication of a heart condition. For a while the doctors diagnosed Colm with nothing more than syncope—a vasovagal disorder—in which his blood pressure dropped with changes in temperature, pain, and other autonomic reflexes. No blood could get to his brain, and he simply fainted. But typically those who faint regain a heartbeat as soon as they fall into the supine position, and blood can make its way back through the heart to the brain.

The blood never flowed for Colm, though. Everything in his body simply stopped.

Nonetheless, Colm had been released from the hospital three previous times in five years with the same diagnosis: syncope. His mother had been given her own diagnosis: hysteria. However, this time, with so many witnesses on that subway platform who saw him collapse and saw that his heart did not begin beating for several minutes, no one ever could say again that it was just a fainting disorder.

❦ Chapter 3

D R. GASPAR BASU WAS NAMED ONE OF THE COUNTRY'S best electrophysiologist-cardiologists by *U.S. News & World Report,* and after ten years of mostly treating elderly patients with congestive heart failure, smokers with hardened arteries, and obese patients incredulous as to why their hearts were not functioning, a bit of morbid curiosity arose in him when one of his nurses dropped a child's chart onto his desk late one evening.

"Dr. Jakes from Children's Hospital wants you to look at this five-year-old boy's chart. He's been in asystole four times in five years. Came to the hospital DOA a couple of times. And the other times, he was DOA when medics reached him, but they were able to revive with shock. He's been diagnosed with vasovagal syncope."

Gaspar slid his turkey on whole wheat and his grape juice out of the way in one smooth swipe of his forearm across his desk and made way for the chart.

"Doesn't sound like syncope if they had to use paddles. Have the parents set up an appointment yet?"

"Parent."

"What?"

"Just a mom. She hasn't yet. Do you want me to call her?"

"If they can make it, yes, I want to see him. Tomorrow."

"I'll do it now. Then can I go?"

"Sure."

Gaspar spent the remainder of the night looking at the long thin streams of paper that were Colm's EKG readings, measuring out heart rates and searching for the tiniest aberration or dropped beats. He gazed at the films from echocardiograms and marveled at the beauty and perfection of the human heart, even one that seemed to be failing this small boy. He loved the heart in all its wonder, its mystery, even its weakness. For he knew that no matter how many tests, no matter how many diagnoses, no matter how many miles jogged or apples eaten, a person would never know, could never know what the heart would do next, what it was truly capable of doing.

After some time, Gaspar closed the chart and returned to his sandwich. He sat staring out the window at the night sky, noticing only a few small stars overhead that were powerful enough to outshine the city lights. He remembered his life in India, something he allowed himself to do only when everyone was gone for the day. If he closed his eyes, he could almost hear the sounds of young children running and shouting in the streets along with the fury of the carts and animals. He thought of the fateful river that carried with it his entire past. A world away, it still flowed under the same stars that shone above him all the way here in New York City. If he sat long enough in his office, he would see the sky turn to night, the blackness and eerie quiet of a city asleep. He still relished seeing the stars—all two or three of them that made their way through the reflective light and smog of the city. He thought of their electricity, their form, and their matter and how parts of humanity had been a part of the stars at one point, a vast interconnection and exchange of energy. There was such beauty in nature and science, an answer to every riddle in the universe and an explanation for everything. All of it went back to the stars, and in his cardiological mind, the heart.

He finished his sandwich, swiped the crumbs into his hand, and stuffed them in his pocket as he headed out of the office.

Out on the sidewalk, Gaspar dropped the crumbs for a group of pigeons pecking around a fenced ginkgo tree. In that moment, he was reminded how all of it—the stars, the earth, and the rivers that flowed through it and the ginkgoes that grew out of it—had been here so much longer than he, and that they would be there after he and everyone on the planet had ceased to be. And that constancy, that firmness, that rootedness in all of eternity, and his small part in all of it, made it all the more bearable for him to continue his journey home alone.

❧ Chapter 4

I DON'T KNOW WHY WE HAVE TO GO TO ANOTHER DOCTOR. I'm fine," Colm protested. He sat defiantly with his arms crossed as he tried to inch as far away from his mother as he could on the bus bench. It was the last place on earth he wanted to be. Actually, it was the second-to-last place. The last place he wanted to be was where they were headed.

Cathleen knew he was right. There was absolutely no point in shelling out more money for another doctor who wanted to put them through more pointless testing for another vague diagnosis. But since Colm's first collapse, she had had a singular mission in life: to save her son. Any hopes of improving her stalemated career as an interior designer, rekindling romantic prospects with his father, or even finding another man to take his place fell off her list of priorities as soon as the possibility that she might lose her son had presented itself in her bathroom that evening five years earlier. When she had come home later that week with baby Colm laughing in her arms, she had privately vowed to do anything, pay any amount, go anywhere, pray to any saint—any God—whether she believed in him or not, if it meant she could keep her son with her always.

But experience had taught her that this doctor would most likely be like all the others she had met before. He would breeze into the examining room after she had read the whole of a two-year-old *Newsweek,* while listening to him describe yesterday's golf game in a phone conversation that reverberated through the paper-thin walls of the cheerless office. Colm would have climbed up and down the examining table so many times that he would have exhausted himself and might be lying sideways off it—his head hanging midair and upside down while his legs spread out in a V up against the wall. She would hear the rustle of a chart being opened just a second before the doctor came in and introduced himself with a *well, well, well, what do we have here*? And she would have to explain it all over again. And then he would say, *Hmmmm, I'll have to order some tests*. And after a quick listen to Colm's heart, a few brief questions about what Colm felt like before and after he collapsed, she would be at the front desk pulling out her checkbook and scheduling the next appointment. In spite of all this, she knew she couldn't show any doubt in front of her increasingly obstinate son.

"This time it could be different, Colm. This guy is supposed to be the best." Cathleen tried to sound encouraging, despite her own misgivings.

"So why's he seeing someone like me?"

"Because you're special."

"Uncle Sean doesn't say I am special."

"Now I am sure your uncle Sean has said you're special."

"No, I am pretty sure he's never called me special. He calls me a little shit though."

Cathleen gasped, shocked by her son's language, but not by her brother's. She knew him too well.

"Colm, watch your mouth! You know he's kidding, right?"

"Yes. I know." Colm smiled, thinking of his wild uncle Sean.

She could just kill Sean sometimes. But he was the only father figure she could provide for Colm, so she put up with some of the crazy things he said and did because Colm loved him, and he loved her boy.

"Well, you're special-special," Cathleen repeated aloud.

"To you maybe."

"Yes to me. But to this doctor, too. And to lots of other people."

"We'll see about that."

Colm laid his head on the bus window and considered the possibility that his mother might be right. Maybe there was someone out there who might think he was special enough to be worth fixing. Still, Colm had his doubts because surely if there had been something remarkable about him, his father would have come to find him by now. Colm didn't know anything about him, but he knew how sad his mother's eyes looked whenever she answered Colm's questions about why his father and his mother weren't together and why his father was not around.

I thought I could do a better job raising you on my own, that's all. He loved you like crazy. He did. He'd be here if he could. I just do a better job on my own. It's how I do things. You know that, Colm.

Even his five-and-a-half-year-old self could tell there was something she wasn't saying. It made him wonder if his father had taken one look at him and decided he wasn't cute enough or strong enough. He imagined various scenarios in which his father had looked at him or even held him, and then Colm wondered at what point it was that his father had rejected him. *Was it after he collapsed the first time? Was it because he was sick?* Colm thought of every possibility. He combed through the scrapbooks his mother made for him every year for his birthday. He scrutinized every old picture looking for his father's face, anywhere. *Is it this guy, Mama? Is this him? Is he my father? No, Colm, that's your uncle's friend. No, Colm, that's just a cousin.* Colm didn't stop there; he went through her jewelry box and scoured the hidden nooks he found throughout the apartment. Surely, he thought, there had to be some evidence of his father. He had to have met him at some point. At least once, he thought. His mother always explained that his father had been long gone before he was even born, but Colm didn't believe that. If she lied about why he left, he thought, she probably was lying about when, too. Besides, Colm knew it was his fault because *what man would ever leave Mama?*

All he wanted to do was become better, stronger, more wonderful in every way, because surely if he got better, if he was as good as he could possibly be, surely his father would come for him and his mother. And if he couldn't get better, if there was no way to fix him, he knew he had to find his father more than ever. *Somebody has to take care of Mama when I'm gone,* he thought to himself.

When the bus stopped in front of Good Samaritan Hospital, Cathleen grabbed her purse and nudged Colm, who she thought had fallen asleep. Without speaking, he took her hand and followed her down the aisle. As the bus pulled away, they stood on the curb and waved good-bye. When Colm was no more than two, he used to jump, shout, and clap every time the bus arrived and sob when his mother told him it was time to get off. The bus, like the subway, was a magical thing, a home on wheels— large, rumbling, and filled with strangers and so much awkward silence that a hiccup was an event worthy of a stomach-grabbing giggle. For three years, they had kept up their routine, but at five, Colm was much more interested in cars. Cathleen, on the other hand, believed Colm still wanted to and needed to wave good-bye. She had no idea her son had long since stopped crying over the loss of his large steel-framed friend.

"I promise this won't be a long visit," Cathleen assured him.

"You always say that."

"When we're done, I'll go home and make you shepherd's pie—and we can build something together with your Legos."

"You're not very good at it."

"What? Cooking shepherd's pie? I thought you loved Nana's recipe, and the way I make it with extra whipped potatoes for you?"

"No. The pie is good. You're just not good at Legos, Mama."

"Well, I can try."

"No, thanks. I'll just do it by myself."

Cathleen bristled a little, but she didn't want to push him. She knew this was as boring and tiring for him as it was for her, and she knew he had every right to be cranky.

"OK, suit yourself. But I make a mean moat."

Colm knew he was hurting his mother's feelings. He knew

it as the words came out of his mouth. But these days when Colm played, he liked to imagine his father was right there with him building castles or robots. He pretended his father was everywhere, watching everything and telling him what to do, and he was immensely proud of everything Colm did. Colm would smile back at his father, nod, and say, *Thanks, Dad, I couldn't do it without you.* But the most wonderful thing about his imaginary father, Colm thought, was that he was there at night, lying right beside him, telling him not to be afraid, and assuring him he would wake up in the morning, and when he did, his father would be there waiting for him, ready to look after his mother.

"What if this doctor sends us home and says nothing is wrong with me?"

"That's not going to happen. I don't want anything to be wrong with you. But you and I both know, what's been happening to you isn't exactly ordinary."

"I know. What if I don't wake up?"

"What do you mean?" Though Cathleen had spent hours fretting over the same question, she had never heard Colm himself express the same fear. She had no idea he even knew that was a possibility. "Of course, you'll wake up. You always do."

"But what will happen to you if I don't?"

"That's nonsense. You'll always wake up. In fact, this doctor is going to make sure you never ever collapse again. We won't leave his office until we get a straight answer."

Colm didn't say anything. He knew his mother was promising something she would never be able to deliver. But he knew a lot of things, things he couldn't yet explain or tell her, because he knew it would hurt her. There were things, he believed, he just could not say to his mama. He couldn't say he longed to be with his father or longed for his father to come and protect his mama so he didn't have to anymore. He couldn't say that he didn't think his mama was strong enough to live without him. He couldn't say that he needed to find his father to protect them both. And he couldn't tell her his biggest secret of all. The biggest one he knew would break her heart. No, there were thoughts and feelings and deeds that mamas couldn't see or hear or know, because it would break them both and tear them apart forever. Mamas always say they will love you no matter what, until someday the what is just too much for them, for anyone, to bear.

❧ Chapter 5

ONCE THROUGH THE AUTOMATED DOORS OF THE HOS-
pital, Colm pulled away from Cathleen. He knew once
he was indoors and off the sidewalk Cathleen would
permit him to let go of her hand. As soon as he was able, he
broke free and ran ahead. Cathleen chased after him.

"Slow down, Colm. This is a new hospital. We don't even
know where we are going yet."

Colm stopped in front of a long row of elevators.

"Found the elevators, Mama! Can I press the buttons?"

"Yes, babe," Cathleen said, digging into her purse for her
notepad with the new doctor's information on it. "Stand still for
one minute, while I figure out where we need to go. I just don't
want to jump on an elevator and not know where we are headed.
We have plenty of time. We're early. There's no need to rush."

In the time it took Cathleen to find her pad and look up, Colm
had jumped through the doors of an open elevator. Just as the
doors were about to slide shut, Cathleen slipped through.

"Colm, don't ever do that again! You scared me half to death."

Colm smiled at her apologetically.

"I didn't mean to scare you, Mama. It's just that the doors opened, and I was ready."

"Well, I wasn't. What if I lost you? Then what would I do?"

Though Cathleen had begun preparing herself to lose Colm after that first incident in the bathtub, a part of her had always felt, from the moment he was born, that she didn't deserve a child as beautiful and perfect as Colm. She knew at any moment that her *thy just punishment* would certainly take him away from her. At one point she also believed it was this thought that was creating the entire drama. *Maybe I am the reason,* she often speculated, but then quickly she would dismiss that thought. Still she hoped for a miracle that would let her keep him. Every night, she prayed and laid hands on his head while bargaining and pleading with God to heal her son. She even looked into going on pilgrimages, like to Lourdes to bathe Colm in the healing waters of St. Bernadette's unnatural spring or Assisi to bless him in the healing quarters of San Damiano, but she didn't have enough money to make such trips. So instead she prayed and prayed. *Please God, don't take my son from me. I'll do anything. Anything.*

"Colm, we have a few minutes. We're a bit early. Why don't we go find the chapel and pray a bit."

"Aw, come on, Mama. Do I have to?"

"God gives you seven days and nights, and you can't give him a few minutes?"

Colm had heard it all before and dropped his head and rolled his eyes. There would be no arguing with her now. It was done. He had to go.

"All right, Mama. Just a few minutes," he said in a resigned voice.

Cathleen smiled at him. She knew how he felt. Raised Catholic, she and her brother were dragged to Sunday Mass by their own devout mother and forced to attend all the requisite holy days of obligation and to pray in every available chapel too. As children they were taught how to be devout, but Cathleen never *felt* devout, especially as a child. She never truly believed all she was supposed to and as superstitious as she seemed to those around her now, even her own brother and son, who watched her dip her hands in the holy water, light daily candles, and genuflect before the Blessed Sacrament, Cathleen had a rather complex understanding of God and how prayer operated. Life had taught her some things, and she suspected that most of what one wanted in life was left largely to chance. Her prayer was motivated more by her belief in something C. S. Lewis had once said: *Prayer doesn't change God, it changes me.* Cathleen seemed pious to others, but she actually found solace in the fact that everything in life was random. God was not responsible for all the chaos in the world. God simply stood by and watched. No matter how much one prayed, it wasn't up to God. Praying was an end in itself because it gave her respite in an otherwise chaotic world. All she could do was endure and make herself stronger through it all.

She came to this realization in college after years of reading Nietzsche, Camus, Wiesel, Solzhenitsyn, Dostoevsky, and the Stoics. There had been times over the years that she'd tried to embrace a more or less godless, but nevertheless contemplative existence. She often weighed one great thinker against the other and then against her own beliefs—the beliefs she had carried her entire life. She asked herself if she believed as Nietzsche did. Was God dead? Or was she, more like Camus, doomed to endure all of life's sufferings without hope of an afterlife? Dostoevsky, Solzhenitsyn, and Wiesel forced her to look at her own suffering as the path to her ultimate redemption, and to reassert her belief in God. But then she read the Stoics and thought, perhaps the best way to survive it all was to let the natural world take its course and to react dispassionately to all that life presented—both its joy and pain. She had even gone and spoken to a close family friend, Monsignor Benedicto, at St. Patrick's. She grilled him for hours on all sorts of matters of philosophy and theology. Patiently, the monsignor listened, nodded, and, whenever he could, assured her that her doubts were all part of her belief. Finally, he asked her a simple question, "What would bring you comfort, Cathleen? What would ease your mind?"

Cathleen didn't even have to think about the answer. "I want it all to make sense." She continued: "If there were someplace, somewhere far away from here where we could all go, that would help me. When I was a child I thought there was a heaven, full of angels and people I loved—for everyone in the whole world who did not have it easy."

The monsignor smiled at her. "What if you just decided there was such a place and stopped looking for proof? What if you just made up your mind there was a heaven and a God? Would that help you?"

"I guess."

"Just try then. Try to believe."

"But it's so hard. My head is telling me something completely different."

"Do you know where the word *believe* comes from, Cathleen?"

"No."

"It's from the ancient Latin word *credo*, which literally means 'I give my heart.' What does your heart tell you, Cathleen?" The monsignor knew it was a bit of a loose interpretation, but many priests before him had used this old standby on unassuming doubters, so he went with it, hoping Cathleen wouldn't know better.

By the time Colm had arrived in her arms when she was fresh out of college, she had had plenty of time to think, and plenty more experiences—and heart-to-hearts with the monsignor— that made her absolutely certain of two facts: there was a heaven and she would go there someday, and everything on this earth must be endured to get there. Life was as chaotic and random as Madison Avenue on Christmas Eve, but heaven would surely make sense of it all. Because, in her mind, there was no reason that a child such as hers should be born into such screwed-up cir- cumstances, and another child born into better ones. She wasn't naive, though. As dark as some of her days seemed, she knew she was one of the lucky ones. She counted her blessings, and at some point, she followed her heart and began to pray again. It steadied her like whiskey steadied a drunk's nerves. She knew it was no panacea, and in the end, too much of it might even delude her, but it was a quick fix nonetheless, and it got her through the day.

When she had become pregnant, she needed prayer more than ever. She had lain awake one night rubbing her swollen abdomen and feeling the taut flesh that covered the small bumps that were Colm's feet kicking madly, forcefully. He wanted out, and she very much wanted him out too. She put the rosary on her belly and counted her Hail Marys and Our Fathers and occasionally looked over her shoulder to the clock and then the phone. If she prayed one more, she convinced herself, *he* would call. If she prayed two more, *he* would show up. She had already spent the better part of nine months moving the beads through her fingers, but Pierce had still not changed his mind.

There were times, wonderful times, she thought, when he would call and say he was ready for the responsibility, that he wanted to be a dad. She would spend an hour in the bathroom, showering, shaving, blow-drying, tweezing, all of it to prove once again how much more beautiful she was than the other girl he had left her for months after she told him a baby was on the way.

But the nights always ended the same. She would find herself alone, crumpled on the floor of her bathroom moaning over how stupid she was. There seemed to be no reason for his change of heart. He had told her he loved her. They were happy, and then one day, he wasn't anymore. At first she blamed herself. She wasn't pretty enough. Skinny enough. She hadn't complimented him enough or been a good enough listener. But hadn't she? She tried over and over to figure out how it had all changed, how it had all come undone. And there seemed to be no singular reason. Love was as random as God or life itself. If love came quickly and easily, she assumed it could disappear in just the same way. She never deserved it in the first place. It was then that a persistent, overwhelming fear lodged itself deep in her stomach. Colm came so easily. Loving him took no time at all.

And like his father before him, he too, Cathleen believed, at any moment would leave her . . . all alone.

In the hospital chapel, Colm stared at his mother in annoyance while she kneeled and leaned over the pew in front of her praying the Our Father. He couldn't possibly imagine what his mother had ever done that was so wrong that she had to spend so much time praying to God to *forgive her trespasses.*

"Mama! Mama! Can we go now? How long do we have to sit here and pray?"

"We still have a few minutes."

"Please, Mama. Can we just go? I really, really have to go to the bathroom," Colm whispered loudly.

Cathleen knew he was lying. And he knew she knew. Cathleen grabbed her purse and took Colm's hand. "OK. We'll go. How about we go find the gift shop and kill some time?"

"Sure! Can I get something?"

"We'll see."

After Cathleen bought Colm a Matchbox car from the gift shop, they found the elevators again. When they arrived on the seventh floor, Colm tried to make a run for it, but Cathleen gripped Colm's hand tightly before he could and they walked together down a wide, brightly lit hall, following signs to the Electrophysiology and Cardiology Department.

✂ Chapter 6

As expected, Dr. Basu's waiting room brought few surprises to Cathleen. While she signed in and handed over her insurance card to the unfriendly receptionist, Colm climbed up on the only available vinyl chair. On either side of him was an elderly gentleman. The man to his right had a tube running from his nose to a large oxygen tank on wheels sitting between his legs. He rested his hands on the tank as if it supported his entire upper body. To the left, the other elderly man grumbled to himself as he read aloud from the form he was filling out: *high cholesterol, yes; high blood pressure, yes; short of breath, yes.* Cathleen looked over her shoulder and saw her son, sitting between the two old men, and flashed a goofy look his way. She thought immediately of the *Sesame Street* song and asked herself: *One of these things is not like the other ones, which one doesn't belong?*

When Cathleen began to walk toward the chairs, the older

gentleman with the oxygen tank feigned movement and asked her if she would like his seat.

"Oh, that's quite all right. I'll just sit in my son's chair. He can sit on my lap. Right, Bud?"

Colm didn't say a word, but he turned his back to her and lifted his arms so his mother could sit down and scoop him up as he slid effortlessly onto her lap the way all children do.

"It won't be long before you'll be too big for this," Cathleen whispered into Colm's ear.

"I'm already too big for this," Colm grumbled, surprising himself—and his mother—with his honesty.

The man without the oxygen tank, now finished with his forms, looked over at Cathleen and sat up a little straighter. Cathleen felt his gaze and ignored him. But Colm caught the old man looking, and he knew why. His mother was beautiful. When he was very small, he thought he was the only one who thought his mother was the prettiest woman in the world. He had loved to hold her face in his hands and stare at her green eyes. And he often ran his dimpled hands through her long black hair and wrapped his small arms around her neck, his fingertips barely touching because his arms were so small. He could stay there forever, smelling the faint perfume of her shampoo. It had been a while since he had hugged her in that way, but now with the old man ogling her, he snuggled into her and glared, as he often did, at her adoring fans.

He wanted desperately for the nurse to call his name, to take his mother away from these men. The old man with the oxygen tank made his move and touched Cathleen's thigh. Colm swung his leg and knocked the man's hand with so much force that the man pulled back and gasped.

Cathleen quickly wrapped her arms around Colm, while apologizing to the old man. "Oh, I am so sorry. His leg must have just slipped."

Colm glared at the man, while clinging tightly to Cathleen.

"You're too young and pretty to be here. You seeing Dr. Basu too?" the old man asked.

Cathleen smiled and said a quiet yes. She kept her eyes down-cast, focusing on the boy's kneecaps, so she didn't have to share any more information.

"COAL-M Magee," the nurse called, mispronouncing his name.

Cathleen let out a sigh of relief. "That's us, Bud."

The old men looked at each other as Cathleen scooted Colm off her lap, and he ran through the door. She corrected the nurse's pronunciation of his name as she passed her.

"It's Col-um. Pronounced like a newspaper column."

"Sorry 'bout that."

"No problem. It happens all the time."

Again, exasperated, Cathleen and Colm waited for another half hour in the examining room. Colm climbed up on the doctor's chair and looked out the window, staring down at the small cars and people below. He leaned his lips against the glass and blew air through his cheeks, making puffing sounds and laughing.

Cathleen, just as bored as Colm, watched the clock. She had missed another day of work. There would be no explaining another day off to her boss. She had been hired just out of college as an office assistant to the head interior designer with the promise of advancement. At the time she was pregnant already, though still not showing. It was a miracle she got the job at all and that they didn't fire her the minute they found out. She knew legally they couldn't do that, but firing someone in design, pregnant or not, was never hard to do in New York City.

She promised them that she would work harder than anyone after the baby was born. But once Colm had actually arrived, she could never keep up with the interns and junior designers, who were more able to put in extra time to prove their worth and whose ideas seemed fresher. She was always so tired and usually distracted by some crisis at home, whether with Colm or her brother, to ever contribute. Sometimes, when she was over-tired, she took five minutes to feel sorry for herself, bemoan her sacrificed career, her wasted youth. She knew she wasn't the first woman to give up her career for her child, or for someone else's needs. She reminded herself that a paycheck was a paycheck, whether she was designing or booking conference calls. She re-minded herself that the sole purpose of work was to provide for her son, and it didn't matter what she did as long as she kept doing it. But she knew if she kept this up much longer, she might not have a job, let alone a career. This was the third doctor's visit this month, not counting the day and night she had already spent in the hospital this week after Colm's collapse on the subway platform.

She heard the faint sound of an Indian accent through the walls and could hear the predictable doctor-patient banter. She tried to reassure herself that she would be able to keep her promise to her son. This would be a different doctor. There was hope. There was always hope.

She heard the rustle of papers behind the door as Dr. Basu grabbed Colm's chart from the inbox that hung outside the door.

"Well, well, well, what do we have here?" He never looked up from the chart as he shook Cathleen's hand. Cathleen's heart sank as the usual scene began, but then she looked up at the tall man who stood before her. He looked surprisingly young to be a doctor. But she guessed that he was most likely in his mid to late thirties, perhaps early forties. He was handsome and fit for a doctor too, she thought. Dr. Basu was impeccably dressed and wore expensive cologne. She caught herself staring at him and quickly shifted her gaze to his hands, where she noticed the lack of a wedding ring on his left finger.

"Nice to meet you, Dr. Basu. I heard great things about you from Dr. Jakes," Cathleen said as she smiled and held out her hand to shake his. But the doctor seemed to ignore her.

Cathleen noticed Dr. Basu look toward her son, who was still standing by the window. Colm turned around, smiling widely. As Cathleen continued speaking, she realized the doctor was not hearing what she was saying.

Staring at the boy, Dr. Basu felt a small, but violent rumble in his stomach. His hands began to sweat, and for a second he saw the face of another small boy, Dhruv, his own son. He looked at the chart for a moment, trying to regain his composure, but when he looked up again, instead of Colm's large green eyes, he saw Dhruv's. They had been Dhruv's mother's eyes before they were his. When Dr. Basu's parents told him that the woman they had arranged for him to marry was the jewel-eyed Niranjana, he could have run through the streets of his town shouting her name, forgoing all dignity, all pride, all composure. He had fallen in love with her before sunset on their wedding day. He knew few Indian men who could say the same. And the same thing happened when he held and saw Dhruv—he had loved the boy instantly.

"Dr. Basu, this is my son, Colm," Cathleen introduced the boy.

The doctor gathered himself, smiling at Cathleen, whom he immediately noticed had the same green eyes as the boy, and as his own Niranjana. Struck by her beauty, he felt himself begin to blush, so he quickly turned away to give all his attention to the boy.

"Hello, Colm. That is a nice name. My name is Gaspar." Dr. Basu said, holding out his hand to introduce himself to the boy. "Do you know the story of the Three Wise Men from the East?"

Colm nodded, eager to share what he knew: "Gaspar was one of the Wise Men and he brought gifts to the baby Jesus."

Dr. Basu laughed. "Do you know what else Gaspar did?"

"No. What?"

"Why, he saved Jesus's life. Don't you know?"

"No, he didn't," Colm said back defiantly. "No one did. He died, remember?"

Cathleen wondered aloud, "What are you talking about, Dr. Basu?"

Dr. Basu smiled at Cathleen and turned to the boy to finish telling him the story of Gaspar, the Wise Man.

"In my old country, my father worked for a prosperous Englishman, Gaspar, and that is who he named me after. This man was a Christian, and my father often returned home at the end of the day with stories that he had heard from the man. My favorite was, of course, of Gaspar—the Wise Man from India. He told me that Gaspar and the two other Wise Men saved Jesus from death as a child. Legend says that King Herod, hearing of the birth of Jesus, sent the Wise Men after him. They were told that when they found him to return and tell Herod. The Wise Men followed the special star to Jesus, but when they got there and saw the baby and his mother, they knew he was a special sort of child, and they knew they would not tell Herod, who would have most certainly killed the baby Jesus. He and the other Wise Men protected the baby. So . . . if it weren't for Gaspar and the other Wise Men from the East, *who knows . . .*"

Dr. Basu shrugged his shoulders when he said *who knows.* And Colm smiled at him, because Colm knew that if there was anyone, anyone in the world who was going to save him, it would be a man named *Gaspar.*

"So, my boy, you know what my name means. Now, what does yours mean?"

"It's sort of silly. Not cool, like your name, Dr. Basu."

"Go on, tell me. I'd love to hear it. I am sure it is cool, as you say."

"Dove."

"Ah, Dove. Why do you think you were named after a dove?"

"Dunno."

Cathleen interjected. "I named him that because the name *Colm* is the Gaelic form of dove, which is the symbol of peace. I can't explain it, but from the moment I felt him swimming and leaping around in me, I felt nothing but peace." Cathleen noticeably blushed, but Dr. Basu was moved by her confession.

"That's a tall order, my good boy. I hear you're causing some trouble, Dove, for your mother. Disturbing her peace, is that true?"

"Yes, I fall down sometimes. It scares everybody, especially my mama."

"Do you know when this is going to happen to you?"

"Sometimes. Sometimes I start to feel real sick, and the world gets fuzzy and I can't see or hear so well."

"How do you feel when you wake up?"

"Pretty bad. Heavy, like someone is sitting on me and I can't get up."

"It takes him a long time to speak, Doctor. He stares up at me for a long time, and it's like he doesn't really know me. He seems so far away."

"Hmmm. I see," Dr. Basu said, all the while using his stethoscope to listen to the boy's heart.

"I think he needs a pacemaker, Ms. Magee. That should do it," he said, wrapping the stethoscope back around his neck.

"Excuse me?" Cathleen said, incredulous.

"A pacemaker. It's a minor operation really. I do them all the time. It will take no time, and we'll fix this once and for all. Everything will be A-OK," Dr. Basu said as he made the OK sign with his fingers.

Cathleen couldn't believe what she was hearing. And she couldn't believe she was going to say what she was about to say. She thought she wanted to hear this. She wanted to hear something decisive. For years she had been ordered to take Colm to other hospitals for other tests, where she would then be told, if she was told anything at all, that the tests found nothing out of the ordinary and there was nothing anyone could do. All this time, she thought she wanted someone who would fix all this and make it all go away. But suddenly she had her doubts about this man. He seemed too relaxed, too sure of himself, too together. She felt the anger coming, the way she always could, like someone took a rope and tightened it around her throat. She tried to fight back the urge to explode, but she couldn't.

"Do you mean to tell me, you've been with my son for less than two minutes—you found out what his name means and what he feels like when he collapses—and you want to operate on him? Are you out of your . . . excuse me, Colm, don't ever say this word . . . your goddamn mind?"

Dr. Basu stared at her without speaking. Her response was not exactly what he had expected. He was used to gratitude from his patients. Yet here was a young woman, pretty, too, wearing a crucifix and swearing at him.

"Excuse me. You misunderstand what I am telling you. Your son needs a pacemaker. It will keep his heart from stopping arbitrarily."

"And how do you know this, Dr. Basu? Have you ever seen anyone or treated anyone like my son? Tell me, Dr. Basu, how many of your patients flatline for several minutes at a clip and miraculously wake up? How many don't?"

"How much time do you have?" Dr. Basu said back to her smartly, trying to crack a joke, but he could tell she was in no mood for his humor, and he immediately tried to reassure her.

"Ms. Magee, I have been at this a long time. I assure you pacemakers work and that with the right medicine, I can keep your boy vertical."

Cathleen's face flushed hot. She couldn't tell if she wanted to smack him or hug him. She wanted Colm to stop collapsing, to live a normal life. But for some reason she couldn't quite explain, she didn't believe that the solution to her son's problem was such an easy fix. How could it be? *After all these years this doctor has been right here, under her nose, and she hadn't heard of him? There weren't other doctors who could have suggested this? Why now? Why him? What was the difference between praying for a miracle and asking a doctor to perform one?* Her mind was raging, but she spoke slowly and deliberately. She couldn't put her finger on it. She was confused by her own anger, and then she suddenly remembered something her mother often said—*anger is nothing more than your fear screaming.* She stopped herself and recognized the cause of her anger—the fear rising inside her. But what was she so afraid of anyway? This was the answer. Finally, an answer to her prayers. *Maybe prayers did work after all?*

"I don't know, Dr. Basu. This seems awfully fast. It seems like you're just pulling this procedure out of a hat. It doesn't even make sense. You don't even know Colm. You haven't even ordered any tests. You don't even have a diagnosis."

Cathleen couldn't believe she was suggesting ordering more tests. They were the last thing she wanted for Colm.

"I assure you, Ms. Magee, I stayed up well into the night reading most of the information in Colm's hefty chart that Dr. Jakes sent me. There is only one explanation for your son's condition. I don't think the other doctors were too far off with their diagnoses. He has dysautonomia. You see, the part of his brain that sends automatic messages to the heart to continue beating is malfunctioning. Your son's heart stops beating, and when he collapses, his body lies flat, and the blood can eventually get back to his brain, which starts sending messages again, and your son's heart begins beating again. It's a magical thing really. The heart can't operate without the signals from the brain, and the brain can't produce the signals without the correct pumping action of the heart. People often treat them as two completely independent organs, but they are not—they are interdependent. The brain and the heart must coexist peacefully to keep the body functioning. There is no peace in Dove's body today, but if we put the pacemaker in him, then when his brain starts acting up and his heart rate drops below a certain number of beats per minute, the pacer will step in and do the work for the heart and brain."

Colm looked at his mother and then back at the doctor.

Cathleen popped up, grabbing her purse as she rose. "Thank you so much for your time. You must be very busy. We won't keep you any longer."

Cathleen headed for the door, grabbing Colm's arm as she went.

"You don't want to schedule the surgery?" Dr. Basu asked in a surprised voice, thinking he had convinced her.

Cathleen stopped, dropped Colm's arm, and turned to the doctor.

"There is no way in hell I am going to let some doctor I barely know cut open my son, insert a device that may or may not work, based on an idiomatic love story between the heart and the brain! It's clear to me, and everyone else who sees it happen, that once Colm collapses he does not wake up right away! He lies there for minutes without a heartbeat—nothing. And all of you 'doctors' say the same thing to me. I am sick of hearing about this dysautonomia and vasovagal. Not one of you can explain why he stays out so long!" Cathleen snapped loudly.

"Please, just listen to me. You have to trust me. I don't know if I can explain why Colm stays unconscious for so long—which I admit seems beyond my own comprehension—but I think I can prevent his collapses from happening in the first place."

"I need to think about this," Cathleen said, softening a little. After all, Dr. Basu was the only one who had ever offered to help, the only one who didn't ask her if she was giving her son drugs, or ask her if she was depressed or lonely and trying to make her son collapse to get attention from the boy's absent father. He was the only one who said he had looked at Colm's chart, had studied it even, and had offered her a way to heal him. He seemed to be, if she thought about it, the answer to her prayers.

"Of course, absolutely. Although I recommend the sooner, the better. Here are some pamphlets with all the information. Here is my card and the nurse's card. When you're done thinking about it, call my receptionist and we'll set up another appointment."

Colm had never seen his mother so angry. And he had seen her angry—plenty. As his uncle Sean would often say, "That's her MO, kiddo: always POed. If you know what I mean." Colm always laughed, but he had no idea what his crazy uncle meant.

Colm had decided he liked Dr. Basu from the moment he had walked in the door and began to speak directly to him. No other doctor had ever done such a thing. Doctors always pretended that he wasn't in the room.

As Cathleen left, Dr. Basu bent down on one knee and looked at Colm. Colm could smell the doctor's breath mint and the musky perfume emanating from his hair.

"I will see you soon, Dove. I am sure of that. In the meantime, try to stay standing—and alive."

"Yes, sir."

Colm laughed as the doctor rubbed his hands through his hair. Cathleen came back into the room and snatched Colm's hand before heading out the door.

On the bus ride home, Cathleen pulled the straps of her purse back and forth. She was finishing the heated argument with Dr. Basu in her head. She was really sticking it to him. Colm had seen her do this many times before. Cathleen could never muster the nerve to tell people *all* that she really thought. Instead she grumbled, mumbled, and had little wars inside her own mind.

"I like him, Mama," Colm admitted. "I have a feeling he knows what he's talking about."

"We'll see about that. I have to talk to your uncle Sean first."

✣ Chapter 7

C ATHLEEN SAW HER BROTHER ONLY ONCE A WEEK, when his shift schedule or a hangover didn't get in the way. She and Colm joined him on most Sunday mornings at St. Patrick's. Since their mother had died more than six years ago the two had an unspoken pact that this was how they would honor her. Granted, they had given the woman her fair share of grief over her daily attendance at church, but now the ceremony rooted them in their past, in their present, in their future, even if they didn't believe everything the church espoused. Church was like a name, or a neighborhood, or a sibling; it was theirs, good or bad, because it was all they had ever known.

They rarely missed a Sunday, even around Christmas, when the streets were packed with tourists. Afterward, they fought through the crowds and took Colm to visit the Metropolitan Museum, the American Museum of Natural History, or to the Central Park Zoo, or even to the Times Square Toys "R" Us.

Uncle Sean always bought Colm something from the Lego section and later helped him build it. Colm couldn't get enough of playing with Sean, and Sean was always immensely proud that he could do this one thing for his sister. Even if he couldn't make her happy, he could make her son happy.

When mother and son arrived at St. Patrick's on the following Sunday morning after visiting Dr. Basu, Colm immediately spotted Uncle Sean waiting for them in the back near the gift shop. His tall, broad, uniformed body was hard to miss. Colm broke away from Cathleen and leaped into Sean's large arms. Together the three walked down the center aisle and took their regular spot in the pew.

Colm started to say something, but Uncle Sean put his finger over the boy's mouth to remind the boy where he was. Uncle Sean was usually all fun and games. There was no limit to the noise they could make—wrestling, dancing, and chasing each other around his apartment. Colm loved to turn on Uncle Sean's stereo as loud as it would go and dance on the coffee table and the sofa. Life with Uncle Sean was always a party, and Colm loved to watch his uncle move his hips and slide his feet across the floor, swaying to the music, sometimes stopping only to swig his beer. "You move like Timberlake," Colm often heard his mother say. Colm had no idea what that meant, but he loved to watch his uncle and mother dance around the living room as if they were floating on clouds. It was the most wonderful place in the universe, he thought, and he often vowed that when he grew up, he would be as free as Uncle Sean, except he wouldn't bother with church.

For the life of him, Colm never understood how his uncle, who was so unrestrained outside the walls of the church, could be so different inside them. Church was such a letdown for Colm, and the worst part of it was sitting still. Colm believed his mother and uncle chose to take him to the world's longest Mass—with a choir that sang every response, with a priest who seemed to go on and on during the homily and who talked with his mother after every Mass. Colm didn't get it. Why did people come to church? What was the point? But then he quickly reminded himself, he knew something that the others didn't. He glanced at his mother, who at that moment was staring up at the windows above the altar. She looked to Colm as she had often described the angels in heaven—a glowing blast of radiant light and beauty. But Colm knew better.

His mother was beautiful, but she was no angel.

Despite all evidence to the contrary, Cathleen never paid much attention in church. The rituals had become so ingrained, her body moved without knowledge it was moving. Her lips spoke without awareness of what she was saying. She didn't feel the words in her mind, heart, and spirit as she spoke them. She let her imagination run. She sat and admired the beauty of it all, the work that had gone into designing these magnificent buildings for the glory of God, all to give humans a piece of heaven here on earth.

Sean had assured her that the cathedrals in Italy made St. Patrick's look like an ersatz copy, but she had never been to Europe, so to her, St. Patrick's was the supreme church. Sometimes after Mass she took a moment in one of the side chapels with her mother's stack of prayer cards—a collection the older woman had earned by visiting various wakes and funerals of friends, relatives, and firemen—and began to recite them. The first card in her mother's deck had an illustration of St. Florian, the patron saint of firefighters. On the back of the card was the Firefighter's Prayer and imprinted on the bottom was her father's name and a date: *Michael Patrick Magee, June 15, 1985.*

Sean and Cathleen's father had died when a backdraft caused a warehouse floor to collapse, crushing him and another firefighter instantly. Their mother, an Irish immigrant, thousands of miles from her own family, was left all alone. Dressed in a black maternity dress and carrying her nearly three-year-old daughter on her hip, she marched behind an engine carrying her young husband's coffin to St. Patrick's while bagpipes echoed down Fifth Avenue. Cathleen always thought it was a blessing that her mother had died before Sean became a firefighter. She knew her mother could have never survived the possibility of losing another loved one. Cathleen could barely handle it herself.

After Mass, as they headed out of church, Sean and Cathleen grabbed Colm's arms and swung him. Some people, the *regulars,* Sean called them, glared at them. But some of the older people who still had memories of their own children smiled at the three of them, thinking quietly to themselves: *What a happy, young family.*

People often mistook Sean and Cathleen for husband and wife. Sean looked nothing like Cathleen. He had auburn hair like Colm's and blue eyes. He was lantern jawed, like his own father. And unlike Cathleen and his mother who were tall and slight, Sean's body was a massive bulwark—wide and seemingly unbreakable. When Cathleen was a child, she found a picture of their father standing next to their young mother. She couldn't imagine how a building could have ever crushed the man. Like Sean, he seemed like Atlas to her; he could carry the whole world on his shoulders and never succumb to its weight. Cathleen had been looking for that same strength in a man her entire life.

"How did the visit with the new doc go, Cate?" Sean asked as soon as they were out on the sidewalk.

"It wasn't like all the other visits. He didn't order any tests."

"I thought you hated all the tests."

"I do. But it all seems to be moving really fast. He says he wants to put a pacemaker in him."

"What's wrong with that? I thought you said you wanted someone who would help Colm."

"You agree with this guy?"

"From what you're saying, he's the first one so far who seems more worried about fixing than diagnosing. Let's face it, Cate, most people go through their entire life not knowing what it is that is killing them."

"So you think we should do it? I'm just so torn . . . I . . ." Cathleen stopped when Colm began pulling on her arm.

"Now what, Colm?" Cathleen was annoyed, and she didn't know why. Church with Colm always tried her patience though. As a child she would never have behaved the way he did in Mass, with all of his fidgeting, climbing, and sighing. She was tired of being constantly tugged and called. Motherhood was an endless stream of unsolicited nudging and urging on, when all she really wanted to do was stay put.

Sean saw what Colm was trying to do, and he reached in before Colm hit the ground.

"Oh, crap, here we go," Sean said audibly, although mostly to himself. It came on so fast, Sean could barely make sense of it. Although he knew Colm had done this four times before—he had never seen it firsthand.

He rested Colm's body on the ground as a small crowd began to gather on the sidewalk in front of the cathedral. Using his paramedic training, he felt for Colm's pulse and checked to see if he was breathing, but the boy had already stopped. As he started chest compressions, Cathleen yelled out for help as she dug through her purse, trying to find her phone.

As Sean pressed on Colm's chest over and over, all he could think was that he had no idea how his sister had managed it all these years. Despite all the emergency calls he had made during the past two years as a firefighter, Sean wasn't prepared to watch someone he loved die in front of him. Worst of all, he knew he was powerless. No amount of training could save Colm once his mysterious heart stopped beating.

As Colm's face lost its color, Sean started, for the first time in several years, to pray, really pray. In his head, with every compression he repeated over and over: "Hail Mary full of grace." Press. "The Lord is with you." Press. After a minute of praying, he began to beg God to not let Colm go. He bartered with God. *Take me.* Press. *Take me instead.* Press. Sean thought how much easier it was to lay down one's life for a friend, or even a stranger. As a firefighter, he had put himself in a fair share of sticky situations to save people he had never met, and he had even been called a hero for it, but suddenly he knew saving lives was the easy part. It was nothing like watching someone he loved die. The heroes were the ones who were left behind, who endured it all. He had known from the beginning of his own life that death was always felt more by the living.

Five minutes later, after the paramedics arrived and took over, they told him to stand back and take care of his sister. Sean began to shake uncontrollably and reached for Cathleen's hand and took it. She looked at him, feeling the fear in his body rise in her own. The monsignor worked his way through the crowd and came to stand beside Cathleen, taking her other hand and praying out loud. Cathleen didn't even notice. Her mind was on only one thing—her son.

"Where could he be?" Cathleen whispered to herself, staring blankly at the scene before her.

The monsignor and Sean said nothing.

The paramedics worked on Colm a long three minutes before they grabbed the shock paddles and jolted him several times. Each time, Cathleen jumped, as if she could feel the electricity and pain running through her own body.

Suddenly, Colm's eyes popped open. Above him, he could see the dark shadows of people standing over him and behind them the towering steeples of the cathedral and the blast of morning light pouring through. He closed his eyes again.

Cathleen lunged for him. "Colm, come back!"

One of the paramedics explained how they had to get the boy

to the hospital and that they might have to intubate him to keep oxygen flowing to his brain. The boy had a pulse, she said, but it was weak, and he needed help breathing.

Another paramedic asked Cathleen and Sean, "How long do you figure he was out before we arrived?"

"At least five minutes before you started working on him—I guess that means about ten minutes total," Sean said.

The paramedic looked at Sean. She didn't have to tell him what she was thinking. Sean already knew. It was too long.

He is most certainly brain-dead, Sean thought quietly to himself.

"Can we ride along?" Sean asked.

The paramedic nodded, and Sean and Cathleen broke away from the monsignor and climbed into the ambulance. In the ambulance, Cathleen held her son's hand and glanced quickly out the window only to see the monsignor's worried face and the church behind him grow smaller as the ambulance sped away.

❧ Part II

Something happens in this room, something unmentionable: here the soul is yanked out of the body; briefly it hangs about in the air, twisting and contorting; then it is sucked away and is gone. It will be beyond him, this room that is not a room but a hole where one leaks out of existence.

—J. M. Coetzee, *Disgrace*

❧ Chapter 8

WHILE THE AMBULANCE MADE ITS WAY UP THE avenue, Cathleen pulled out the card Dr. Basu had given her just a few days earlier in his office. She handed it over to her brother.

"Will you please call him, Sean. Can you see if he can meet us at the hospital?"

"I thought you didn't trust the guy?" Sean looked at her confused.

"I am willing to try anything at this point. I don't think Colm can go through this again. I know I can't. I can't even bear the thought of going into another ER today."

Hospitals still terrified Cathleen and left her feeling cold despite all the modern design attempts to use warm colors and decorate with inoffensive artwork. Of all the hospitals she had been in over the years, she had preferred the Midwest Heart Clinic the most. The white walls, concrete floors, steel sculptures, crosshatched abstract art, and gargantuan tank of cleansing water were all put there to remind patients they weren't home. She appreciated its honesty.

She and Colm had spent an entire day there the year before, moving from one long test to another—hemodynamic testing, Q-SART analyses, heart rate variability studies. She waited two hours to meet with one of the best electrophysiologists in the country to go over the results, but he had canceled their consult. Again, she went all that way for no answers. Exhausted by the process and feeling hopeless, she never called to follow up. *Surely, they would have called,* she thought, *if they had found anything at all.* She was certain the hospital was doing something for other people . . . just not her son. As she followed Colm from the ambulance to the emergency room, she realized that all she wanted and maybe all she needed was one person, just one, who could help her and her son.

When the ambulance arrived, Dr. Basu was waiting for them. As Cathleen stepped out of the truck, he could see that her soft face was tense with fear. She was clutching Colm's hand, and he noticed that Colm was unconscious and had a breathing tube down his throat. At that moment, Dr. Basu was inclined to act more like a worried family member than a doctor, but he resisted the urge to rush and he walked in calculated, paced steps toward Cathleen, Colm, and the uniformed man he saw standing next to them.

"You don't have to worry, Ms. Magee. I will take care of Little Dove," Dr. Basu said when he reached the gurney that the medics were pushing into a curtained room. He patted Cathleen softly on her back. His hands felt warm, steady, and surprisingly strong to her. He was shocked he had made this gesture and that he was unable to resist the compulsion to comfort her.

Cathleen's eyes filled, and without thinking, she folded her body into the doctor's arms. He held her, and for a moment he was surprised by her remarkable about-face, from her anger on Friday to her complete submission today. But then he understood. He knew the feelings well. *Fear makes people angry, and grief never ceases to transform.*

Dr. Basu said nothing, and he let Cathleen gradually untangle herself from his embrace. As she pulled away she did not look him in the face, embarrassed by her sudden rush of emotion.

"How did you get here so fast, Dr. Basu? I thought my brother, Sean, just called you in the ambulance?" Cathleen asked the doctor, while pointing to her brother as a way of introducing them both.

"I am on call and was already here. The message service contacted me and let me know you called and were on your way. I just had to come down from the seventh floor. So what happened?"

"We were walking out of church this morning, and he just went down. He was gone at least a good ten minutes; Cathleen says it's never been that long," Sean told the doctor, while holding out his hand to shake it and introduce himself. "Sean, Cathleen's brother, by the way."

As the paramedics, nurses, Sean, and Cathleen moved Colm's gurney down the hall and into a room, Dr. Basu walked with them, while trying to get as many details as possible. When they all reached the room, Dr. Basu stopped Cathleen and Sean at the doorway and asked for a moment alone with the nurses to examine the boy.

Cathleen was startled. "You mean, I can't stay?"

"Just for a few minutes, Cathleen. I want to be as thorough as possible, but I'll try not to be too long. We'll come and get you as soon as we're finished. Why don't you both get some coffee or something to eat?"

Cathleen wanted nothing to eat; all she wanted to do was stay with Colm. Sean could sense his sister's urge to start an argument and stepped in between her and the doctor.

"I'll take care of her, Doctor. No worries. We'll be back in a half hour."

"That should be more than enough time. Thank you, Sean."

Colm lay on the gurney, hooked up to wires and IVs. Cathleen could hear the slow *blip, blip, blip* of his weak heartbeat. She kissed Colm softly on the cheek, squeezed his freezing hands, and whispered something no one else could hear. She knew, no matter where he was, no matter what realm she had thought he entered into, he could hear her words loud and clear, "I'll be right here waiting."

After Cathleen and Sean left the room, other doctors, interns, and residents stepped in. Together they discussed scheduling various tests to measure the boy's brain activity. After so much time without oxygen, they had to consider that he might be brain-dead. Although Colm was alive for now, Dr. Basu knew that this was most likely temporary. Decisions had to be made. After the test results came back, he'd most likely have to tell the boy's mother the unthinkable. He was slightly angry with himself for not being more persistent with her the other day, and for not reminding her how serious her son's condition was. He had always had trouble expressing or even realizing the appropriate sense of urgency. *How could I have made the same mistake twice?* he berated himself.

After Dr. Basu examined the boy, he pored over his massive chart, hoping to find something, anything, that he could have possibly missed. And there it was. Dr. Basu found a short letter from a physician at the Midwest Heart Clinic buried under hundreds of other forms and lab reports. The head of the electrophysiology department there had written in his medical consult notes: *Diagnosis—progressive, degenerative neurological disease. Do not rule out multiple system atrophy (MSA). Prognosis for MSA—Terminal. Treatment—Symptom maintenance and pain management.*

Dr. Basu read through the letter, which detailed how all the tests at the clinic pointed to one thing: Colm's central nervous system and, consequently, multiple other systems were failing. He had an inability to regulate his heart rate and his body temperature, and eventually he would lose control of his muscles, his speech, and his ability to swallow. Dr. Basu read it over and over. There was no known case of this disease in a child—ever. Its incidence in the population was so rare it was all but unheard of. It was a disease attributed to old people—in their sixties and seventies. Not a child. Not a young lively boy.

Dr. Basu pushed his hands through his hair. *There either has to be a mistake or there has to be another explanation. A disease like this in a child would be the equivalent of a five-year-old coming down with Alzheimer's—an impossibility.* But then he thought of any number of aberrations in nature and science. Yes, he told himself, deviations and variations in nature are the rule. All things are possible. The universe itself was thought to be an aberration. He knew this. He looked again at all the tests, and he too concluded what the clinic had. Why hadn't he put all the pieces together himself? Why had he missed all the telltale signs? The boy's central nervous system was imploding. His body failing. If he didn't hit his head falling down during a syncope episode, he'd eventually die of an embolism, pneumonia, heart failure, or malnutrition after his body stopped absorbing nutrients. There was a long list of ways he could go—and it wouldn't be long—ten years max—before he finally did.

Why didn't anyone tell this woman? Why didn't anyone call? Who sends—and receives—a consult letter like this one without a phone call to the patient? Damn these massive hospitals, he thought for a moment. But then he composed himself and remembered how easy it was for papers to get lost, for patients to fall through the cracks. He himself only found the letter now. None of it mattered, he realized, because in the end there was no cure. Nothing anyone, not even a doctor, could do to change it all. The only thing that mattered now was that somehow he had to deliver all this terrible news to the family—to Cathleen.

As he was looking up more information on the disease on his laptop, a nurse poked his head through a crack in the curtain.

"There is a priest here in the hall who says he knows the family," the nurse said to Dr. Basu.

"What does he want?"

"He is waiting to speak to Colm's mother and uncle."

"Very well. I will let them know, thank you."

When Cathleen and Sean returned to the room, they saw Dr. Basu leaning over the boy's bedside—gently patting his head.

"Dr. Basu?" Cathleen said, stepping into the room quietly and startling the doctor.

"Oh good, you're back," Dr. Basu said, smiling at Cathleen and trying to disguise any hint of bad news. "We have more tests, but for now I think he's resting."

As the lie came out of his mouth, Dr. Basu cursed himself for it. It would be harder now to tell her and for her to believe it. He couldn't explain why, but he wanted Cathleen to like him, to trust him. He usually didn't care much about what his patients thought of him, but Cathleen was not his patient and Colm was unlike any patient he had ever had.

"Do you mind if I have a moment with him?" Cathleen turned and looked at Dr. Basu and Sean.

"Certainly," Dr. Basu said, backing out of the room.

"I'll be right outside, Cate, if you need me," Sean assured her.

Cathleen sat down next to Colm and took his hand. Sean and the doctor looked back to see Cathleen slump forward over her son's body as if pressed by the weight of the world.

Dr. Basu slipped the stethoscope into his white lab coat pocket. He whispered to Sean, "Do you have a moment?"

"Sure."

Dr. Basu's smile disappeared and he seemed grave. "I have a few matters to discuss. I need you to help me explain these things to your sister. When I spoke to her on Friday, I got the feeling she didn't trust me, or any doctor."

"Well, Doctor, she has her reasons."

"Yes, she has every reason to doubt us," Dr. Basu said as he inhaled deeply and thought of the letter from the clinic.

The doctor's solemn expression frightened Sean. "What aren't you telling me and my sister?"

Dr. Basu inhaled deeply again and began to explain to Sean what he thought was wrong with Colm. "I think Colm's problems are not limited to his heart alone. I was on the right track. I explained this a bit to your sister on Friday. But now I have reason to believe your nephew is suffering from a degenerative disease that is attacking his central nervous system, which controls his heart and brain, among other things. Of course, I, and the other doctors whom I have consulted, could be wrong. Illnesses of this nature are never clear-cut. But if it is indeed what I think it is, it will only get worse. Some people call this Shy-Drager. Some people call it MSA—multiple system atrophy. Most people only live ten years with the disease before dying. It is extremely rare, and even rarer, if not unheard of, in children. And it's incurable. Unless we've made some error, or unless Colm makes some miraculous turnaround, he will die. His brain and heart seem to be warring with each other. It is as if the part of the brain that controls his autonomic functions is attacking, and the heart is responding by shutting down. The result, however, is that he collapses. In short, his body is slowly dying. We can give him medications and we can install a pacemaker to help alleviate some of the symptoms, but I am afraid there is not much hope. If your nephew does wake up, you will need to convince your sister to put the pacemaker in as soon as possible, and he will have a difficult road ahead. You all will."

Dr. Basu stopped talking. Somewhere in his explanation he knew he had lost Sean, whose face had gone pale.

Sean straightened up and stood tall. He nodded a small thank-you, and they both turned and walked back to the examining room where they stood quietly watching Cathleen smooth Colm's hair over and over. Several silent minutes passed before Sean noticed the doctor staring at his sister. He could see the pain in the doctor's eyes, and to Sean, the doctor seemed afraid—afraid to tell Cathleen what they both knew.

But Sean's impression was wrong. Dr. Basu was not afraid. He feared little. Life had served up his worst possible nightmare already. All he felt was compassion for this woman, this stranger, who had come into his life. He seemed to know, more than anyone in the world, what it was like to be a parent who had to raise a child that was not for his keeping.

"Dr. Basu, you mind if I go in and see Colm and Cate?"

"Please, go on."

Sean began to walk away, and then Dr. Basu remembered.

"There is someone here waiting for you and Cathleen. A priest from your church stopped by. He told the nurse that he knows the family and would like to talk to your sister. Would that be all right? He is in the waiting area."

"Oh, sure. It's just my sister's friend, the monsignor."

"I'll have one of the nurses go get him," Dr. Basu said.

❧ Chapter 9

MONSIGNOR FRANCESCO BENEDICTO HAD KNOWN the Magee family for nearly forty years. He had married Maureen and Michael over thirty-five years ago and had buried Michael a few years later. He had baptized Cathleen, Sean, and Colm. He was especially fond of Cathleen, who had been somewhat of a rebellious teen and young woman but had matured into a loving, capable mother. He saw her at Mass regularly now. And after her own mother's funeral and before her son was born, she had stopped by the rectory often seeking counsel. He understood that Cathleen saw him as a father figure—a man with answers—and he had tried, throughout the years, to do whatever he could to prove her right.

Now as the monsignor walked into the hospital room, he saw Cathleen with her head down on her arms folded on the bed. He thought of a small child saying her nighttime prayers, *Now I lay me down to sleep, I pray the Lord my soul to keep.*

"Cathleen?"

Cathleen lifted her head and saw him. "Oh, Monsignor. Thank you so much for coming."

"How is he?"

"He hasn't woken up yet. This is the longest he's ever been out. He was gone for ten minutes this time. And he usually comes back to me right away—well, at least after a few minutes. Some of the nurses and paramedics, and I can tell even Sean, think that this time is it. It was too long. He's never, ever been gone this long."

"Oh, Cathleen. Do you want me to administer the holy oil—the sacrament of the sick?"

"Do you think he's gone? Do you think this is it?" Cathleen asked in disbelief.

"Oh, no. There is always room for miracles, for faith. Little Colm has proven God's benevolence time and time again. He can still come back bright as day. You must believe, Cathleen. He needs you to believe now more than ever."

"Then why do you want to give him his last rites if you think there is still a chance for a miracle?" Cathleen was pleading with him.

"No. You misunderstand. Remember, the anointment is not just for last rites or for the dying—it's for the sick as well. Would you pray with me?"

"Yes, Father."

Cathleen looked past the monsignor's shoulder at her brother leaning against the door frame with one foot in the room and the other out. Sean thought all of this was a bunch of hooey, but he knew his sister needed him to be strong for her. And so he stepped forward into the room and took Cathleen's hand. Dr. Basu stepped back and stood where Sean had been in the doorway and looked on. He had seen this ritual many times while working at Good Samaritan.

Cathleen and Sean made the sign of the cross together, and then the monsignor pulled out the oil from a little pouch he carried. After he placed the pouch and the Bible on the table beside Colm's bed, he dipped his fingers in the oil and then made a small cross on Colm's forehead. Cathleen and Sean could smell the sweet oil. The same kind they smelled on the day of Colm's baptism.

"Through this holy anointing may the Lord in his love and mercy help you with the grace of the Holy Spirit," the monsignor chanted.

"Amen," Sean and Cathleen whispered, their eyes closed as they fought back tears.

Just as the monsignor reached for the boy's palms, to make the sign of the cross on them, and began saying, "May the Lord who frees you from sin, save you and *raise you up*," Colm's eyes opened wide. He looked terrified and confused. Through the oxygen tube he tried to cry out: "Mama? Mama?" But nothing came out of his mouth.

"Colm!" Cathleen screamed and began to cry with relief.

Sean chimed in too. "Jesus H. Christ."

"It's a miracle. Jesus, Mary, and Joseph, thank you for the many blessings you have bestowed upon your child Cathleen and her son, Colm," the monsignor prayed aloud, glaring at Sean for taking the Lord's name in vain.

Dr. Basu, incredulous himself, came to Colm's bedside.

Colm was trying to talk but couldn't with the tube down his throat. His eyes were moving back and forth, trying to take in his surroundings.

Dr. Basu stepped up to the bedside now. He had immediately pressed the nurse call button when he saw Colm's eyes open. Now he began to check the boy's vitals while directing the nurses to begin removing the breathing tube. As they worked on him, they could see he was alert and awake and in no way brain-dead as they had all feared.

Throughout it all, Cathleen spoke gently to Colm, moving around the bed to stay out of the way of the doctor and nurses, but never letting go of his hand.

"You gave us quite a scare this time, Colm," she whispered softly to him. "You were gone for a long time. We thought you were on your way to heaven, sweetie. We were worried you might never come home."

"That's silly, Mama. I'm never going to heaven," Colm whispered scratchily.

Dr. Basu took out a penlight and looked in Colm's eyes. Though Colm's throat hurt, he continued to try to talk to reassure his mother that he had no intention of going anywhere.

"See," the monsignor said confidently, "God provides. Nothing to worry about."

Dr. Basu glared at the priest. He wanted nothing to do with this superstitious talk. There was clearly a medical reason for Colm's collapses, for his revival, and none of it had to do with God, he thought.

"Oh, thank you, Monsignor. Thank you." Cathleen hugged the priest and shook his shoulders. "I am so glad you came."

"It wasn't me. It was the Lord," the monsignor admitted while raising his face toward the heavens.

The monsignor believed without question that the hand of God played a role in every miraculous intervention, but there had been brief moments in his life when even he had had his doubts. When he saw people like Cathleen, and Cathleen's mother before her, suffer, he wondered where God was in all of it. He struggled with the question of suffering, as many priests did. He had been trained well in the seminary not to try to explain the age-old dilemma—doing so only brought with it more questions and doubts. He simply believed that God had a purpose for all that he did and that God alone knew what was right. When Cathleen had challenged him that day long ago, instead of being angry with her, the monsignor had said a prayer for her. He prayed that she, and others like her, would come back to God. Then with the death of Cathleen's mother, he thought God had answered his prayer. He thought Cathleen had come home to God when he saw her praying so solemnly at her mother's funeral. He had no way of knowing then how far away she really was. How she would leave her mother's apartment, because she was unable to stay there all alone—without her mother—with only the memories of her death. The unbearable loss. No, Monsignor wouldn't see Cathleen for months after that day. He had no way of knowing she would move into her boyfriend's apartment shortly after the funeral, and within months become pregnant with her sickly son, Colm.

The resurrection of Colm brought a newfound hope to the monsignor. Through him, he thought, the Lord God had come and laid his hands on the child and brought him back to life.

The monsignor could hardly contain himself and shouted out in exaltation to the boy: "Colm, you're a modern-day Lazarus! Once dead and now alive!"

Dr. Basu reprimanded the priest. "Please, sir, not now. I don't think we quite know what is going on here. I don't think we should jump to conclusions."

"Oh, come on, my good man. This is a miracle, plain and simple. There is no scientific way to prove it otherwise."

Dr. Basu was angry, though his reserved demeanor did not show it. The priest was speaking out of turn. He had no idea what was at stake—he was giving this poor mother hope—hope he had no right to give. He looked at Sean, who knew what the doctor knew.

"May I have a moment alone with you, Cathleen and Sean?"

Dr. Basu followed Cathleen out of the room and explained to Cathleen what he had told Sean earlier about Colm's condition. As Dr. Basu gently spoke the words he had just said to Sean—*degenerative, terminal, multiple system atrophy, prognosis, pain management*—Cathleen tried to block it all out. She refused to hear it. She shook her head in disbelief, over and over, all the while looking at her son through the glass.

"Why should I believe you? Or those doctors at the clinic? Those tests were taken a year ago. What's any of this have to do with my son now, today? You've seen him. There is nothing else wrong with him. I don't . . . I won't . . . I can't . . ."

She would not believe that her son could be dying. *Hadn't he just come back? I just saw him resurrected. It was a sign from God.*

Logically, Cathleen knew resurrection was impossible. But after all the doctors, after thinking her son was really gone, *this time actually brain-dead,* she was beyond logic, beyond knowing what the natural and medical world could do for her son. If she had to wager which one would save her son—God or doctors, she was going to go with God today. She had seen it for herself five times and she wondered, who was she to doubt it?

Sean couldn't believe what he was hearing. His sister—his intelligent, bullheaded, predictable sister—was starting to lose her grasp on reality.

"Sis, you gotta listen to the doctor. He knows what he's talkin' about."

"No! Colm is special. I've been waiting for the medical world to figure this out for years, and I've had it! There is no answer for me or Colm in this hospital or in any hospital. It's somewhere else, Sean. I have to believe that. I can't lose him. Don't you get it? I'm not going to lose anyone else. I won't."

Cathleen broke away from the doctor and Sean, going back to Colm, where she found him sitting up and listening to the monsignor telling Colm he should say prayers of thanksgiving—for the miracle of his revival. And that starting today, he should pray without ceasing for a cure.

"I am sure you will eventually be healed. I trust in God. And so should you," the monsignor said as he patted Colm's hand.

Colm looked past the monsignor at his uncle, who was now standing behind his mother in the doorway and shaking his head. Colm never loved his uncle more. At least someone in the room was on his side, Colm thought. Colm wanted to scream: *Just get me out of here, please. I want to go home.* He felt like crying. Why did his mother have to invite the priest, who didn't know how to give a short homily, to *his* hospital room?

Cathleen looked at the monsignor talking, and even she recoiled a little at his fervor. Then she looked at Colm, still so pale and small in the bed. Suddenly her own passion faded. Part of her still wanted to put her whole heart in God's hands—but she hesitated and waffled again. *What if I am wrong? What if the monsignor is too? What if Sean and Dr. Basu are right?*

"Monsignor, thank you so much for coming. I really appreciate it, but I think Colm needs his rest now. The doctor just told me he wants to put a pacemaker in Colm tomorrow and get him on medicine. We have a long day and night ahead of us. I really appreciate your coming all the way over here, especially on a Sunday. It's just, well . . . I think Colm needs his rest."

"Yes, certainly. God's work is done here for the day anyway! You know where to reach me if you need anything, kids!" the monsignor said brightly as he walked over to Colm's bed and kissed his forehead. "God blesses the little children. Mark my words, this boy's a living miracle," he whispered quietly to himself.

Cathleen heard the monsignor and smiled at the thought of it. *Yes, perhaps there were some miracles, after all.*

After the monsignor left the room, Colm looked at his smiling mother. She was happy, he thought. He didn't want to ruin her smile with his own news. He knew it would break *her* heart.

Meanwhile, Monsignor took the long way to the rectory. He meandered through the park and marveled at all the living miracles running past him, flying above him in the trees, growing out of the ground. Everywhere he looked he saw the hand of God at work. He had really only had one singular prayer his entire life:

that the entire world could see what he saw—God in everything on earth and in heaven—from the largest, strongest, most beautiful cathedrals to the smallest and frailest children. "Miracles did and *do* happen," he said aloud. Yes, yes they do. He was sure, just positive, that all he had to do was pray—and his poor Cathleen, who had her fill of life's pain and loss, would have her one wish, this one miracle.

❧ Chapter 10

Later that same evening after Colm was stable and settled into a room upstairs in the hospital, Dr. Basu urged Sean to take Cathleen home. She was visibly exhausted and needed a good night's rest. "Tomorrow Colm will be operated on. It will be a long day," he reminded them. He assured Cathleen he would take excellent care of the boy and would not leave his side. Cathleen could not believe his dedication.

"What about your other patients, your own family? Don't you have to go home?" Cathleen asked.

"Well, I am on call. And, to be frank, I do not have a family. Don't you worry about me. I don't have anything else I'd rather do. Nothing whatsoever."

"Thank you, Doctor. We will see you in the morning then." Cathleen whispered softly into the sleeping child's ear, "Sweet dreams, my little one," and kissed Colm good-bye.

After Cathleen and Sean left, Dr. Basu walked past the sleeping boy to stand at the window. Immediately, he found the North

Star; *the polestar—constant, never changing,* he thought. He had named Dhruv for it. He didn't believe Dhruv was up there looking down on him though. Dr. Basu had long since put such fanciful notions to bed. But he looked nevertheless, thinking that this time, there would be a way—there had to be a way—to save this child.

Colm woke up and saw the doctor. "Dr. Basu? Is that you?"

"Yes, Dove. How are you feeling?"

"Why do you call me Dove?"

"That is what your name means. In India, some people think a name determines one's future."

"But my name is not Dove. It's Colm."

"There is a funny thing about people in India. We give everyone we love a special name, sometimes lots of names. That is why I call you Dove or Little Dove."

"Do you like me, Dr. Basu?"

"I like all people."

"Am I like all people then?"

"Yes, but you're special."

"So does that mean you still like me?"

"Yes, of course."

"I knew you did. I could tell you were different the moment I saw you."

"You are special indeed, Little Dove."

"My mama says I am special."

"She is right."

"Dr. Basu, can I tell you something? It is something I haven't told anyone—ever."

"Yes. Go on."

"You won't tell Mama or Uncle Sean, and especially not the monsignor?"

"Of course, not ever."

"When I am gone, I know everyone thinks I am dead. I know my heart stops beating and part of my brain stops working. I have heard people say that. And today, I heard everyone say that my brain died . . . that I was *gone*."

"Yes. You know a lot for a young boy."

"If I am dead, shouldn't I be in heaven? Shouldn't I see the angels Mama told me about? Shouldn't I see my Irish nana? And my grandfather, the giant fireman?"

"Some people believe there is a heaven, Colm. Yes. Some people, after they die for a bit and come back to life, think they have been to heaven."

"I don't believe them, Dr. Basu."

"No? Why not?"

"I know what happens when we die."

"You do?" Dr. Basu was fascinated.

"I don't see anything when I die. There is nothing, but a black, black world. There is no God, no heaven, no angels, no people. There is nothing. Do you think it's because I am a bad boy that I can't make it to heaven? Do you think God has forgotten about me?"

"No. You are a good and brave boy."

"Then why don't I see God when I am dead? Doesn't he love me? Doesn't *God* even want me?"

"What is this *even* stuff? Everyone wants you. Everyone loves you."

"Not my real dad."

"Oh. I see," Dr. Basu said, exhaling. *What a terrible burden for a child to carry,* he thought.

"I am not good enough for him either."

"Now, listen here, Dove. I do not know the answers to such questions about God. They are big questions for a boy—for a man. But I know you are wanted and you are loved. I also may not be able to explain God, but I can explain this: if you are alive right now, that means that most likely you were not *really* dead. I know there has been a lot of talk about you being dead, and I know that must sound very scary to you, but I want to explain something. May I?"

"Yes."

"When a certain part of your brain is resting—the part that sends the messages to the rest of your body to work—it doesn't send your heart the messages it needs to beat. Without that certain part of your brain your heart doesn't work. Do you understand this?"

"Yes, I heard you tell my mama the other day."

"Yes, you are a good listener. When your heart can't pump, it can't get blood to the rest of your brain. If your brain doesn't get blood, it doesn't work very well either—so that is why you can't see *anything.* It's very difficult to understand, I am sure. Do you follow me?"

"Yes, I do."

"For some reason, Colm, your brain stays asleep for a long time. A very long time. It's unique and special, like you. But I am sure there is a reason, and I intend to find out why. I am sorry I can't answer your questions about God. I can't explain why you don't see him, but as a man of science, a doctor, Colm, I can tell you this: if you're really not dead, then perhaps that is one reason why you can't see God."

"Do you believe in God and angels and stuff like that, Dr. Basu?"

"I used to. When I was a child, I prayed to many gods. But when I became a man, I came to believe in other things."

"I don't believe in God, Dr. Basu. If I tell my mama, she'll be mad."

"No, she won't be mad. She loves you no matter what. You would be surprised how strong a mother's love is. It's stronger than anything in the world—even doubt."

"You won't tell her though, right?"

"My lips are sealed."

"Thank you, Dr. Basu."

"You're very welcome, *son*." Dr. Basu didn't even notice he used the term.

But Colm heard the word and treasured it. He held it close to his heart. "Son," Colm repeated softly so the doctor couldn't hear, and then louder he said to Dr. Basu, "Thank you for fixing my heart, too," Colm said.

"I will try my best, Little Dove. Does it hurt you? Are you in any pain tonight?"

"My heart hurts me all the time. The pain never goes away."

"I see. Can you point to it?"

Colm pointed to the center of his chest.

"OK. I am going to try to make you better."

"Thank you, Doctor."

"You're welcome. Now get some rest."

Dr. Basu pushed himself away from the boy's bed and began to make his way out of the room.

"Don't go, Dr. Basu. Will you stay with me?"

"Yes."

Colm closed his eyes and began to fall asleep. As he drifted off, his face relaxed, and Dr. Basu noticed a broad smile come across the boy's face. *If I didn't know better,* the doctor thought to himself, *the angels in heaven are making the boy laugh.*

Chapter 11

CATHLEEN WAS GRATEFUL HER BROTHER WAS THERE with her in the apartment, even if he had drunk himself to sleep by sneaking swigs from her old, dusty bottle of whiskey that he snagged while she was in the kitchen fixing them something to eat. He didn't think she could see that he stashed the bottle between the pillows on the couch where he now lay. He didn't think she saw him pour the whiskey into the club soda she had poured for him. Any other night she would have said something—gotten into a serious fight with him—but she was tired, and she was relieved he was there. It was the noticing, she thought. The tiny moments that she noticed that no one else did that were constantly undoing her, them. Although she wished he was awake so she wouldn't feel so alone, she was happy to hear him breathe in the room. His presence was enough. It would have been unbearable to be there alone.

She walked by Colm's room and stood in the doorway look-ing at all the evidence that her little boy resided there. A tall robot built out of Legos lorded over an assortment of precisely lined up cars, a wrecking crane, a fire truck, and a rumpled, well-hugged bear. His hooded Yankees sweatshirt hung over the chair beside his bed, and the books she had read to him the night before were stacked on the floor beside the messily made bunk bed with fire truck sheets. She bent over to straighten the pile of books, thinking about which ones she should take to the hospital for him—*If You Give a Mouse a Cookie, Where the Wild Things Are, No Matter What.* He had outgrown *Oh My Baby, Little One,* but she still kept reading it to him and could, after five and a half years, recite the words by heart. She loved the illustrations of the mother bird and her son, and Colm loved looking for the hidden hearts on each page—inside the mother's collar, underneath the boy's cap, curled around a coffee cup. No, it didn't matter where the two birds—the mama and the baby bird—went, their love was *everywhere.* Yes, on every page, Cathleen thought, Colm was looking for a crisp, whole, beautifully shaped heart.

It was all she could do to stand up. The exhaustion and heartache seemed to settle in every joint, muscle, and bone. She was the oldest twenty-seven-year-old she knew. She moved around the room, absentmindedly straightening and picking up small toys off the floor and putting them in the appropriate sorted baskets on the shelves along the wall. When she was done, she looked back one last time at Colm's empty bed and tried not think *what if,* hit the light, and headed across the hall to the bathroom.

As she closed the bathroom door behind her, she caught herself in the mirror and winced at her reflection. She thought she looked awful—her hair was a mess, and her eyes, showing signs of wear and age, stared blankly back at her. She could barely stand the sight of herself; no wonder, she thought, no man could either. Cathleen had no idea how men perceived her. She only measured her beauty by the one man who had rejected it, rejected all of her.

She had grown accustomed to her single life, and she often told herself that she could live the rest of her life without a man. It had been nearly six years since she had been touched by someone other than her son or brother, but she didn't feel the absence of intimacy. Had she known then what she knew now, she would have tried harder to remember her whole life before, to hold on to it for all time. She only remembered how Pierce's lips felt on her cheek; she did not remember how he had looked when he kissed her good-bye. She had pretended to be asleep, and she did not know it would be the last time. If she had known, she would have made one last plea for herself, for their unborn son. When she woke later that morning, she found a note that he'd left on her mirror. There was no apology, no good-bye— just some lyrics of Bob Dylan and Joan Baez's "Mama, You Been on My Mind" scribbled on a piece of paper, asking her to look inside her mirror each morning, and to remember that even though he wouldn't be there, he would be able to see her so clearly, and he wondered if she, Cathleen, could see herself as clearly as he did, when he had her on *his mind*.

Could he really see her? See her now? She hoped not. She hoped he would only remember her as she once was. She could barely see him now. The memory of him was fading for her every day. Something for which she was secretly grateful. He took up less mental space, less heartache with each passing moment. His absence left more room for Colm, she thought. She did not let herself waste too many moments thinking about what might have been. Instead, whenever she became nostalgic or began to miss him, she tried to think of what Monsignor had said to her when she went to him to tell him that she was seven months pregnant and that Pierce had left her.

"Sometimes we love the wrong people, Cathleen."

Monsignor's words struck her. Yes, she had loved Pierce. It *was* real. And the purpose of that love produced a child. But just because it was real, it didn't make it right. It didn't mean it would last forever. Her head knew that, but her heart felt an entirely different thing. She missed him. She imagined various scenarios in which he, with his guitar slung behind his back, would surprise her by arriving on the doorstep of their apartment or by meeting her at the same subway station where he first saw her all those years ago. She dreamed he would touch her cheek, smooth the hair on top of her head, and slide his hands over an escaped wisp and tuck it behind her ear as he gently kissed her. If she closed her eyes, she could feel it, almost believe he was real. He was there and he loved her. But when she opened her eyes, he was gone and it was her own hand tucking her hair. And it hurt all over again. She had to believe the pain of his leaving her, of his leaving their son, would subside someday. It just hadn't happened yet. Yes, it hurt considerably less than it did all those years ago, but at any moment the pain asserted itself—a note to the *parents* of Colm Magee, a homemade Father's Day card from the day-care center that went to no one, a Dylan song on the radio. Yes, whenever Cathleen felt the familiar sting, she reminded herself of the words the monsignor spoke often, "These things take time, dear. Let your heart heal. No reason to get back out there right away. You have Colm now to love—that's all you need now."

She reminded herself of his wisdom as she brushed her teeth without looking up at herself again in the mirror. Then she turned out the lights and headed off to her bedroom. If life had taught Cathleen Magee anything, it was this: No matter what, the morning always came and whatever it brought her—a note on the mirror, a trip to the hospital—she would survive as long as her brother and son were by her side.

❧ Chapter 12

S EAN WOKE UP ABRUPTLY FEELING THE VIOLENT, burning surge lurching up his esophagus. For a second he had forgotten where he was—on Cathleen's couch— so when he stood up and headed toward what he thought was his own bathroom, he tripped over the coffee table, causing his half-filled glass of club soda and whiskey to spill across the table and soak Cathleen's *Elle Décor*.

"Shitgoddammitall," he said, stumbling over the table, ignoring the mess. He knew he had only seconds to get to the bathroom.

Once down the hall, he slammed the bathroom door shut behind him and began making a loud retching sound that echoed in the toilet.

Cathleen sprang out of bed immediately and screamed out, "You all right in there, Sean?"

"Yeah, fine. Nothing to worry about," Sean whispered, staring into the bowl. Without looking, he reached behind himself, grabbed Cathleen's bath towel, and wiped what he thought was the usual clear liquid dripping out of his nose. When he pulled the towel away, he noticed a mixture of fluorescent-colored bile tinged with blood. He stared for a second and then stood up in front of the mirror. He looked for cuts on his lips, but then he realized the blood was coming from his stomach. The thought of this made him gag again, and when he looked at the vomit in the bowl, he saw the green and red swirl.

"Never, ever again," he whispered to himself. "Never."

"Seriously, Sean, are you OK? What's going on?"

"Nothing, don't worry about me. You've got enough to worry about. Nothing a solid Bloody Mary won't fix." He laughed, trying to make an ill-timed joke.

"Geez, Sean."

"I'm joking. Come on! It's nothing."

"Well, hurry up in there. I want to get ready and get to the hospital before Colm wakes up," Cathleen said, shaking her head and trying to hold back her usual tirade against his drinking.

"Give me a minute," Sean said as he wiped down the bowl with the towel and then ran it through the cold water under the sink. The blood wouldn't give and soaked deeply into the fibers. There was no way to hide it from her, he thought. He looked at the window and back at his reflection and shook his head, saying to himself, *You're a first-class idiot.*

Without waiting another second, he quickly opened the window and threw the blood-soaked towel out, promising himself he would swing around the alley and pick it up later. He was shocked at how adept he had become at hiding how excessive his drinking had become again. Even if he knew he wasn't fooling anyone, least of all his sister, it made him feel better to at least pretend he had it under control. This, he thought, was the worst part—the tiny deceits. The little lies he told to get through the day, to get out of the bathroom, because of the shame and embarrassment of it all.

After he shut the window and flushed again, he opened the door and stepped out. "It's all yours, madam."

"You look like hell, Sean. When are you going to knock this off? I thought you were going to start going back to meetings?" Cathleen said to Sean, who pretended to look surprised that she could tell he had been drinking.

"Naw. That shit's for quitters. But when I do go back, you'll be the first to know . . . and the first to bitch about that, too."

"I give up," she said, exasperated, and threw up her arms.

"Love you too, Ms. Morning Sunshine."

Cathleen hated to do it, but she cracked a smile. He always had a way of disarming her—by reminding her of who she really was—a royal pain in the ass to him.

Sean walked into Cathleen's bedroom and noticed her laptop open on the bed. She had been up late, he could tell, probably doing research again. If he had been awake, he thought, he could have stopped her from this, stopped her from driving herself mad with worry.

"Hey, Cate, mind if I check my e-mail?" Sean shouted through the door.

"Go ahead. Computer is open. Just wake it up," she said, turning on the shower.

He walked over and sat on her bed and clicked. He had no

intention of checking his e-mail. He was curious about what his sister was up to—what she found out. Sean pulled down her history and could tell by the amount of sites she visited that she spent the better part of the night stressing herself out by looking at medical journals dedicated to dysautonomia, pacemakers, MSA, heart defects, and brain ailments.

He started clicking through all of her sites and stopped suddenly when he saw a Favorites tab open, which contained a link to a website named "Miracles Happen." On the site was a forum for all sorts of people who had died and come back to life—and all who attributed their revival not to science but to miracles. And several people claimed that while they were dead, they had been to heaven and had seen proof of an afterlife. Physicians from the University of Pennsylvania Near-Death Study program, the president of the International Association of Near-Death Studies, and previous near-death survivors were all quoted or cited. Priests, reverends, pastors, rabbis, theologians—all came together on the issue to talk about the veracity of God, and how near-death experiences always served as proof of God's miraculous interventions, proof of his existence. Scientists and researchers who explained how the body works, some explaining that near-death experiences were nothing more than the final stages of brain failure—the cells, slowly dying, creating a dreamlike twilight just before it all ends—were discounted and refuted as quacks. Science couldn't possibly hold all the answers. Miracles did and do happen.

Sean looked up from the screen, shook his head, and said, "Please, tell me she is not buying this bull." Everyone, it seemed to Sean, had a story, had a way to rationalize, explain, and defend the afterlife—and not one of them had a clue, a real clue, what they were talking about.

In the bathroom, Cathleen stepped into the shower and marveled at how things had started to turn around. Despite the horrific diagnosis Dr. Basu delivered yesterday, she couldn't explain it, but it felt, dare she say, "good" to know that this wasn't all in her head—or in her son's. That there was now a name for what was happening to Colm—and that there was a real enemy, something, anything, to actually fight against. More than that, after reading information on all the sites, she was convinced that all these doctors, scientists, and theorists were just wrong about her son's prognosis. There was always a cure. There had to be. And yes, there were limits to what science could do, but not to what the heart could do—not to what God could do.

Buoyed by the stories of miracles on the newly discovered Miracles Happen website, she felt more certain than ever that God was on her side for once, and that perhaps the monsignor and the website were right—miracles *do* happen. She was even a little surprised by Sean's ability to step up yesterday. He actually stuck around all day at the hospital and stayed with her last night. He called in sick to work too. He had never done that for her before. She had always been the one caring *for him*.

When they were teenagers living with their mom, he was always so distracted by his studies that she stepped in and took care of the details he let slip. He seemed to be so driven, drunk then only on the possibility of flight. He had had a singular purpose, and so while he was off studying or volunteering, she did his laundry, signed his forms, arranged for his tuxedos for the proms. When he was applying to college, she set up a calendar with due dates and wrote the checks for his SATs and college applications, things her mother, who never went to college, had no idea how to do.

But then when things didn't go as planned, and even later still, after he became a firefighter, she still kept helping him, *enabling* him, one of his old AA sponsors once accused her. She opened his bank account and had the rent pulled automatically to make sure they never lost the rent-controlled apartment his mother left him after she died. She ran interference with certain friends, asking them to call her if they ever saw Sean at certain bars. Sean didn't think his sister knew that he spent a good amount of his paycheck at Eamonn's across the river, but she was always one step ahead of him. She kept the account numbers and pass-words for herself, and when she or his friends hadn't heard from him for too long, she could log into his account to see where he had been the night before. She never went looking for him or embarrassed him by dragging him off a barstool, but she was always vigilant.

For the first time in years, she felt relieved that she didn't have to handle something—anything at all—on her own. She exhaled and felt good, surprisingly rested and fresh, despite the lack of sleep. She felt like she was finally turning a corner, and beyond it were some answers, some ways to fix Colm. She turned off the shower and reached for her towel. Her hand slipped out from behind the curtain and slapped the cold metal bar as she fumbled for it, and then she pulled back the curtain and looked around.

"Where in the hell . . . Hey, Sean! Would you grab me a towel from the hall closet? I don't know what happened to mine."

Startled, Sean slammed the laptop shut and ran to the hall to grab his sister a towel, and he slipped it through the door.

Cathleen wrapped her hair, put on her robe, stepped out past him, and slid into her room.

As she was about to shut the door, Sean yelled back at her, "Wait a minute, Sis."

"What?"

"Don't get mad, but I was snooping around on your computer."

"I'm not mad. I don't have anything to hide. And I'm the last person who should be mad at you for snooping."

"I saw you were probably up half the night—and I saw that crazy site—the one you tabbed."

"What are you talking about?"

"Miracles Happen."

"So?"

"I just don't want you setting yourself up . . . for some . . . I don't know . . . some heartbreak."

"Don't be ridiculous, Sean. I was just doing some research, that's all."

"I know you though. I know what you're thinking. You're the person who thought praying would cure Mom's cancer. You're the one who thought praying was going to make that jackass father of Colm's show up at the hospital and actually give a damn about you two. You're the one who thought all I needed to do was accept that there's a Higher Power, and I'd quit the sauce. It just doesn't work that way. You can't go hide out in church. You can't go buying that crap the monsignor is selling—wholesale.

He doesn't know what he's talking about. He just doesn't. That's all I am saying. For whatever it's worth, I hope you listen to me for once."

"Wow, you don't know anything about me. You don't know anything about Monsignor. What do you know about faith or miracles or anything? Huh? You can't get through a day, let alone a Mass, without taking a drink."

"Hey, it's not my fault they serve the sauce there. What am I supposed to do—*not* drink it?"

Cathleen cracked a smile; he was quick, that was for sure, she thought. But she remembered again what she was angry with him about. "Sean, you have no right to judge me. You're one to talk. You don't know anything that you haven't gotten from a bottle!"

"Well, I may drink my stupid, but you get your stupid someplace else altogether. Your son is sick. Sick! And you're praying for miracles instead of listening to the doctors. Instead of getting ready . . . preparing yourself for the wor—"

"Shut up! Shut up! Don't even say it."

Sean looked at her and felt like getting sick again. He didn't know when to stop, when to shut up.

"I'm sorry, Sis."

"You're not sorry. You're not sorry for anything. You're just a . . . a . . . I don't know what! You can't just give me this. This one wish. This *one* thing. You can't get better for five minutes to help me—to be there for me. For Colm. It's always gotta be about you."

Sean didn't want to go down this road. Every fight they ever had always led to her begging him to stop drinking, to get his act together, to go back to meetings, to sort his life out for her sake, for Colm's, for his own.

Cathleen saw in Sean's downcast eyes that she had gone too far again, and she stopped and tried to calmly speak and bring the conversation back to who it was really about—Colm.

"Sean. I'm sorry. I shouldn't have said that. I know you love Colm—me. I'm just tired. And I just don't know how or why Colm comes back, whether it's because of a miracle or science, or a doctor or a priest, or God or Colm himself. Listen to me, Sean, I only care that he *does* come back, and that someday, somehow, he'll never, ever die on me again. For now, I'll just say my prayers because they make me feel good and get me through the day, and if I just keep at it, maybe they'll work and Colm can stay with me forever."

Sean listened to her and understood his sister in a way he never had. For the past six years, all he saw was her genuflecting and cross signing and praying. She looked downright robotic to him, as if nothing was going on in that once vibrant mind of hers, and now he saw her in a new light.

"OK, enough of this shit. Sorry, Cate. I get it."

"Let's get dressed and get out of here. Dr. Basu's taking Colm into surgery in a couple of hours, and I want to be there before he wakes up."

"OK. You go get ready then."

"Hey, Sean?"

"Yeah?"

"Would you mind making me some coffee while I finish up? I'd really like to get going."

"I'll take care of it, Sis. You just do what you need to do."

While getting dressed Cathleen's mind raged. Throughout her life the battle between what her mind was capable of knowing and what her heart was capable of feeling waged on. She admired people who knew for sure whether they did or didn't believe in God or in heaven. She was drawn to Monsignor because he had such confidence in his own opinions. But she couldn't align herself with any one category. She heard equally the voices of faith and reason. Dr. Basu, who believed just as steadily that science and the natural world held the answers, echoed in her head as loudly as the monsignor. For her, belief was something she had to take like some people took sobriety, one day at a time. She knew she could be so easily swayed by one way or the other. The only constant in Cathleen's life was her ability to love—the father she couldn't remember, the mother who she never fully understood until she gave birth herself, the son she feared would leave her, the man who took her heart, the brother who challenged her but who knew her better than anyone. Her love was so different for each person, but miraculously her heart had room enough for all of them. Even when her faith and reason failed her, love did not.

❧ Chapter 13

WHILE CATHLEEN DRESSED, SEAN DID HIS BEST to make up for passing out on her couch the night before and yelling at her this morning. He rushed to throw out the ruined magazine and tidy up the living room, folding the blankets and arranging the pillows. He grabbed the empty bottle of whiskey, rinsed it out, and dropped it in the trash, hiding it under the other garbage. Then he remembered to make the coffee he'd promised Cathleen. While it brewed he washed the few dishes and cups in the sink from Colm's Sunday breakfast that Cathleen never had a chance to clean herself.

Sean didn't want to be useless. He didn't want to be the burden he knew he could be to his sister. There were so many things he didn't want out of his life right now, and he didn't even know how to begin to change it all, or how to make it all better for himself or his sister. So he tried to make amends one dish at a time.

From the kitchen, Sean heard Cathleen leave her room, head

back into the bathroom, and switch on the blow-dryer. He poured a cup of coffee for himself and took another down to her room and set it on a coaster on her dresser, placing it next to the picture of him on his graduation day from the Fire Academy. He was holding Colm, just a toddler then.

Sean shook his head as he looked at the picture and then at his reflection in Cathleen's bedroom mirror. He was the last person on earth anyone thought would grow up to be a firefighter. Even though his father had been a fireman, Sean had never had any intention of following in Michael Magee's footsteps. Sean had decided when he was a boy about Colm's age that he would do everything in his power to make his mother happy and never to give her cause to grieve. He'd grown up in the shadow of his mother's loss of his father and that was enough.

Like his older sister, he was intelligent, but he also had a daring, fearless side. While Cathleen sat on the couch reading or drawing, he ran around the apartment with his arms outstretched, pretending to soar above the earth. He wanted to see the world from above it, and he had marked the globe his mother had given him for Christmas with flags and stickers on all the places he wanted to go and see when he grew up—Ireland of course, Italy, France, Germany, England, the Great Plains, the Rocky Mountains, the wild American West, the Pacific Ocean. He had plans to see the world, but after that awful September day, his thoughts moved from this world to another. He thought only of one thing: *How could God let this happen?* Why was there so much evil in the world? Why and how could people who say they believed in a god, any god, cause so much pain, suffering, death?

In college, he immersed himself in a liberal arts education, preferring classes like philosophy and theology, which surprised him. He had been required to take them, but he ended up enjoying them more than any of the others. The more he read, the more something slowly started to change in him. Unlike his sister, who had begun to resist God and the church when she went to college, Sean felt oddly at home in the texts of Aquinas, Aristotle, and Augustine. A strange force pulled on his heart, and he found himself spending hours on his knees in prayer. It was the closest he felt to being weightless, almost as if he had been levitated, like he often felt after a night of drinking when he lay on his bed and watched the ceiling spin into infinity. For a brief moment, before the alcohol settled in his blood and made him sleepy, he could clearly see his purpose in life. But after the drink dissipated, so too did the feelings of certainty. And when he woke in the morning, he always felt more lonely and wanting than ever before. Praying didn't have the same effect on him that alcohol did. There was no letdown afterward. He knelt for hours, feeling as if the walls around him had disappeared and he could fly over the entire Earth and see all of its beauty, just as he always hoped to do as a boy. It was his dream come true after all. He tried, weakly, to explain it to a girl he had been seeing, but she thought he was trying to let her down easy. He was dying to tell someone who understood. He was certain that he was ready to spend his life drunk on God. It had all the benefits of alcohol without the hangover.

Sean spent hours in the dark, stone crypt below the Byzantine-style basilica on campus. He preferred it to the large upper basilica because he thought the larger one too garish.

Most of all, he hated the mosaic of what he called the Giant Aryan Jesus—a blond, he-man-like figure who lorded over the entire altar. The image disturbed him and made him think of his childhood imaginings of what God might look like when he finally came to Earth—a gargantuan man, larger than the entire universe, who tore open the atmosphere like ripping a piece of paper and who appeared before everyone all at once so that no one could deny his existence. While he feared the God who could tear the sky in two, he secretly wished that everyone would know the God he did—the way he did.

Then late one night his sister called, ending his two-month-long bender with the Lord. He had just come home from church and was eager to begin studying for his final exams, so happy to have finally finished his first semester of college and ready to get on with the business of studying to become a priest. He knew from Cathleen's tone, from the words she stumbled over, what she was about to say. He knew with his whole body that his mother was gone.

"How did she die?" He said it so matter-of-factly, as if a part of him, the part that made him feel, was gone too.

Through broken speech and long controlled pauses to fight back her own tears, Cathleen explained to Sean how she had taken their mother to the doctor a few months earlier, after she complained of severe back pain. The doctors ordered blood tests, and they found out shortly after that she had an aggressive form of leukemia, but no one, not even her doctors, expected her to go so fast. They had planned on telling him after his finals, after he finished his first semester of college, but there wasn't enough time. Sean told her it was all *bullshit,* that he had every right to know what was going on. But Cathleen and her mother knew how Sean operated—if things didn't go perfectly or according to plan, he'd invariably quit and turn to the bottle. Or worse, he would have felt bad for his mother and would have given it all up altogether just to be with her. He would have easily sacrificed his career as a priest, if it had meant he could stay near her.

He wanted to be angry at Cathleen for keeping this secret from him, but he could tell she was hurting too. They only had each other now. There would be no one else in the world for them. He'd told Cathleen he would try to get to her as soon as possible.

After Sean had hung up with his sister, he cried for his mother, he cried for the father he never knew, and he cried for himself—his lonely, sad, adult-orphaned self. He cried because he was angry. His anger surged and rose through him, like a heat wave that evaporated the moisture off the city streets and made steamy waves that obscured his view, making everything look blurry. Nothing came into focus. He sat alone with his questions for a long time. *Why was everyone's life filled with so much loss and pain? Why did the people we love the most have to go?*

Eventually he threw open the window of his dorm room and let the cold blast of air wash over his face and body. Finally, it seemed, he woke from the dream. Yes, as quickly as his newfound fire for God came, it left him like a powerful gust of air, a massive backdraft, fast and forceful, consuming him completely without a moment to inhale or to know what hit him before it all went black. He didn't know it then, but he would look for that fire everywhere, eventually settling for the real thing as a firefighter just two years later.

Sean quickly packed and turned off the lights in his room for the last time. Through the open window, the blue mosaic dome of the basilica shone underneath the moonlight. It seemed absurd to him now to think he would have ever said Mass below that dome. Everything around him seemed a cosmic joke, and for the first time in months he felt the ground beneath him, the cold air, and the ache in his chest and head. The light had gone out of him, and all the wonder and awe that had filled him until that moment just disappeared. In its place was a gaping hole in the middle of his chest that no amount of prayer or drink would ever fill. His life would never be the same. There was no one to please. No one to try to make proud. No one, except for Cathleen, left to worry about him—or to protect him.

Sean closed his eyes. Even though he was supposed to be a man, he still felt like a boy, the same boy who soared through his mother's apartment, running with his arms outstretched while warning, "Look out, look out! Here I come, Mama!" He felt sure that at any moment she would appear before him, and she would, he was certain of it, catch him midair, swing him over her shoulders, and tell him the entire world was his for the having.

But when he opened his eyes, he remembered he was not that boy anymore or the man he was supposed to be today. Who was going to hold him now and tell him it would all work out, that everything would be just fine?

His mother was gone.

When Cathleen stepped into her bedroom while brushing her hair, she found her bed made and the hot coffee set on her dresser next to her brother and son's picture. She smiled and shouted down the hall, "Thanks, Sean."

"Does it taste OK?"

"I meant thanks for everything—for the coffee, for staying over, for being here, for helping with Colm yesterday. All of it. Thanks. And I am sorry. About before. What I said. I really am."

"No big deal, Sis. Hurry up, so we can get out of here," Sean shouted back. Sean wasn't big on scenes. Besides, he knew she wasn't the one who should be saying sorry to anyone, especially to him.

❧ Chapter 14

L ATER THAT SAME AFTERNOON AFTER COLM HAD
woken up from his surgery, his mother and uncle were
there waiting for him. Cathleen looked tired, and Colm
could tell she had been crying.

"Did I do it again?" He looked at Uncle Sean. But his mother
answered him.

"Yes, dear. But it wasn't so bad this time. The pacemaker is
already helping."

"Where is Dr. Basu?"

"He had to leave for a bit. He has other patients he needs
to see."

"Oh," Colm said, disappointed.

"Are you feeling OK?" his mother asked while gently rubbing
his cheeks.

"I'm tired."

"I bet you are. Does it hurt?"

He felt a sharp, heavy pain when he breathed in and his shoulder ached. He reached across his chest and felt the bandages. A tiny, hard disc protruded from his chest wall.

"This feels funky."

"I bet it does," Cathleen said, feeling it for herself.

"Do you think it will work?" Colm pleaded.

"We already think it does. Your heart stopped beating for a little bit, and the pacemaker seems to be able to rev it up. I think the worst is over," Cathleen said as she smiled, trying to remain calm for the boy's sake.

"Mama?"

"Yes, Colm?"

"I love you."

It had felt like forever since he had spoken those words to her. It had only been days, but it dismantled her. She fell apart inside, but she knew he shouldn't see her cry. She smiled and said it back with a goofy cross-eyed face and grin: "Love you too, Bud."

Colm giggled and immediately felt a surge of pain from the movement. He cried out.

"Just rest, kiddo," Sean said. "We have all day. No rush. The insurance company is even gonna spring for another day. How do you like that? You get another day off of Cut and Paste Land."

"But I want to go to school," Colm argued. He was so sick of hospitals—even school seemed like a better alternative.

"Hon, there will be plenty of time for school. Right now you have to get better," Cathleen assured him.

Just then the monsignor walked into the room, and catching the last bit of their conversation, he added, "Your mother is right, Colm. Our first order of business is healing you."

Sean cringed and snapped back, "*Our, Our, Our first order of business.* Who invited you, Padre?"

"Excuse me? Sean?"

"Why are you even here? Did you come back to give God credit for 'healing' my nephew? Did you come to fill my sister's head up with more nonsense about praying for miracles? Save it."

"I am sorry, Sean. I don't know what you mean. What's this all about?"

"Sure you do, Father. Sure," Sean said disapprovingly and shook his head.

"Sean, please. Not now. Not in front of Colm," Cathleen pleaded.

"No, I got this guy's number, Cate. Believe me, I know what he's all about. He forgets I was almost one of his types—before I wised up," Sean said while looking at Cathleen, and then he walked over to the monsignor. The monsignor could smell the alcohol coming through Sean's pores and the acrid smell from his mouth. *He must have been sneaking drinks all day,* he thought as he braced for Sean's attack. He had heard about them from his sister.

"Does it make you feel good, Pops? Does it fill your heart up with love and good shit to know you're serving God? Do you think that God stopped whatever he was doing to fill your precious heart up with love for him? You think I don't know? That I don't get it? What you and your *people* are all about? Give me a break, old man. Go sell your crazy to someone who buys it. That crazy feeling you get when you pray or think God is talking to you—you know what that is, Monsignor? A chemical reaction in your brain." Sean was pointing at the middle of Monsignor's head.

Cathleen shouted, "Sean, please stop!" But Sean was on a roll.

"You get high off it, don't you, Pops? You're no different than a junkie or a drunk. You just get your juice from a different kind of bottle. Trust me, I know allllll about it. And let me tell you something else, Monsignor, he's *ours*, Colm's *ours*."

"Not in front of Colm," Cathleen said, cutting Sean off. She couldn't take it anymore.

"Mama, what's Uncle Sean talking about?"

"Nothing, Bud. It's just silly, stupid adult stuff. They're both cranky and tired."

The monsignor was obviously flustered by Sean's tirade, but he was more angry at the way Sean had reduced his faith to nothing more than the old *opiate of the masses* line. He had spent the better part of his life arguing with skeptics that the God he believed in was real and heard and saw everything that everybody did and said—even doubters like Sean. Even though he wanted to tell Sean how disturbed he thought he was and how, at some point in this life, he would cry out for God, the monsignor held his tongue. There would be no use in trying to explain it all to someone like Sean, he concluded. If Colm's miraculous revivals couldn't prove it, the monsignor thought, then nothing ever could.

"Sean, we all want Colm to get better, that's all I am saying."

"What's this *we* stuff, Pop? The only *we* here is Cate and me. Got it?"

"Stop!" Cathleen screamed. "Leave Monsignor alone. He's

only here to help. And you're right, there is no *we*. *I* am Colm's mother. And *I* want the monsignor here. He's our family, Sean. He's the only one we've got left now to help us. If you don't like it, *you* leave. Just get the hell out of here. I can't stand to look at you right now."

Sean felt a stabbing pain in his chest. The air completely left his lungs. He felt like the wet, bloody towel he had thrown out of a window. *An embarrassment. Discarded and forgotten.* He leaned in without thinking and kissed Colm's head and then started for the door.

"That's right, Sean. When the going gets tough, the tough get drinking. Have one for me, why don't ya?" Cathleen said it quickly and drily, hoping it would cut him deep.

Sean stopped himself at the door. He wanted to slap her, but more than anything, he was embarrassed because she was right. As he left the room he never looked back.

Cathleen couldn't believe she'd said something like that in front of other people. She and Sean often argued, but not in front of Colm. Her mouth and contrary disposition always made things so difficult for her and for those around her. She knew she had no right to speak to Sean that way. Her mother's final request had been for her to take care of her brother. And hadn't Sean been so good to her these past two days? She had just gone for the jugular, and now she regretted it. From the look on Colm's face, she could tell he was as disappointed with her as she was with herself. Maybe even angry with her. He adored his uncle.

"Mama, that wasn't very nice. I wanted Uncle Sean to stay."

"I know. I was wrong, Bud."

"You should say sorry so he forgives you."

"I will. I promise."

Dr. Basu was in the hallway on his way to see the boy when he saw Sean walking briskly toward the elevator.

"Sean! Where are you off to in such a rush? How is the boy?"

"Gotta run." Sean pushed past the doctor, knocking his shoulder as he went by. He only wanted to get out of the hospital. To get away from everyone. There was a bottle of Jameson, Sean thought, and it had his name on it. The elevator door opened, but Sean turned around. "Hey, Doc!"

"Yes, Sean?" Dr. Basu headed toward him, meeting him halfway.

"Watch out for that priest. He's filling my sister's head with crap. And he's trying to convince her he can heal Colm—by praying and shit, if you know what I mean."

"Yes, he seems very, how should I say, vigilant."

"My sis has gotta be prepared for what's really going to happen. There is nothing worse, believe me, than having death sprung on you without any chance to prepare for it."

Dr. Basu nodded in agreement, remembering that awful day from long ago.

"I think your sister has been preparing for a long time to lose him. She has a bit more practice than most."

"I know, I know. But you heard him yesterday. He's giving her hope that he has no right to give."

"Hope isn't a bad thing, Sean. It will get her through the worst of it."

"But it's a lie, Doc. A lie. I thought you were a smart guy. You know as well as I do hope isn't going to save Colm."

"I think it's best not to get involved with what helps people in times like these. I have found that it is my job to fix what is broken, and do no harm. I can't control how people will react, and how they get through it."

"Keep your distance. I get it. That way you hurt less. You're a lot smarter than I thought. Takes one to know one, Doc."

"Wait, that's not what I . . ."

"No worries, Doc. Your secret's safe with me."

Sean patted Dr. Basu's shoulder and headed back toward the elevator. As the doors were about to close, he said something the doctor could barely make out.

"I've seen the way you've been looking at my sister and my nephew these past two days, Doc. You're not fooling anyone. You may think you're tough and nothing bothers you, but I see it. I know. They're getting to you. *She's* getting to you." Then the elevator doors closed and he was gone.

The doctor, unnerved by what Sean said, moved toward the boy's room and bumped into Cathleen, who'd just stepped out.

Dr. Basu looked at her and smiled. She was so beautiful. He wondered if it was as obvious to her, to everyone, as it was to Sean—how fond he was becoming of her and her boy.

❧ Part III

Make me an instrument of your peace;
where there is hatred, let me sow love;
where there is injury, pardon;
where there is doubt, faith;
where there is despair, hope;
where there is darkness, light;
and where there is sadness, joy.
O Divine Master,
grant that I may not so much seek to be consoled
*   as to console;*
to be understood, as to understand;
to be loved, as to love;
for it is in giving that we receive,
it is in pardoning that we are pardoned,
and it is in dying that we are born to Eternal
*   Life.*

—Prayer attributed to St. Francis of Assisi

Chapter 15

BY ALL COUNTS THE SURGERY HAD BEEN A SUCCESS. The boy had not died once in the entire year since Dr. Basu put in his pacemaker. Colm and his mother came in every six weeks to see the doctor, although he knew this many visits was a little excessive. Most pacemaker patients only came in every six months and could phone in their readings every three months. It could all be done remotely—saving the doctor and his patients time and money. But Dr. Basu looked forward to seeing Colm and Cathleen. It was the highlight of his day, of his life really, which had found a new purpose since the day the two had walked into his office.

But more than his personal reasons for seeing the boy and mother, the doctor was fascinated by what he observed. The boy's heart was, he thought, like that of a healthy ninety-year-old woman's—strong, but slow, barely pumping on its own, and unpredictable. No one knew when it would stop. He was surprised the boy could stand up, let alone bounce around and fidget the way he did when he was in his office. The boy was so full of energy and life. *How could he be dying?*

He had many frank conversations with Cathleen. The pacemaker was working, but he warned her he didn't know how long that would last. He reminded her to be consistent with Colm's medications, and to watch for other symptoms of distress, things the boy wouldn't naturally notice himself. Was he urinating too much during the day? Was he eating OK? Were there other signs that things might be going awry? He took careful notes and documented everything. Any of the tiniest changes or shifts in behavior or activity, he noted. Colm was a curious case. There was so much to take note of, in fact, that his receptionist started to block out an hour of time for Colm's visit. Most of that hour, Dr. Basu would spend talking with Cathleen. Not just about Colm, but about ideas and theories. "The human body is already a mystery on its best day, unfathomably complex on its worst, Cathleen," he said once to her, launching them into a discussion in which Cathleen became completely enthralled. She connected with Dr. Basu and couldn't wait to find out what he was thinking next. Like him, she wanted to understand it all. He too was determined to find some way to stop the disease from playing out. Every time he saw the two in his office, he set about looking for clues, symptoms, little revelations that might lead to some scientific breakthrough.

But Cathleen only noticed two things different about her son—his hands, usually so steady, now shook constantly. And his body, which she once thought often seemed to be on fire, had now turned cold and numb, especially his head, hands, and feet. When she went to hug him, his middle still felt hot—as if he had no ability to sweat or output heat. He seemed to contain it all. But she noticed his nose and face were freezing. "Like there is no blood in them, Mama," he would say.

He was impossible to keep comfortable. He had taken to wearing a navy blue New York Yankees hat that covered his eyebrows, ears, and most of his auburn hair, which wisped out the sides and along the nape of his neck. He had to take it off when he was at school, but as soon as he was able he put it on, day and night, everywhere he was—even in the apartment. At night when she sat on his bed watching him sleep, she took his hat off to brush his long hair away from his eyes and to feel the strands in her fingers. She could never bring herself to cut his baby curls, which had long since grown into messy, wavy strands. She always put the hat back on—to keep his head warm and to keep him from knowing she had been there. Sometimes she would pull the blankets up from the end of the bed, take his small, smooth feet in her hands, and rub them—attempting to warm them—but nothing seemed to help.

Colm's handwriting was also a mess. His teachers sent home pleasant notes asking Cathleen to work with her son on his penmanship, but he could only stop his hands from trembling by making a fist or shoving his hands into his pockets. When he built with blocks, she noticed he got frustrated when he was unable to steady his hands long enough to place one block onto another. Still he persisted in building whatever it was he set out to make.

Dr. Basu did not like these reports. Though such things were expected if the diagnosis of MSA was correct, he still didn't want to hear that they were happening. It meant that Colm's brain was taking over—winning the battle against his heart and body. He prescribed more medication to help alleviate the symptoms and monitored Colm closely for changes. He called neurologists, the world-renowned Drs. John Jager and Joseph Wilson, two of the wisest and most published men in the field of autoimmune and autonomic disorders, as well as young medical students, residents, and research assistants to review the boy's chart, hoping that one of them could offer new insights. Many of Dr. Basu's peers wanted him to publish his findings about the boy's previous collapses and revivals, but Dr. Basu refused. There was nothing to report—yet. He still had no idea what caused the boy's curious condition. *Idiopathic. No known origin,* he would say. No one could know for sure what was happening. No diagnosis seemed absolutely precise.

Colm was one of a kind.

Meanwhile, Cathleen needed a way to diminish her own nervous energy, so as always, she prayed and on Sundays, she took Colm with her to Mass. He hated going. It was a slow form of torture for him. The church was cold, and he had to take off his hat. He couldn't move or try to warm himself. He never said anything to his mother, because he knew she would make an excessive fuss—like she had before when she would use the familiar line, "If you're too sick for church, let's just stay home today. I'll call your uncle and tell him to pass on the museums, too. It's more important that you get your rest." He didn't want to miss out on going with his uncle Sean, so he knelt while he silently cursed church. *It is all so stupid,* he thought. He could have been warm, sleeping underneath his mountain of covers instead. He could have been playing with his toys, his imaginary father, doing anything else but praying.

One day after Mass the monsignor came to Cathleen in the pew, just as she was about to get up and leave.

"I have some amazing news, Cathleen! Do you have a second to sit here with me?"

"Yes . . . for a second—we're meeting Sean today after he gets off duty."

"Yes, it won't take long. I just wanted to let you know that an anonymous benefactor wants to send you, Colm, and Sean to Assisi on a pilgrimage for healing!"

Cathleen stood dumbfounded and confused.

"What?"

"You don't have to do it. Someone in the parish offered to send you. They went on the pilgrimage last year, and I told them about you and Colm—and they want to send you."

"Oh, that's awfully generous. But I don't know. I'm not sure Colm will be up for traveling." She was working through the obstacles in her mind.

"It's only a weeklong trip. You would love it, Cathleen—and so would Colm. I have heard many stories of healings at the Friary of San Damiano. Thousands of people have gone there seeking healing and have found it. I am certain that if you take Colm there, he will be transformed."

"Monsignor, this is so kind of you. But why? Why us?"

"Because, Cathleen, people are generous—and God is good. Don't think too much about it. It's a trip of a lifetime."

"Oh, Monsignor. Thank you so much. That's very kind. Let

me give this some thought. Colm's been doing well—no collapses, but you know his trembling and temperature control is a bit off."

Colm could see his mother thinking and seriously considering the trip and was waiting for her to say no.

"Yes, I have heard that anything is possible on these sorts of trips, but of course, there is no guarantee."

"Well, I have to talk to Colm's doctor, and I have to talk to Sean. I need to see what they think."

Chapter 16

DESPITE ALWAYS LOOKING FORWARD TO SEEING CATH-leen and her son, Dr. Basu was shocked when he heard his nurse say that Colm's mother was in the waiting area. The boy didn't have an appointment for another two weeks. Dr. Basu asked nervously: "Is everything all right with Colm? If there is an emergency, why didn't she take him to the ER?"

"Relax, Dr. Basu. I don't think anything is wrong with Colm. He's not even here. Cathleen's here alone. She said she is here to see *you*." The nurse winked at him, implying she knew he had a crush on the young woman. Dr. Basu, embarrassed by the nurse, pretended to ignore her and fidgeted with the files on the desk in front of him.

"Very well, then—does she look angry about anything? I don't know why she would just show up. It's not like her to come without an appointment."

"No, Dr. Basu." The nurse laughed. "I don't think she's here to complain about anything today. She seems to be in a good mood."

Over the past year, Dr. Basu and Cathleen had had their fair share of ups and downs and had not always seen eye to eye on Colm's treatment. In moments of panic or anger, she had often called demanding to speak to Dr. Basu. He would always take her call, and he was always kind and patient and ready to assuage her. However, she was never easy to convince—*Can we please put him on a beta-blocker, Cathleen? I think it would be best.* No, she'd say, armed with research she'd found on a medical website. *Have you read about these side effects, Dr. Basu? I want to make him better, not sicker. Studies are finding that these drugs are ultimately ineffective. Find something else.* He couldn't figure out why he, with his degrees and his proven track record caring for her son, had to debate her every time he wanted to change any little thing, while the monsignor had persuaded her so easily that Colm could be cured with a miracle if she just prayed. Eventually he won the battles over Colm's treatment, but he just wished she would make it easy on him. Just once.

The doctor pressed his nurse. "Did we call in the boy's prescriptions? Did we screw up his time at the pacemaker clinic?" He had heard these particular complaints before.

"I'm telling you. She's not angry. I think she even has a present in her hand."

"When it's not even my birthday or a holiday?"

"Who knows. Maybe she's just trying to be nice?"

"OK. Go get her. I'll see her in my office, please. I'll be there in a minute."

As soon as the nurse left, he went to the examining room sink and splashed cold water on his face before taking a quick look at himself in the mirror. His hair was still thick and mostly black. His skin, a golden caramel color, was smooth. Dr. Basu's face, like Cathleen's, belied his age. While Cathleen was an old twenty-eight, he was a young forty-five. On a good day, after a good night's sleep, he could even pass for being in his midthirties.

He looked over his clothes, straightened his white lab coat, and made sure his tie was straight. He stood up straighter and stretched his neck to make himself look taller. He tried to smile and show his teeth, but it seemed so unnatural, he thought it best not to smile when he saw her. He practiced. *Hello, Cathleen. What a surprise!* He grimaced. It was hopeless, he thought.

Cathleen was sitting in the chair in front of his desk already, with her back to the door, when Dr. Basu walked into the office. Her hair was swept back in a ponytail away from her face. He noticed a small, almost invisible tattoo on the back of her neck. It was odd—most tattoos he had seen were black or pigmented, but hers looked white. He had never noticed it before, even though he had seen her several times in his office with her hair swept back. As he approached her, he made out that it was indeed white, a small white dove. He tried to get a closer look as he passed her to get to his desk. When he did, she looked up and smiled. She was fiddling with a red bow that was wrapped around a rectangular golden box.

"Hello, Cathleen! What a surprise!"

"Hello, Dr. Basu. I hope I am not disturbing you."

"Nonsense, I always have time for you—and your son. Where is Little Dove?" The doctor winced as he said it. He overpronounced the *t*'s in *Little*. He hated when he did that.

"He's at school today. He's fine. He started the first grade last week."

"Wonderful! Then to what do I owe this special visit from you?"

As he spoke the words, he knew he sounded too uptight and proper—too Indian, pronouncing every syllable and emphasizing every other word in a singsongy fashion. He had tried for so long to rid himself of the accent, but it was so much a part of him. He was trying to impress her.

"I came to give you this." Cathleen slid the present across the desk.

"For me? Why? What did I do?"

"It's for all you have done for Colm . . . for me over the past year." She twisted her hands in her lap and avoided his gaze. "I know I don't make it easy, but I know you only have Colm's best interests at heart. He adores you. When I told him I wanted to get you a gift, he said he knew exactly what he wanted to get you. He saw it at the Natural History Museum gift shop and thought of you. He asked me to bring it to you as soon as possible. He was so proud of it!"

Dr. Basu ripped into the paper like a child on Christmas morning. He could not remember the last time anyone, a patient or otherwise, had given him a gift for any reason other than an organized office party.

He opened the box and pulled out a midnight-blue-colored tie. On it was the pattern of the constellation Ursa Major, which pointed to a bright white North Star. He gasped.

"What, you don't like it?" Cathleen asked.

"No, no. I love it. Why? Why did he pick this tie? For me? *How could he . . .*"

"It's because you told him your first name was Gaspar—one of the Wise Men who followed the bright star to the baby Jesus. Don't you remember our first visit?"

"Oh, why, yes. Yes. Of course that's why. Of course."

"What did you think he meant by it?"

"Oh, nothing at all. I was just surprised. It's beautiful. I love it. I'll put it on right now. I'll wear it every day, right here, close to my heart. Please tell him."

"OK, I will."

"Thank you."

"Dr. Basu?"

"Yes?"

"I have a favor to ask you."

"Whatever it is, I promise I will do it."

"But you don't even know what I am going to ask."

"I would do anything for you . . . for Colm."

Cathleen blushed. She felt guilty now for coming, for giving him the gift. Even though she meant every sentiment behind the gift, she had brought it knowing that she needed this favor from him.

"Dr. Basu, I need your opinion on something."

"About Colm?"

"Sort of. It's about a possible treatment—sort of treatment."

"What? Did you find something new you would like me to try?"

"No, the monsignor says there is a benefactor at my church who wants to send Colm and me to Assisi, Italy. There is a friary there where miracles have been said to happen. This benefactor went himself, and I guess a miracle took place. I guess the monsignor had told him about us, and he wants me to take Colm."

"I see. And what type of miracle are you looking for?"

"A complete cure, of course. No more doctors, medicine, pills, nada."

"I see." Dr. Basu closed his eyes and tried to think of the best way to say just how crazy he thought she—more aptly the monsignor—was.

"I know you must think I'm nuts. But I'm at my wit's end. I'll do anything. Anything at all for Colm, if I thought it might help. That's all. But if you think it would be dangerous to even put him on a plane and take him, then I won't. Just say the word."

"I do think it seems like an awful lot for him to go through. Traveling is exhausting, and I am not sure—it would be—how should I say this . . ."

"Worth it?"

"Yes. Worth it."

"I know. I have the same doubts, and so does Sean. In fact, Sean says the only way he would let me get on a plane with Colm was if you were on it with us. Isn't that funny?" Cathleen giggled and looked at Dr. Basu to read his reaction.

Dr. Basu was totally taken aback. He barely knew the woman or her son. Yes, he had spent time with them and come to know them through their visits to the office and hospital, but could he be hearing her correctly? Was she asking him to go on a pilgrimage—for all intents and purposes, a vacation—with her?

"I know it sounds crazy, I can tell by how you're looking at me," Cathleen said as she began to ramble. "But, you see, Colm can be completely cured. I have been praying for a miracle—for some time. But I am not crazy. I know I have to be responsible, too. I need to have a doctor with me, just in case something terrible were to happen on the plane or what have you . . . I know it's a lot to ask, but would you please, please consider it?"

Dr. Basu could barely contain what he was thinking any longer.

"Why, Cathleen, this is all ludicrous!" Dr. Basu couldn't believe he said it.

Cathleen stiffened and immediately started for her purse. "I'm sorry, Dr. Basu. I made a terrible mistake. I knew you wouldn't understand."

"No, *I'm* sorry. I didn't mean to offend you—or your beliefs. I want to understand. I do. I just don't know if I am the right, or the best, person to help you. What is it exactly you want me to do?" Dr. Basu didn't really want her to go on, but he didn't want her to leave, either.

Cathleen hesitated and then started to explain. "I'm grateful for all you have done, Dr. Basu. Truly. But I can't help but wonder whether there is something else out there. Something else we ought to try. Colm is an angel. He's special. I know most moms say that or feel that. But I mean it. I always thought that, from the first moment I held him. What if he knows something we don't? And I have been thinking about this for a while—ever since that day in the hospital when the monsignor was reading Colm his last rites and he woke up. We all thought he was brain-dead— you did too—but the monsignor prayed over him, and wham-o, Colm woke up. And then I got to thinking. Every time Colm collapsed before that time I just started to pray. I'd pray like crazy, and he eventually just woke up. So I have to believe that maybe, just maybe, a miracle is not out of the question."

Dr. Basu sat silently listening to her as she went on. He knew every mother felt her child was an angel without wings—a miracle with messy hair, scratched knees, and dirty fingernails. He knew every mother would be willing to believe anything or do anything if it meant saving her child. So even though he could not believe what he was about to say, and every fiber in his being knew that it was a lie, he admired and understood her enough to say it anyway.

"You could be right. I will go. I'd go anywhere with you for the boy. If it means that much to you, I will go. I will begin to make arrangements."

"Oh, Dr. Basu, that's wonderful! And you don't have to worry about money. Monsignor says the benefactor has plenty."

"So this benefactor—what does he get out of this?"

"What do you mean?"

"I am just curious. Why would an anonymous person spend a lot of money to help some people he barely knows—and to pay for someone who doesn't even believe in the same things he does?"

"I guess, the same reason you're a doctor."

"Excuse me?"

"What do you get out of healing, fixing, and treating people day in and day out?"

"For one, doctors get paychecks."

"Yes, but so do I. Why do you get your paycheck by saving other people's lives?"

"Because, I suppose, it makes me feel good. Like I have a purpose."

Cathleen smiled. "See."

"See what?"

"You understand what a benefactor is."

"I do?"

"Yes. A benefactor just wants to do good—just to be good. Someday I'll pay whoever this person is back—tenfold. I believe that. And I think this person has enough faith in me to know that I will, but he doesn't expect it. That's what the monsignor says."

"Do you think this anonymous benefactor is the monsignor, Cathleen?"

"No. Oh, I don't know." Cathleen squirmed. It hadn't occurred to her. But it made a lot of sense now. "Even if it was him, he obviously doesn't want me to know, and he wants Colm to get better. He wants that for me."

"I know, Cathleen. I know." Dr. Basu nodded with his eyes closed. He could hear her desperation.

If nothing else, Dr. Basu's intellectual curiosity was piqued. What was this magical place where people could be healed? More than anything, he worried about Colm. His mother was not thinking straight. She was so determined to cure him she was willing to try anything—believe anything. He had seen it all before. He had done it himself at one time. He didn't want anything to happen to Colm. He knew someone with common sense had to be standing beside him. More over, he knew Colm would not be happy about any of this.

In her excitement at his acceptance, Cathleen went on, "Thank you so much. I am sure it will thrill Colm to know you'll be with us."

"Will your brother come?"

"I'm working on it."

"Oh, so he hasn't agreed yet? Why not? I thought you were all so close—and the boy is so fond of him."

"Colm is. It's just that we, Sean and I, disagree about some

things. He doesn't believe in all of this. I mean he goes to church.
Don't get me wrong. I just think he's employing Pascal's wager . . .
hedging his bets. Besides, I don't see him much now. He comes
over sometimes to see Colm and take him out on day trips, but
things are different between us."

"That's too bad, Cathleen."

"You'd think, because of my faith, I should love everybody.
I should love people no matter what they think or believe, even
if they think differently. But it's hard sometimes to be in the
same room with someone who doesn't think like you or feel like
you or see the world the same way you do. *Even if they're family.*
Sean just doesn't get it. He has issues with the church—some of
the people running it—with God, with everybody. Besides, he's
already been to Italy."

"Really?"

"He went there right after he left college, after our mom
died. I thought he was going to pursue his vocation at the North
American College. That's what he told me anyway when I wrote
out the check for his airfare."

"Excuse me?"

"His vocation. When he was a freshman in college, he thought
he was called by God to become a priest."

"What did he do instead?"

"Drink . . . mostly . . . from what I gathered. And he's at it
again. Seeing Colm collapse was hard on him, and of course,
there was our fight. I said some hurtful things to him that day."

"Now you can't blame something like that on yourself. He has
to take some responsibility for how he behaves. Has he always
been a drinker—even before Italy?"

"He definitely had his moments. I guess, thinking back, it really all started in high school—even before my mom died. He was always the starry-eyed type. You know—with his head in the clouds. Literally. He wanted to join the navy, become a Blue Angel. Then 9/11 hit, and something changed in him. I don't know what. I think it sort of sunk in that joining the military was more than flying fast planes and going to far-off places. I don't think he was afraid for himself; I just think he didn't want to hurt my mom or cause her worry."

"Did you ever ask him why he made such a decision?"

"Oh, sure. We talked about it one day shortly after. I told him it was very brave of him—to give up his dreams for our mother. But he shrugged it off."

"From what little I know of your brother that doesn't surprise me. But how does one go from wanting to join the military to being called by God—and then a firefighter? Seems like an unlikely progression."

"When the military fell through, he decided on college—one that would make my mother happy, of course, and one the monsignor could help him get scholarships to—the Catholic University. We were all so proud of him, but he was so ashamed. He kept comparing himself to all of his friends, especially the ones who chose to sign up for the military right after graduation. I remember the first time I ever saw him drunk was after a buddy of his told him that he had enlisted."

"So he went to this Catholic University and that's where he was called by God, as you say?"

"Yes, he even called our mom shortly before she died to tell her that he wanted to be a priest. Then after Mom passed away, he dropped out of school. Took off for Italy shortly after, and that was the end of the Sean I knew as a boy. When he came back home, he was so cynical. So mistrustful. So full of anger. He was drunk all the time, but I got him in treatment and he was OK for a while—long enough to get selected to go to the Fire Academy. But I can tell he's back at it."

"Have you talked to him about it?"

"No. Every time we try, we end up fighting. He tells me I'm brainwashed, and I call him a drunk. It never ends well."

"Well, are you brainwashed? You seem to have good reason to call him a drunk; does he have good reason to think you are brainwashed?"

"No. I'm not excluding any possibilities—that's all. Maybe Saints Francis and Clare in Assisi can heal Colm. Maybe you could. I don't care who does. I just want Colm to get better."

"I know why you want Colm to be better. I understand that. You are his mother. But I must ask you, why does the monsignor care so much? Aren't you the least bit skeptical about why he seems so eager for you to drag Colm to Italy? I just don't follow. I don't know what he gets out of all this."

"You sound like my brother now."

"I am sorry, Cathleen. I don't mean to upset you. I am just having trouble understanding all this. These customs are, how shall I say, *new* to me. And I tend to side a bit with Sean, to be honest with you. Sean seems to be a grounded young man, his drinking notwithstanding. Most important, he seems to have your and Colm's best interests at heart. And don't you think he's just being cautious for your sake?"

"Are you saying now you don't want to help?"

"No, Cathleen. I want to help you. But I just need you to help me understand this. I have told you, Colm is ill. There is no cure for his disease, and no known cause or reason for his long collapses. I just don't want you setting yourself up for disappointment or worse. I don't want you giving up on medicine altogether because the monsignor convinces you that miracles are the answer to Colm's disease."

"Dr. Basu, I'm trying to trust both of you. Like Sean, I have to cover all my bets. Like I said, I have to do whatever it takes. And to answer your question about the monsignor, I don't think he has an agenda. He doesn't. He just wants to help me—and my son. I think he believes more than anyone I know in the power of prayer and God. In my eyes, he is the saint. He's just a selfless person who wants to help me and Colm."

Dr. Basu closed his eyes and nodded. Cathleen thought he was agreeing with her—that indeed the monsignor was a saintly man who wanted only to help her and Colm. But Dr. Basu was not nodding in agreement with Cathleen. He was reassuring himself that yes, he had to go to Italy, now more than ever. Someone had to look out for them both. Someone had to protect them. Yes, from the sound of things, Dr. Basu could tell that Cathleen would need someone she could trust; and Colm would need a doctor, not a miracle, in Italy.

Chapter 17

ALTHOUGH CATHLEEN HAD NEVER LEFT THE COUNTRY before, she had never considered herself unprepared for the excitement and promise of travel. Over the years her brother had explained much of what he saw in Europe in exact detail. Besides, she was a design major. She had spent hours studying with professors, experts, and peers in the field of interior design, architecture, and fine art. She was well read and knew her fair share of history—American, world, church, and otherwise. She thought, like most New Yorkers did, that there were few surprises, barring her son's illness, left for her in the world. Her worldview was not unlike the famous Saul Steinberg iconic illustration that showed a map of the United States, which the artist drew from the perspective of an onlooker in an apartment facing the Hudson River—everything beyond it seemed small and insignificant compared to the colossal New York, the most important city in the world. The print hung over her makeshift bookshelf and the infinite stacks of books in her bedroom. As far as she was concerned life really didn't even exist much beyond her beloved city.

She was actually a bit disappointed when she landed in Rome. The airport, a drab, outdated building with low ceilings and grungy floors, reminded her more of Port Authority than of an international airport. Cathleen was the farthest from home she had ever been, and she wasn't sure it was the best place to be.

As soon as they gathered their luggage, she, Dr. Basu, and Colm climbed into a small minivan that the pilgrimage leader, Brother Rocco, had arranged for their trip to Assisi. When she handed her luggage over to the cabdriver, Massimo, he kept staring at her, and calling her *Bella, Bella, Bella,* in a rich Italian accent that sounded like someone was turning the dial up on the volume every time he ended a word with a vowel—which in Italian was every other word. Cathleen, exhausted from the long flight, could barely muster a *grazie.*

"Something better make this trip worthwhile," she said.

During the past ten hours, she had had a hard time rationalizing the trip. Perhaps her brother had been right. *This was crazy.* The trip had already proved exhausting for her and Colm. He froze on the airplane. He was uncomfortable, and he complained that his pacemaker was kicking in too much and making his heart beat fast. Dr. Basu monitored him and confirmed what the boy had said—his heart was beating well over a hundred beats per minute, leaving him breathless and tired. He couldn't sleep, couldn't rest. He climbed, fidgeted, pulled, and prodded. Cathleen felt for him, but she was tired too. It was all she could do to keep awake, let alone keep Colm quiet and comfortable. She kept chanting to herself: *This is going to be worth it. It has to be*. Meanwhile, Colm wanted only one thing: to go home to his room, to his toys and his imaginary father. The farther he got from New York, the farther he felt from him and the prospect of ever finding him. He worried that while he and his mother were gone, his father might show up at their apartment, and he would miss him.

As the car weaved its way through the countryside, the hot afternoon sun poured through the back window. The boy, finally comfortable, snuggled up to his mother, and the two of them fell asleep. Dr. Basu was relieved to see them finally at rest and sat back himself to enjoy the view. Two hours later, Dr. Basu whispered to Cathleen and Colm, "You have to see this."

Cathleen and Colm rubbed their eyes, uncertain of what they were looking at. They saw what appeared to be a shimmering, pink medieval castle nestled inside a long hillside. As they drove closer, cutting through the olive groves and vineyards that lined the Spoleto Valley, the magical kingdom revealed itself to be a small, intricate town hewn of a rough, rosy stone. The outlines of individual homes with shuttered windows and window boxes filled with cascading geraniums and honeysuckle appeared before them. A large fortress wall surrounded it all, and two colossal churches acted like bookends holding up the entire city. It all overlooked an endless stream of olive groves and grape vineyards that spread across the valley below.

His voice still cracking from sleep, Colm asked Cathleen, "Where are we? Is this heaven?" He thought quietly to himself, but only briefly, *Have I finally made it? Perhaps there is such a place.*

Cathleen looked out the window and said, "No, Bud. But we're close. We're in Assisi."

Massimo sped up the narrow road that led to the crest of Assisi, forcing Cathleen to grip the door handles as the car wound around steep cliffs. When they reached the tallest point of the hill, the paved road ended and they began to descend the narrow, cobblestone streets toward the town center. Pedestrians barely flinched as the large minivan whizzed past them. Cathleen began to feel sick to her stomach, but Colm's eyes were wide with excitement. It was the most fun he had had since he went on the rides at Coney Island with his uncle Sean and his mama the summer before they stopped taking him on field trips together. Suddenly Massimo hit the brakes. They all lunged forward. Massimo shouted, *"Eccoci qua!"*

"Here we are," Massimo said again in English.

"Where? Here? This is it?" All Cathleen saw were white doors in a tall four-story stone building. There were no signs above the door, only a small cornerstone engraving that said: *Casa Papa Gianpaolo.*

"This is where we'll stay. It's the *pensione.* Some nuns—Franciscan sisters—run it, and the attached bookstore is for pilgrims and those who come to be healed," the pilgrimage leader explained. "They have everything you'll need—beds, baths, and a chapel to pray in. You'll love it."

Cathleen didn't want to seem ungrateful. She could never have made it here if she'd had to pay for it herself, but she was dying to lie on a comfortable bed, take a hot shower, and relax. When she heard the words *nuns* and *chapel,* she wanted to get back in the van. Though she knew in advance that this was part of the package, suddenly it all seemed too much, even for her. She couldn't imagine what Dr. Basu was thinking or what Colm must be feeling. Even though she was there to receive God's blessings and save her son, she really didn't want any part of the overzealous religious piety that went along with it. Her old internal battles, the ones of her youth, were starting to flare up; and she was beginning to doubt her decision with each passing moment.

At the door Brother Rocco and the nun embraced and spoke for several minutes in Italian as they walked together into a small room where the nun kept the keys to the rooms. While they were gone Cathleen, Dr. Basu, and Colm explored the small, unadorned chapel to the right of the entrance and the bookstore filled with books, postcards, and Franciscan ornaments and trinkets—tau crosses, rosary beads, golden crucifixes, and ceramic statues. *The complete Catholic kitsch works*, Cathleen thought. She was grateful Sean wasn't here to say something cutting.

While he waited Colm began to feel weaker than ever. He didn't want to admit to his mother how exhausted and hungry he was, how badly he wanted to get to his room.

A small nun handed Dr. Basu and Cathleen the keys to their rooms, then led them up the smooth, worn marble stairs. After four flights with two suitcases in tow, Cathleen was not expecting much of the room.

In the hallway, the nun reminded them that they were all welcome to join the rest of the sisters for dinner in the dining room if they weren't too tired. Dr. Basu agreed to meet them, and Cathleen looked at Colm to see if he was up for it.

"Are you hungry, Bud?"

"I'm starving," he said weakly.

"We'll see you in a couple of hours then. I think we'll just take a little rest."

After Dr. Basu disappeared, Cathleen found her room and opened the door slowly. And for the first time all day she was thrilled she had come. Before her was a large, open window that spanned half the width of the far wall. The shutters were wide open and before her was the entire valley—she could see the golden afternoon sky in all directions, and the small red-roofed villas, groves, and vineyards below. She could smell the honeysuckle that grew up the side of the building and wafted in with the warm breeze. But her moment of peace lasted just a second. Colm climbed up on the desk that was pushed up in front of window and leaned out.

"Hey, Mama, look how high up we are!"

"Colm! JesusMaryandJoseph!" Cathleen screamed.

Colm knew better. "Sorry, Mama. I didn't mean to scare you. It's just so cool here."

"I didn't fly all the way to Italy to have you fly out of a window, Bud. Got it?"

"Yes, Mama." Colm hopped off the desk and spread his body across the bed.

After Cathleen unpacked, she drew Colm a bath. She turned the water on as hot as she could get it without burning him. He took off his clothes, not quite embarrassed yet of his nakedness in front of her. She knew the time would come when he would not want her nearby, but until then she relished washing his long hair, running her fingers through it and lathering the soap. Colm loved feeling his mother's nails gently scratch and massage his head, so he closed his eyes and held his head back, leaning into her. After he washed himself, she asked him to stand up so she could rinse him. She marveled at how he had the same long, angular body as his father. He was cut exactly in his image. His hands, his feet, the curve of his back—she recognized it all. She stood up over the boy and poured the water over his head and body.

While she looked for a towel he stood in the bathtub shaking. He was trembling uncontrollably, his body already cold. She took the large white towel she had found in the wardrobe and wrapped him up tightly. He would be seven that December, just three months away. But she could still—like she had done when he was a baby, a toddler, a preschooler—swaddle him like a newborn and carry him over to the bed.

By the time she reached the bed, Colm's eyes were closed.

For a split second Cathleen thought he wasn't breathing, but before she could panic, she heard a deep sigh and saw his chest rise and fall gently.

He had fallen asleep again. She pressed her head to his and inhaled deeply. She could smell the lavender from the handmade Assisi soap and the mint from the shampoo. She thought of dressing him while he slept and putting him in the bed. But she didn't want to disturb him. Instead, she positioned herself on her bed—pushing her back up against the pillows and the wall—and held the boy. She could not explain what came over her, but she began to sing "Mo Chuisle" in her mother's Gaelic and remembered the time she asked her mother what it meant. Her mother had responded in her quiet, lilting brogue, *A chuisle mo chroí, pulse of me heart, dear, pulse of me heart.* Cathleen sang it softly to the sleeping boy, mimicking her mother's accent, just as she had when Colm was an infant—back before it all began, back before she had any idea, any real concept of how difficult and unpredictable life could really be as a mother.

As she sang, she tried to remember the last time she had done such a thing. Mothers can never know the last time they will rock their children to sleep, sing them a final lullaby, pick them up and carry them on their hips, or even bathe them, she thought. Babies grow into children without notice. They grow out of such habits without mention, without mourning their passing or loss. No one ever seems to remember the last times. *It is a good thing a mother doesn't remember, doesn't know when she is holding her child that it will be the last time,* she thought. She knew she wouldn't know how to let him go.

Down the hall, in his own quiet room, Dr. Basu had also admired the view, showered, and freshened up. But instead of making him sleepy, the shower had woken him up, and he decided to explore the beautiful village. He knew he had promised to have dinner with Cathleen and Colm, so he only went out to the piazza, which was just a short walk from the hotel. Scores of tourists sat under umbrellas in the outdoor cafés while children ran and chased each other around the large fountain in the center. He gazed at the cloudless late-afternoon sky before stopping for a moment and closing his eyes. He tried to listen to everything, the murmur of conversations in various languages, mostly Italian, the water cascading out of the font, the soft patter of small children running past him, the *whoosh* made by the wings of birds flapping as they took off and landed on the fountain ridge. He kept his eyes closed, feeling the sun upon his face, and he tried to remember a time like this when all the world seemed at once perfect, beautiful, and alive. When he was finished, he turned away from the crowds and walked briskly up the steep hills that wrapped around the ancient buildings until he found himself back at the doorway of the *pensione*. After greeting the nun at the front desk, he made his way to the dining room, where he saw Brother Rocco and a nun eating. Dr. Basu tried to hide his disappointment that Cathleen and Colm were not there and that he would have to eat alone with the strangers.

"Hello. Just went for a quick walk. Did I miss dinner? Where are Colm and Cathleen?"

"We've been waiting here for a while and haven't seen them. Perhaps they retired early. They must be exhausted. Here, sit with us, Dr. Basu. We promise to be good company," the pilgrimage leader said as he lifted a glass of red wine up toward Dr. Basu as if to toast him.

"That's kind of you," Dr. Basu said. "But would you mind if I just went upstairs and checked on them first, just in case?" Dr. Basu knew how physically drained he felt after stepping off the plane, so he could only imagine how the boy was feeling in his weak condition now.

Dr. Basu left and ran up the wide marble steps, two at a time. When he reached Cathleen and Colm's room he stopped. Through the door, he heard Cathleen's voice, softly singing a foreign, ancient-sounding song.

He stood for a moment, trying hard not to breathe or make a sound. His head fell softly against the door to listen closely. With every note, he fell deeper and deeper into the past until Cathleen's voice became his own Niranjana's. It did not seem so long ago that he had heard his wife sing as he held his child in his arms, their chests touching, and feeling the rhythmic thump and pulse of each other's hearts.

❧ Chapter 18

B Y HER SECOND DAY IN ASSISI, CATHLEEN HAD BEEN
lulled into a state of serenity she hadn't experienced
since she was a child. She could not remember a single
time in her adult life when she had been able to relax—when she
hadn't had to worry about her mother, her brother, or her son.
She often wondered what it would be like to be so carefree, so
utterly adrift, to *never ever* have to think about what someone
else needed. In the twelve hours she had spent in Assisi, most of
it asleep, she had had a glimpse of what it must be like to completely let go of life's cares.

She and Colm could have taken their time waking up with
no schedule other than the loose itinerary of church sightseeing
that Brother Rocco had given her upon their arrival, but she
was too excited. She had left the shutters open the night before,
but she still hadn't woken even once during the night, so when
the bright sun shone through at dawn, Cathleen was stunned.
The light was nearly blinding. When she jumped out of bed, she

tripped trying to get to the shutters to close them. But when she reached the window, she stopped. The entire valley glistened below the sun. She felt an overwhelming desire to leave the room and head toward that magnificent light. For the first time in more than six years, she felt full of hope and pregnant with possibility.

Colm had been woken by the light too, so Cathleen asked him if he was up for a walk with her to the piazza for a café Americano for her and a brioche—maybe even with chocolate—for him. Colm leaped up. Realizing he was still in a towel, he laughed. They quickly dressed, brushed their teeth together at the sink, and practically ran down the stairs. It had been years since she felt that free and spontaneous. She pretended to tackle him when they jumped out onto street, and she nuzzled his neck. Colm loved her in Assisi.

As they ran toward the piazza, Colm grabbed his mother's hand to get her attention. Cathleen slowed, worried that something was wrong. But he said, "Look, Mama!" He pointed out a nun on a Vespa, her long gray habit flowing behind her as she passed.

"A nun on a motorcycle! Can they do that, Mama?"

"I guess so!" Cathleen said as she laughed. It seemed like such a funny, improbable thing. But then again, Cathleen was hoping that Italy was full of the impossible.

She was counting on it.

In the piazza, old women were coming from their morning Masses from all directions. Assisi was small, but it had fourteen churches in the village and surrounding areas, not to mention the tiny chapels and hidden altars throughout the city. Natives, tourists, and pilgrims already filled the café chairs. In one of the chairs, sipping a small cup of espresso, Dr. Basu sat all alone, admiring the ornate fountain, once an old well for drinking, now a birdbath.

Colm spotted him immediately and ran to him. Dr. Basu saw the boy coming. He kneeled down and opened his arms wide to accept him. As they embraced, the doctor stood and lifted Colm's feet off the ground. For a second, and only a second, Dr. Basu forgot that Dhruv was gone. For one ephemeral moment, he remembered with his entire body what it was like to be something other than Dr. Basu. For a moment, he was *Papa*. And then Cathleen spoke, breaking the dream.

"Dr. Basu! What a wonderful surprise. You're up early today."

"Yes. I couldn't sleep. It's so bright here, no?"

"I'm so sorry about dinner last night. Did we miss anything? We didn't mean to stand you up."

"No problem. You needed your rest. Can I get you something?"

"Some brioches would be wonderful—and a coffee, please, for me and juice for Colm."

"Whatever you wish," Dr. Basu said, smiling and moving toward the counter.

Colm and Cathleen settled into their chairs. On the table was a small gift book about the life of St. Francis.

"Is he reading this, Mama?"

"Yes, I imagine he is. He's probably trying to figure out why the heck we've come all this way."

Colm stared pointedly at his mother. "Why have we, Mama? Exactly?"

"To fix you. You know that."

"But how does coming here make me better? I thought Dr. Basu was doing that."

Cathleen wondered how best to answer her boy. How could she explain such mysteries to a child who, she thought, understood so little of the world?

Dr. Basu came back with the coffee and brioches.

"Thank you!" both Cathleen and Colm said in unison.

"Doing some reading?" Cathleen asked, as she lifted up the book.

"I like to do my research, I suppose. I have not read of any miracles attributed to Francis yet. Where is it in the story that he heals the sick?"

"Have you reached the part of the book where Francis feels like he has been called by God—to go and rebuild his church?" Cathleen asked.

"Yes, but there is no building yet. Right now in the story, he seems to be preoccupied with irritating his poor father, embarrassing him, and publicly denouncing him," Dr. Basu responded.

"Yes, he and his father had some problems," Cathleen admitted.

Cathleen continued the story for Colm and Dr. Basu.

"Francis sells all that he has. He even steals some of his father's things to sell and begins to beg for money so that he can buy enough stones to build the church of San Damiano. He did it right here on these streets, where we are sitting right now. This city, this piazza, is exactly, stones and all, like it was when St. Francis was alive eight hundred years ago. But eventually Francis figured out it wasn't San Damiano that he had to rebuild—it was the entire church—the world really. He spent the rest of his life teaching people how to pray, and be peaceful, kind, and good to everyone, especially the lepers, and others who were too poor or ill to care for themselves."

"He's sounds cool," Colm said, licking the chocolate from his fingers.

"He was—that's why you have his middle name, too," Cathleen said as Dr. Basu and Colm smiled at each other.

"I get it," Colm said.

Dr. Basu listened as Cathleen talked to the boy. She was a wonderful mother, he thought. She would have traveled to the far ends of the earth to save her boy. She protected him fearlessly, mightily, but she was, above all, his teacher and his friend.

"But what happened at the church? Why do people think miracles happen there?" Colm asked.

"We're going there today, I think. First we'll go see St. Clare, Francis's friend, for ourselves."

"She's still alive?" Dr. Basu asked in disbelief. "I'd like to see that," he said drily, knowing full well of its improbability.

"Her remains are under her cathedral—Santa Chiara. You can see her body, clothes, and even her hair."

"Ewww." Colm made a long, tortured face, though he was morbidly curious like most young boys.

"When she became a follower of Francis, she cut all of her hair off, as a sign of devotion, a sacrifice, a *tonsure*, they call it."

"Really?" Dr. Basu said. "Fascinating."

"That's what the sisters, the abbesses, did back then," Cathleen added.

"Colm, did you know that in India, women and men cut their hair as a sacrifice to the gods too?" Dr. Basu asked.

Colm shook his head. He did not.

"See, Dr. Basu, we are more alike than you think," Cathleen said with a wink. "St. Clare took care of many sick people and performed several miracles herself at San Damiano. Now people from all over the world like to go to the room in the friary where she lived. It's there that priests try to heal people. They use a special oil and prayer. Brother Rocco will bless you there today."

"If Clare and Francis were so good to the poor and sick people, why did they have to perform miracles, too? Wasn't it good enough for people that they were nice? That they took care of them when no one else would? Isn't that special enough?" Colm asked his mother.

Dr. Basu's eyes widened and he said, "Dove, you are a wise little boy."

Chapter 19

IN THE CHURCH OF SANTA CHIARA, CATHLEEN, DR. Basu, and Colm meandered through the building and walked down the stairs to the museum portion. Quite unexpectedly, they walked right up to a nondescript wall and peeked behind it, thinking they were about to see some more of Clare's clothing or her hair, when suddenly they found themselves staring at the corpse of St. Clare, which was sealed behind glass. Cathleen rushed to grab Colm and turn him away. She didn't plan on actually taking him to see the body of Clare. But Colm fought her off. He wanted to see for himself what all this saint stuff was about.

"Is she really in there? Is that really her?" Colm asked.

"Yes, let's go. We don't have to look at this. Come on. It's silly."

"But I want to. I want to know if that is really her. Is that what people look like when they are dead?"

"It's what is left of her, Colm—her clothes, her bones. That clay mask over her face preserves her. But it's not real. She was thought to be *incorruptible*. That means her body never decayed, or broke down, Colm. But it has since. When a body dies, it is supposed to return to the earth. But a lot of saints' bodies don't decay. And a lot of saints are exposed like this so people can see them. But that's not what's important. What's important is that St. Clare's soul is up in heaven with the other angels," Cathleen explained.

Colm cocked his head. He was doubtful. "This is sort of gross, Mama."

"Yes, it is," she agreed. "Now let's get out of here."

"Why do they hold on to the bodies if they believe the soul is up in heaven?"

Dr. Basu stood quietly, waiting to hear Cathleen's answer.

Cathleen knew the answer, of course, and she could imagine what her brother would have said on the matter. She had heard it all before. *Follow the money, Sis. There is a whole reason behind the hubbub in Rome, in all of Europe, and it all has the faint whiff of cash. I saw it for myself.* She knew that in the Middle Ages, relics were a huge commodity. With relics came visitors, and with visitors came money, lots of it. Thanks to those relics, Assisi still stood magnificent, well cared for, and visited by millions eight centuries after Francis and Clare had lived.

"I don't know, Bud," she lied. "I guess people still want to hold on to the dead. Want to see the miracles for themselves, just like we do."

Colm stared at the dead body of Clare for a long time. He wondered what he would look like when he was dead, when he was on the other side where it was all black and lonely. He hoped no one would take his body and put it in a glass room for people to look at. He didn't want to scare anyone. He especially didn't want to scare his mother anymore. He hoped his mother could get her wish, that he would live forever—never die, decay, end up like Clare. He knew what was waiting for him on the other side of that glass. He wanted to stay here on Earth, with his mother, his uncle Sean, and now his friend Dr. Basu, and someday with his father.

Dr. Basu and Cathleen began to move on, looking at pictures of little children tucked into the grates along the wall by parents who also left with prayers and petitions to save their lives. Cathleen wondered how many Clare had helped to save and how many mothers went home to bury their children.

When Cathleen looked up, Colm wasn't with her, but she found him still staring at the dead Clare.

"You all right, Bud? You feeling OK?"

"Mama?"

"Yes?"

"Don't put me behind glass."

"What?"

"When I die. Don't put me all alone in a glass room. I don't want people to see me dead."

"Colm, stop it. You're not going to die."

"You don't know that. You don't!"

"Colm, oh baby, I am sorry. I shouldn't have brought you down here."

"That's why we're here, right? Because you think I'm going to die? What if it doesn't work, Mama? What if-what if-what if-I end up . . . like her?" Colm pointed at the corpse, and Cathleen gasped. She reached for him and pulled him close, burying his face in her stomach. He knew so much more than she ever imagined he did. He was so wise, and it was pointless for her to hide any longer how scared she was—to pretend she didn't know how terrified he must be.

He sobbed, and Cathleen was ashamed of herself. In her attempts to heal him, to help him grow old and be with her for all time, she had forgotten he was just a little boy.

Dr. Basu watched as Colm cried in his mother's arms. He wanted to reach out, to envelop them both and promise them that he could make it all better, but he could not. He knew well that he, of all people, did not have the power to heal Colm completely. He went toward the stairs that led to the chapel where they were all supposed to meet Brother Rocco.

Brother Rocco had been waiting upstairs in a side chapel of the upper church, pacing in front of the famous San Damiano Cross.

When Cathleen reached the nave, a nun ran over to her shouting in Italian and waving her arms wildly. Cathleen was shocked, and Colm shrank against his mother as the nun closed in, making a fist and speaking rapidly.

Brother Rocco suddenly left the visitors and rushed over to Cathleen, shouting, "A shawl! A shawl, Cathleen! You need to cover your shoulders!"

"I'm so sorry!" She took the sweater that she had wrapped around her waist and slipped it over her arms.

"Of all the things to get worked up about," Cathleen said exasperatedly. "Isn't Jesus up on that cross naked? And we women have to cover our shoulders?" she asked the nun, pointing to the cross. The nun had no idea what Cathleen had said in English and walked away from her making the sign of the cross as if praying for Cathleen's immortal soul.

Colm laughed at what his mother had said. He laughed even though his face was still wet and red. He had never seen his mother reprimanded like that before or his mother say anything so funny about Jesus—about anything holy. For a second, he forgot about the dead body in the room underneath them and about why they were there.

The guide apologized in Italian and glared at Cathleen. "I have brought you here first, because I thought it best for all of us to say a prayer—to get us in the right frame of mind. I wanted you to see the beauty of this special cross that hangs above us here. I wanted you to see what Francis and Clare saw. I want you all to pray for Colm. God will hear you. God is here with us today. Prepare your hearts for Colm to be healed."

Cathleen composed herself, remembering why she had traveled all this way. As she entered the pew, faith filled her, chasing out any doubts brought on by the long journey. And she quickly pulled down the kneeler and began to pray. Colm sat down right next to Dr. Basu, inviting the doctor to wrap his arm around Colm's shoulders. They stayed together quietly, watching his mother pray to the God Colm and Dr. Basu didn't believe was listening.

Later that afternoon, after lunch and *reposo*, Cathleen, Dr. Basu, and Colm followed their guide down a long hill and staircase leading to the Friary of San Damiano. It was exhausting for Cathleen and Dr. Basu; they couldn't imagine what it was doing to Colm.

They noticed Colm trailing farther and farther behind them. Dr. Basu turned back, taking the long steps—two at a time in certain places—reaching the boy and lifting him up on his shoulders. Colm hung over the doctor's head, and Dr. Basu grabbled the boy's ankles to support him and hold him as they descended the long staircase. Cathleen turned and saw what the doctor had done.

"Thank you, Dr. Basu. Do you think he's going to be OK?"

"He's very tired, Cathleen. Do you think this is really necessary?" Dr. Basu asked in a concerned voice.

Colm groaned a little. He was so tired, he could barely muster the energy to say thank you or even complain.

"We'll be there shortly, Cathleen," the guide assured. "I promise you, it will be worth it."

When they arrived at the friary, the guide spent a long time explaining the history and significance of the place as well as all the miracles attributed to it. Meanwhile, pilgrims and visitors filed past into the friary where the sisters of St. Clare had once lived.

Dr. Basu could feel the boy's weight much more on his shoulders. He was tired, but he could tell the boy was growing heavier with exhaustion, so he didn't want to put him down.

The doctor finally spoke up. "Do you think we could go in now, perhaps take the boy out of the sun?"

"Oh, yes, of course. I got so wrapped up! I'm sorry."

Dr. Basu took the boy off his shoulders, and they entered the friary. They were all relieved to be in the shade of the cool building. It was dark, and Colm grew frightened and clung to Dr. Basu's leg. Dr. Basu reached down for him again and hoisted him up on his hip. The boy rested his head on the doctor's shoulder, as a baby would, and the doctor could feel the warmth of his cheek and hot breath on his own neck.

The guide led the way up the narrow staircase, and Cathleen followed close behind. The doctor and Colm fell behind considerably, as other visitors who were much faster passed them in their haste to get out of the dark, tight passageway. By the time Dr. Basu and Colm arrived upstairs, Cathleen and the guide were already waiting in the upper room where, the guide explained, Clare herself had died.

The room was filled with other pilgrims and their accompanying guides; some were priests and some, like Cathleen and Colm's guide, were Franciscan brothers dressed in their gray, black, or brown habits. Brother Rocco signaled to Colm, Cathleen, and Dr. Basu to move toward the middle of the room and announced: "Here is a good place. I feel positive energy from St. Clare. We will do it here."

Cathleen stood upright; she was so excited. This was it. This could be it for them. If this worked, Colm could be healed and everything in her life, in his, would be different, she thought.

The guide pulled out a vial of oil he had in his pocket. He spoke to Colm directly.

"Are you ready? Have you opened yourself to the healing power of Christ?"

Colm looked at the doctor and his mother. Although he knew this couldn't possibly work, he wanted something to happen. He did not want to end up like Clare.

His mother urged him on. "Go on, Colm. Say yes."

"Yes, I guess."

"Good, my boy."

Brother Rocco rubbed the oil on his thumb and asked them to bow their heads, then kneeled down in front of the boy and made the sign of the cross with the oil on the boy's forehead and chest. He chanted:

> *Here in this most sacred space may you know the heal-*
> *ing power of the crucified Jesus through the intercession*
> *of the Lady Clare.*

Then Brother Rocco said, "Now all of you join me in saying the Lord's Prayer."

The four joined hands. Dr. Basu did not know the words, so he stood silently as the other three prayed the Our Father. When they were finished, the guide spoke a long prayer that he said St. Clare wrote about gazing upon, considering, and imitating God. Finally the friar said,

> *In the Book of Life, your name shall be called glorious*
> *Among all people.*
> *Now go in peace, knowing you are loved and healed.*

When he stopped speaking, they broke the circle with their hands. "Now what?" Colm asked, looking up at his mother.

"Now we wait," Cathleen said, patting him on the back.

"Wait for what?" Colm asked.

"To see if the miracle takes," she said.

"What? Like medicine?" Dr. Basu asked.

"Yes, something like that," Cathleen whispered so Brother Rocco wouldn't hear.

The walk back to the *pensione* was brutal for Colm. Dr. Basu carried him back up the staircase and through the hilly streets. Cathleen couldn't take her eyes off Dr. Basu holding her son, who had fallen asleep again and was nestled close to Dr. Basu's chest. Watching him carry her son, her heart filled with gratitude. When they reached the room, he set the boy down on the bed and helped his mother tuck him in.

"Thank you," Cathleen whispered. "Thank you so much, for everything."

"I hope, for your sake and for the boy's, Cathleen, that it works."

"So do I."

"Do you have a moment, Cathleen? I'd like to show you something."

"Where? I can't leave Colm."

"It's just outside your door, just a few steps down the hall. There is a terrace atop the adjacent roof, and it overlooks the valley as far as the eye can see. I went out there last night. The view is magnificent. You can see every star in the sky."

"I'd like to come, but I'm so tired and I need a shower. Plus—I am just not sure about leaving Colm here alone in the room by himself."

"I'll tell you what, you take a shower, rest a bit, and I will go get us a meal. We can eat on the terrace, and I promise you, Cathleen, Colm will be safe. We're just a few feet away. And there is no one here but you, me, Brother Rocco, and some nuns. Please. You must take care of yourself—and eat something, relax."

"You drive a hard bargain. Can I meet you there in an hour?"

"Absolutely. I'll be there."

Dr. Basu left the room exhilarated. He loved being with Cathleen even if it was under such bizarre circumstances. He wanted to make this evening something extraordinary.

Cathleen had no designs, no expectations for her evening on the roof, but she still primped and wondered how she might look to the handsome doctor. She spent a long time in the shower letting the water pour over her and scrubbing with the Assisi lavender bar. For the first time in years, her mind was completely at peace. Not a thought or a word passed through her otherwise anxious mind. When she was through with the shower, she stood naked in front of the mirror and examined her body, as she carefully brushed through her wet hair and let it flow loosely over her shoulders. She had not looked at herself in years, and she was not disappointed by what she saw. She had remained the same as always—slight yet curvy in all the right places as Pierce once told her. She saw her own face and noticed that it looked rested and reddened by the sun. For the first time in years, she was comfortable in her own skin. She put on a long white sundress and covered her shoulders with a pink sweater. She smiled to herself as she did it, thinking of the crazy nun in Santa Chiara.

Before leaving the room, she stood once more in front of the mirror and hardly recognized the woman staring back at her. Had it really been so long? Nearly seven years? She tried to remember the last time she had shared a meal with someone besides her son or brother. How had her busy life suddenly made her so alone? She shook off the thoughts and kissed Colm before she slipped out of the room.

When she stepped onto the roof, she was delighted. The view was similar to the one from her room, but what the doctor had done was truly amazing.

The table was set with a lit Chianti bottle dripping with candle wax. There were two wineglasses and a bottle of wine along with a loaf of bread and an assortment of cheese and fruit on a beautiful tray.

"What's all this?" Cathleen asked Dr. Basu, whose hair still glistened from his own shower. She could tell he had shaved again by the tiny nick near his unbuttoned white collar.

"The sisters helped me. I said we'd like to eat on the roof tonight. Apparently, we're not the first to have found it."

As she came closer, she noticed layers of candle wax on the stone table. Many people, probably people just like her who had come seeking miracles, had probably sat at the table well into the evening eating, drinking, and sharing their life stories over candlelight.

"Is Colm still sleeping?" Dr. Basu asked as he pulled out a chair for Cathleen.

"I think he's out for the night. It's been an exhausting couple of days."

"Yes. It has."

The doctor poured her a glass of wine. "Thank you, Doctor."

"Please, call me Gaspar."

"Thank you, Gaspar, for everything." As she sipped her wine, Cathleen's cheeks grew pink, and her green eyes shone even more brightly than usual.

The doctor could barely contain his attraction to her. But being around beautiful women only made him nervous and prone to say ridiculous things, so he tried to keep quiet and listen to her.

As the night wore on they grew more comfortable with each other and talked about everything under the stars. Just after midnight they thought they heard the faint sounds of young men singing together as they passed by on the streets below.

"In the book I have been reading about St. Francis, it says that when he was a young man, he did just that, what those singers are doing now . . . he walked through the streets of Assisi carrying on," Dr. Basu commented.

"Young people don't change much, do they?" Cathleen replied. "To be carefree. It's easy to be a rebel when you're young, when there's so much less to lose. I was a bit of a rebel myself for a brief time."

"Really?" Dr. Basu could hardly believe the woman before him, who was so dedicated to her son and her brother, the same woman who knelt in prayer today, could have ever been what she called a *rebel*.

"Well, Gaspar, I did have a child out of wedlock when I was twenty-two. I used to be sure I had it all figured out. You know there was a time when I didn't go to church? When I drove my mother—and even the monsignor—crazy. Man, could my mom and I go at it. She had one hell of a temper, and so did I. But I loved her so much, and then, when she was gone I was so lonely, and things were so hard. Before I knew it, I was already deeply in love, and I didn't care much about anything else. I didn't care about all that my mother thought. I just crashed headlong into love," Cathleen said.

"Do you mean with Colm's father?"

"Yes."

"May I ask what happened? Where is he?"

"I have no idea. Last I heard, L.A. I used to send him letters about what Colm was up to, but I never heard back from him. They were returned unopened. I took it as a sign that he just wanted to be left alone. Besides, I didn't want to make a fool of myself begging him to come back, so I just gave up looking after a while. It's like he just vanished though. Fell off the grid, so to speak. But that is very Pierce. He's the typical artist-vagabond type. Not the 'friend me' or 'text me' type, if you know what I mean. So he's not exactly the easiest person to track down. It wouldn't surprise me if he's still on the street strumming somewhere or performing in some hole-in-the-wall bar. He's a musician. He always said his only hope in life was to create something beautiful. I met him one day in a subway station, right around the time my mother got sick. He was busking for cash, and he started to sing to me—'Mama, You Been on My Mind.' He had a way with women, but back then I didn't realize I wasn't the only one." She trailed off.

"I am so sorry, Cathleen. That must have been very hard for you, for Colm," Gaspar said, reaching across the table to touch her hand. It seemed unconscionable for a man to desert his woman and child—to have a choice in the matter. *To decide to leave them. To decide to live without them.* He could not rationalize the injustice of it all, of the world. A sudden rush of anger seized him, but he forced it back down. He understood now what made her so determined. What made her so careful. What kept her focused completely on her son and his survival.

"Well, you don't get to pick your fortune, do you? That's life, right. No choice but to roll with it," Cathleen lied, pretending to be OK with it all, to be stronger than she really was. "How about you, Gaspar? What's your story? Did you ever think of getting married?"

"I *was* married," he said as he put down his fork and took in a long breath. He wasn't sure he was up to saying it all out loud. He had never had to explain it to anyone, ever. When he left India, he left everything, even the story of it, all behind.

"She, my wife, Niranjana, passed."

"Oh, I'm so sorry."

"She took her own life."

"Oh, my God!" Cathleen gasped. She was sorry to have brought up the painful memory, but before she could say anything else, the doctor began again. He was so matter-of-fact it knocked the breath out of Cathleen.

"She took her own life after our only son, Dhruv, died when he was five. Like many small children in India, he contracted malaria. It kills many children to this day, millions every year, mostly poor children in poor countries—like my Dhruv.

"I should have known something was wrong with him. I should have paid more attention. I dismissed him as a spoiled child, pampered by his mother, when he first became irritable and listless. Those are the first telltale signs of the disease. I wanted badly to believe that my family *was* untouchable and that I had some arrangement with the gods. Like most young people do. But when we got to the hospital, it was too late. He was so dehydrated and so ill that it took no time at all. See, Cathleen, there was a reason he wept and why he cried out in pain. And there was a way to fix him. I just didn't know it back then.

"I foolishly thought that knowledge would bring my wife peace. That she would understand we could try again, and that I would be careful to make sure that it wouldn't happen again. I assured her that her grief would be filled up by the joy of another child. But she didn't want another child. She only wanted Dhruv. I know part of her blamed herself for not being forceful enough with me. I remember the day . . . the day we took him in. She was so angry with me. She would not look at me. She muttered to herself over and over that she should have gone and done it on her own. That there was no use for men. That even as a medical student, I was of no use to her or her son. She cursed me and cursed the gods. I had never seen her so angry. After they covered Dhruv with the white cloth, she threw her body over him and when I went to . . ."

Gaspar stopped and inhaled deeply as if to suppress the tears, his own rage.

"I went to hug her and comfort her, but she said to never touch her again. I said she needed to be held, and that I did, too. But she walked out of the room, and I was alone with Dhruv. I-I-I," Dr. Basu stuttered as if about to break into tears, but he managed to force them back again. "I could not hug him or touch him. I knew he was not there. The only life I had known and loved was gone. The only thing left was Niranjana's rage. It was everywhere; it filled up all of India.

"During the night, before the preparation of *pinda* for the god of death and our ceremonial cleansing, she woke early and went to the river where we'd put Dhruv's ashes. She walked in as if she could follow him to the next life. She never came up again. Many days later, in another village, some people found her body on the bank."

He paused for a moment and tried to blink back the emotion and the memories that came with the story. He didn't want to look at Cathleen in case she judged him and blamed him too. He was still so ashamed. But he wanted to tell it all, finish it—for himself and for Cathleen.

"I left India soon after. I went to New York to finish medical school. I thought I would be able to do something with my life— save someone else's life, since I had been powerless to save or fix my own child's or my wife's."

Cathleen sat breathless. She saw the moments when she first met him in a new light, how he was with Colm during their first visit, how he took to the boy, and how dedicated he was to her— how quickly he agreed to come on this trip.

Cathleen trembled. "Please. I . . . I shouldn't have said anything," he apologized.

"You should have told me everything . . . a long time ago! Why didn't you tell me?" Cathleen pushed herself away from the table and stood at the edge of the roof overlooking the valley below.

"Because I am your son's doctor," Gaspar said, coming up behind her. "It was not my place. A doctor is not supposed to unload his troubles on his patients."

"But I thought you were more than that! I thought . . . I thought . . . we were . . ."

"What?"

"Friends?"

"Oh, yes. Friends."

"No, I mean I thought you and I had come to some understanding; oh, I don't know what I thought."

"I am sorry, Cathleen. I didn't think I was keeping anything from you. I have never told anyone, anyone back at home about Niranjana, about Dhruv. I've never been able to say the words out loud. It seemed too real. Too permanent."

"I understand. I do, I know what you mean. But . . . but I just don't get this. This one thing: How do you go on? I don't understand." Cathleen shook her head, and tears filled in the corners of her eyes and pooled, and finally the droplets gave way down her cheeks in rapid succession.

"I could ask the same of you. You are one of the strongest people I know." Dr. Basu took her hand and held it in his own.

"How can you say that? You lost your son, and now you're helping me save mine. How can you do it?" Dr. Basu stepped toward Cathleen, and she could feel his breath on her face as she looked up at him.

"I only had to watch my son die once, Cathleen," he whispered, and in that moment, she felt as if he understood her totally. She knew she should have been relieved, but instead she felt vulnerable at the depth of their connection. Nevertheless, she felt her body give way to his, and he imagined himself pulling her close to him. But before he could, she thought of Dhruv and pulled away forcefully.

Cathleen thought of the possibility of Colm's death and absently said, "I don't know how you go on. I would have, I would have . . ." She bit her lip, ashamed by what she was about to say, as if accusing the doctor that he showed weakness, rather than strength, by his survival, his enduring of it all.

"It does make life difficult sometimes," Dr. Basu said stoically, stuffing his hands in his pockets and turning away from her.

Cathleen could not explain what came over her as she looked at him standing all alone, but she went to him anyway. Dr. Basu turned back to her, then held Cathleen's face in his hands as he looked into her eyes. He at once saw how heartbroken she was, thinking of Colm and wondering how she would manage in the same circumstance. Her compassion for him came from a pain all her own, and a fear of what would become of her if the unthinkable happened.

Cathleen asked herself if she would be like Niranjana or Gaspar. Would she give in to the heartache or would she endure? She had no way of knowing. But Dr. Basu knew instinctively that Cathleen was different from Niranjana.

"I am not a man of many beliefs and superstitions, Cathleen. I do not believe in much anymore. But I believe this: I don't know who or what is behind this world, but I know you, and the love you have for Colm will keep you strong forever. No matter what happens, you will endure. You will survive, and because of that strength and that love, Colm will too."

Cathleen wept, and the doctor held her without saying a word. When she finally looked up at him, she saw him, *Gaspar Basu*, for the first time. He was the strongest man she had ever met, the man she had been looking for her entire life.

After some time, Cathleen and Dr. Basu stepped away from each other, bashfully adjusting their hair and straightening their clothing, as if waking from an afternoon tryst. They walked back inside together, barely touching as they slipped through the door. In the hallway they looked at each other briefly and parted, making their own way to their rooms. As Cathleen walked away from him, she felt the strings that now connected their hearts stretch and tighten. They made a song she had not felt, not heard in years. It was the song of love, and like it had the first time she heard it on the streets of New York, coming from a tall, handsome boy strumming and singing the lyrics to "Mama, You Been on My Mind," she knew that morning would be too long to wait to see him again.

But Cathleen would not have to wait.

When she opened the door to her room, she cried out, "Colm!" Gaspar came running and before she knew it, he was standing next to her, staring, as she was, at Colm's empty bed.

Chapter 20

GASPAR AND CATHLEEN LOOKED IN THE BATHROOM and the wardrobe. They ran down the hall, screaming Colm's name as they went by each door.

As they passed Brother Rocco's room, the older man came out, rubbing his eyes as he tried to wake up. "What is the matter?" he asked.

"Colm's gone. We can't find him," Cathleen said breathlessly.

"Let me put on some clothes. I'll be right out to help you look for him," he said, already in motion.

The three spread out throughout the *pensione,* knocking on doors and opening closets. The nuns came out of their rooms with their robes on, and Brother Rocco told them in Italian what had happened. The mother's *bambino* was lost. They ran back into their rooms to get dressed and began looking for Colm too.

By the time Cathleen reached the front door, she noticed it was open.

"Colm left!" she shouted up the stairs to Dr. Basu as she ran outside to look for her son.

She went up and down the dark street lit only by small lanterns above the door frames of the homes on the narrow pathway. As she walked toward the piazza, she became aware, for the first time, of the seemingly infinite directions, stairways, and alleys that broke off the main path. *He could be anywhere.*

She started with the piazza, running down toward the fountain. An orchestra that had set up, as they often did in the evenings, was breaking down. She ran up to the dispersing crowd and began asking if anyone had seen the boy.

"I have lost my son. My boy. Have you seen a little boy?"

The Italians shook their heads. Some had no idea what she was talking about; the ones who spoke English told her to relax. She was in Assisi; he could not have gone far. If a child was lost, he would surely find his way back home, they all agreed. And if not, Francis and Clare would watch over him. *He was in the safest place in the world.*

Cathleen tried to take comfort in this, but she was panicking. *What if he was sick? What if he needed his mother and she wasn't there? How could she have left him all alone? How could she let herself go feel love for someone else, for being such a fool? Hadn't she learned anything? Hadn't love only gotten her into trouble.*

All night Cathleen ran up and down the steps of Assisi. She passed Brother Rocco at one point and asked if he had seen anything.

"No, Cathleen. But pray to St. Anthony, the patron of lost things: *Something is lost and can't be found, dear St. Anthony come around.* I am sure he'll show up."

Suddenly, the brother infuriated her. *This is no time for this crap,* she thought. She didn't need St. Anthony. She needed her son. And her son wasn't just *something*—he was *everything.*

By the time the sun began to rise over the valley, Cathleen had been all over the city. She thought of all of the sights they had visited—the chapels and churches. Surely Colm would not return to any of them.

She looked up over the hillside at the Rocca Maggiore standing guard over Assisi. Colm loved to explore. *Could he have gone to this mysterious fortress?* As she walked toward it, she climbed up to a green space that spread out before a gargantuan church. At the crest of the lawn, she saw the defeated knight—a large steel sculpture of St. Francis, which she had read in her book was meant to capture an image of Francis just before he met the leper on the road and realized his life's purpose was to serve the poor. *He was a broken knight who was so tired of fighting too,* she thought.

There on the steps of the massive medieval church, in front a large crowd of men in habits from the Order of Friars Minor Conventual, she saw him. Colm was speaking. She could see his arms rise above his head, demonstrating something and using his entire body to explain it.

She could see that the friars were looking at one another, some nodding their heads and all listening to the boy with rapt attention. Cathleen ran down the long pathway and cut through the crowd of men, trying to get to the boy. When she reached him, she forgot her relief at finding him and yelled.

"Colm! You scared me half to death. Where have you been?"

"Here," Colm said, pointing to the church behind him and then back at the men.

"I spent the entire night looking for you, Colm. Why did you leave?"

"I went looking for *you*."

"I was just outside the door of our room on the roof."

"I didn't know there was a roof. I didn't know where you were."

"What in God's name are you doing here?" As she said that, she realized she should have considered her audience and quickly apologized to the men.

They all smiled and assured her they had heard far worse.

"What is he talking about? Why is he here?"

"He was telling us about what it is like to die," a friar said in English with a faint Italian accent.

Cathleen looked at Colm. She was stunned. "Is that true, Colm?"

"Yes."

"Why, Colm? I'm confused. How did you get here all on your own?"

"I thought I heard singing, and I followed the sounds."

Another friar spoke up to assure Cathleen. "We were singing our midnight prayers just as Francis did when he was alive. The child must have followed us here. We were already finished and heading back when we noticed him. He stopped us, and we began to talk of many things. We didn't realize how much time had gone by."

"You mean to tell me you sat up talking to a boy all night, and it never occurred to you he needed to be home with his mother?"

"He assured us that you would be fine with it because he was at church."

Colm smiled, and all the men laughed. Cathleen blushed hot with anger.

"ColmFrancisMagee you are in deep, deep . . ." she said through clenched teeth. She looked at the friars. "What have you been talking about all this time?"

"Lots of stuff, Mama. Stuff you probably wouldn't understand."

Cathleen looked at the men and back at her son. "Oh, no? What wouldn't I understand?"

"Lots." Colm walked down the steps ahead of his mother.

"Now where do you think you're going, young man?"

"I'm finished here. I thought you came to take me back."

Cathleen nodded. "Yes, right. We're going back right now."

Colm stopped in front of all the friars and said, "Thank you."

An older friar bent down, his habit floating over his spread legs and brushing the ground, and he whispered something only Colm could hear into his ear.

Colm smiled at the reassurance that he would someday meet his father. The friar was sure of it. As Colm walked away, the old friar winked, and all the other men waved good-bye and told him how wonderful it was to meet him, that they were all sure that Colm was a special boy.

Cathleen pulled Colm up the hill and toward the *pensione* while Colm waved and smiled back at all the men.

When Cathleen was out of the men's earshot, she started to yell. "Don't you ever, ever do that again! Honestly, Colm. I don't know what you were thinking. Why did you do that?"

"I just wanted to know."

"Know what? What do you want to know, Colm?"

"Everything."

Cathleen and Colm walked back toward the *pensione* in silence. When they crested the top of the hill, they saw Dr. Basu walking toward them.

"There you two are!" Dr. Basu threw his hands up as if to say hallelujah.

Cathleen walked toward him and said angrily, "He's all yours, Gaspar. I'm exhausted."

Colm could not believe what he was hearing. He looked at the doctor, dumbfounded. His mother had *never ever* walked away from him. Ever.

"Yes, perhaps the boy is hungry. Colm, would you like some breakfast?"

"Yes, I am hungry."

"Very well. Let's get you something to eat. Cathleen, you go and get some rest. I will have a nice chat with the boy. You go back to the room. I'll bring him back soon."

It was all she could do to keep from crying and running down the street as fast she could. Why was he always running off? Why was he so desperate to get away from her? But then she realized he wasn't running from her—he was looking for her. She felt ashamed. How could Colm ever think that she had run off, abandoned him? Didn't he know how much she loved him? She was angry with herself for letting her guard down and leaving him alone. Angry for letting the doctor's ideas make her forget her own. She wanted to scream and hurl something at someone.

As she walked away, she heard soft giggles between Colm and Gaspar. Colm shared his secrets with men—men like her brother, like Gaspar, like the friars. He gave all his love to great, wonderful, and mysterious men, even the father he never stopped asking her about. And here she was right in front of him the entire time. But her love, she thought, would never be enough. She thought of Francis, as she often did these days, and she said aloud the word *asshole*. For all of his love of God and humanity, he didn't have the decency to love and be kind to the people who loved him most in the entire world—even his own mother. *What bullshit,* she said.

When she reached her room, she went to the window and watched Gaspar and Colm walk hand in hand away from her toward the piazza. She closed the shutters, continuing to argue with herself and St. Francis and everyone else she had ever been mad at—her brother, mother, dead father, Pierce, and all the doctors, everyone she could think of who had ever let her down. Then she caught her reflection again in the mirror and realized she had let others down too. *Hadn't her mother asked her to take care of Sean and be kind to him? Hadn't Colm begged her not to go to Italy? Hadn't she left Colm in the room alone?* She felt ashamed and forgave them all, especially Colm. How could she stay angry with him, she wondered as she collapsed on the edge of her bed in exhaustion. Cathleen was done with fighting; she was broken and defeated. Her armor, like Francis the knight, became too heavy to bear and so she slept.

She was tired.

Meanwhile, Dr. Basu took the boy back to the piazza and sat him down on a chair in front of the fountain.

"I will go in and get you some milk and a croissant. Can I

trust that you will be here when I return?" Dr. Basu asked somewhat jokingly, knowing the boy had intended no harm.

"Yes, Dr. Basu. I am not going anywhere. I promise."

"Good. I'll be right back."

While Dr. Basu waited in line to place his order, he examined the boy from afar. Colm's legs were dangling from the chair. He was still so slight. He looked nearly starved.

"Are you feeling well?" Dr. Basu asked when he returned and placed the food on the table.

"Yes."

"You're not tired? Not even a bit?"

"I am always tired, Doctor."

"I see."

"I am mostly afraid. Is Mama mad at me?"

"No. She is not mad. She was just worried about you."

"I was worried about *her*," Colm said.

"Oh? Why?"

"I thought she had left me like my father did. And now she is mad at me. She doesn't want me anymore."

"That's nonsense. Your mother loves you. She's just tired and needs a break. Every mother cracks a bit now and then. Even the best ones."

"But I thought she was abandoning me like my father did."

"How do you know that? How do you know such big words?"

"I just do."

"Did someone tell you such things?"

"No. But I figured it out. My father is a *deadbeat*."

"Where have you heard these words—*abandoned, deadbeat*? Does your mother say such things?"

"No, my uncle Sean does."

"When did he say them?"

"I heard him once say to my mama that if God was real, then he was the first deadbeat dad because he let some other man raise his son and then took all the credit."

Dr. Basu tried not to smile. He could only imagine Sean saying such a thing.

"Colm, I want to tell you two things. First, your mother would never abandon you as you say. She loves you and would never willingly leave you. And second, it is not the child's job to worry. You should never, ever worry about your mother. She can take care of herself."

"I hope so."

"What do you mean, you hope so?"

"I mean, someday, she is going to have to be able to take care of herself. I can't do it forever."

"Oh, and it is you who cares for your mother?"

"Yes. I look out for her."

"I see. I bet you are very good at it."

"I am. But, between you and me, I am a little worried about her," Colm said quietly, leaning toward the doctor like he was telling him something top secret.

"Ah, is that so?" Dr. Basu leaned forward and whispered, "But remember I told you it is not your job to worry about her."

"Yes, but Dr. Basu, you know what I mean. You have to know why I'm worried. You know. You and I both know," Colm said, pointing at the doctor and then back at himself.

"Oh. What do I know?"

"That I am going to die soon. Someday, I am going to die and be gone forever. I won't wake up, and it will be hard for her."

"But you may be healed. You may get better."

"The miracle didn't take."

"No? How do you know?"

"I know because there are no such things as miracles, Dr. Basu. There are no miracles because there is no God."

"Yes, you have told me this before. Perhaps it's time you tell your mother these things. Maybe it is time we just go home and put all of this silliness behind us. Is that what you want?"

"Yes. I want to go home."

"Your mother will understand. Just tell her what you have told me. You're only a child, after all."

"Yes, but she won't be happy."

"Yes, she wants so badly to believe," the doctor agreed.

"I know. But it's not my place to tell people what they should believe. I just know what I know," Colm said while staring off at the fountain as if what he said was something every six-and-a-half-year-old boy in the world would say.

"You are very wise, Dove," Dr. Basu said, in awe at the boy's precociousness.

"Dr. Basu?"

"Yes."

"Will you talk to my mama?"

"About?"

"Do you think we can go home tomorrow?"

"I will see what I can do," Dr. Basu said, patting the boy on his knee.

Colm jumped off his chair and launched himself into Dr.

Basu's lap, snuggling comfortably into his chest. "Thank you, Dr. Basu. Thank you so much."

Overwhelmed, Dr. Basu wrapped his arms around the boy and held him tightly.

"Dr. Basu?"

"Yes, Dove."

"I am tired. Do you mind if I don't eat anything?"

"That's fine, son. Do you want me to carry you back to the room to your bed?"

"Can I just rest here for a while?"

"Of course, Dove. You can stay here as long as you want. I am not going anywhere."

Chapter 21

C OLM GOT AT LEAST ONE WISH IN ITALY. DR. BASU convinced his mother to take him home right away.

Despite having several days planned for other church visits and healing rituals, Cathleen listened to Dr. Basu when he came to return the sleeping child later that same morning.

"My goodness, Gaspar!" Cathleen said, looking at the doctor who was cradling the sleeping boy.

"I'm sorry; did I wake you?"

"Yes, that's fine. I just needed a little nap. No big deal. I feel better now. How long has Colm been asleep?"

"He fell asleep about an hour ago. I sat with him for a while, like he asked me to do. But I think he'll be out for the day. I thought I should bring him back and put him to bed."

"Yes, of course," Cathleen said as she pulled back the sheets so Dr. Basu could lay the boy down.

"Cathleen, Colm has asked me to ask you to take him home soon, preferably tomorrow," he whispered as he pulled up the sheet to tuck Colm in.

"Why? I thought he liked it here. He's been laughing and so

energetic these past couple of days. I swear, he looks fantastic. Sure, he's tired now, but that's only because he stayed out last night. I am sure he's already getting better. I am positive."

Dr. Basu didn't want to crush Cathleen's optimism. She wanted so badly to believe. But he remembered Colm asking him to promise not to tell his mother that he didn't believe in God or in miracles.

"No, it's not because he's feeling badly. He hasn't said anything to me about feeling sick—or sicker than usual."

"Then why?"

"I just think he's homesick, Cathleen."

"Homesick? I am his mother. He's home when he's with me."

"He's just a boy, Cathleen. He misses his toys, his things, his school . . . his uncle Sean."

"He said these things—*to you*."

"Not in so many words. But, yes, he told me he wants to go home. We did do what we came for—didn't we?"

"Yes, but there is so much more we could do . . ."

"Cathleen, please. I know you are only thinking of him. Believe me I do. But I am just telling you what the boy told me. I know you would do anything for him. Anything at all."

"Yes. You're right. We did do what we came to do. I just have to wait and see now."

"Yes. If you like, I can make all the arrangements—change the flights."

"That will be expensive. I'm not sure I can do that."

"Don't worry about it, Cathleen. I'll handle everything. I'll leave now and see if Brother Rocco can take us back to Rome tomorrow to catch a flight home."

"Thank you, Dr. Basu, for everything."

"My pleasure."

The following morning Cathleen, Dr. Basu, and Colm headed back to Rome with Brother Rocco to catch their evening flight back to the United States. But since Cathleen agreed to cut the trip short, Colm and Dr. Basu thought it wouldn't be a big deal if Cathleen got to stop by the Vatican and take a look.

"We'll have about five or six hours to kill in Rome. Why not make the most of it? We can look at the Vatican and maybe even drive by ruins and maybe even throw a coin in the Trevi? Doesn't that sound like fun?" Cathleen asked excitedly.

"Do we have to go to another church, though, Mama? Really?"

"When in Rome . . ." Cathleen said, smiling, but Colm didn't get the joke.

"Colm, I am sure your mother won't take too long in St. Peter's, right, Cathleen?" Dr. Basu said, as if reminding her of their conversation the night before about Colm's desire to leave.

"Yes, sure. Just a quick stop in. It would seem a shame if we came all this way and missed one of the world's most famous pieces of architecture. Besides, Colm, you said you're feeling better, right?"

"Yes, Mama," Colm lied, looking at Dr. Basu.

Brother Rocco took the minivan packed with their luggage to the walls of the Vatican and dropped them off several blocks away from St. Peter's Square. "I will meet you right here in an hour, OK? Then we'll head out for a quick local drive-by tour, before heading to the airport. Sound good?"

After quite an ordeal getting Colm with his pacemaker, not to mention his dark-faced companion, through security without going through the metal detector line, the three finally entered the humongous building. It seemed like an impossible task to take it all in. Colm thought he was dreaming. He stood motionless in the middle of the basilica with his head flung back. The morning light broke through the three windows above the church's central doors and cast huge white streaks of light along the long marble floor that spanned the length of the enormous church. Colm spun in every direction. He looked up toward the altar under the giant, snakelike pillars of what his mother called *Bernini's magnum opus*. Everywhere he looked there were giant things—stone men carrying staffs and wearing large pointy hats, enormous depictions of pictures and stories. After staring for a long time, his eyes burned; he squinted, rubbed them, and continued to look all around.

As they walked toward the central door to leave, Cathleen saw something out of the corner of her eye. She walked across the width of the church as if pulled by some unknowable force.

In a small chapel on the right of the church was Michelangelo's *Pietà*—carved from a large block of white marble. Cathleen stood motionless before it. Her own mother had inherited a small porcelain copy and had it set upon an Irish linen doily on her bedroom dresser. Cathleen had never thought twice about it. Growing up, she saw the replica every day. But she could not believe she was in Rome standing before the real thing. It was the first time in almost three days she felt herself firmly rooted in Italy and in the original reasons for her trip. Suddenly her knees began to buckle. She lunged toward the kneeler in front of the statue. The face that Michelangelo carved—she could tell—he had known well. She remembered from her own art classes in college that Michelangelo's mother, who died when he was only five, was the face of many of his sculptures. For the first time Cathleen contemplated what it would have been like to be a boy a bit younger than Colm's age trying to make his way in the world without his mama. For all these years she had worried about herself. She worried about how she would make it without her son. It never occurred to her that her son, and children all over the world, might have to endure without their mothers.

The first thing Cathleen noticed was the statue's strength. The Madonna sat with her legs wide, supporting her lifeless son's body across her lap. One arm held his heavy head while the other lay open to whatever might come her way. She was young and beautiful, and Cathleen stared at her face tilted toward her son's. She had imagined her as angry or in overwhelming despair, but no. In the real statue, the grieving mother did not look hopeless. She possessed a quiet resignation that her work as a mother was done. That this was the fate she had always known would be hers. She had the rest of her life to live, and she would have to do it without her only son. Cathleen couldn't help but think of Niranjana. She herself had begged for a miracle for her own son. *Please take me instead,* she beseeched.

Colm followed his mother into the chapel and stared at the sculpture of the sad mother and her dead son. He thought he knew what his mother was thinking.

He knelt beside her and held her hand.

"Mama?"

"Yes, Bud."

"I love you."

"I love you, too."

"Can we go now?"

"Yes."

Cathleen pushed her body off the kneeler, took Colm's hand, and walked away from the statue. They left through the center door, stopping briefly to turn one more time to look at the magnificent church. As they exited, the morning sun blinded them, and it took them several minutes to see clearly.

"OK. Let's head back and meet up with Brother Rocco, and maybe he can swing us by the major sites. Maybe we can even get out and see the Trevi fountain and perhaps eat in a café nearby instead of at the airport?" Cathleen said eagerly.

Colm heard all of this and recoiled. He was exhausted, and every joint in his body ached. Every time he inhaled, he felt a stabbing pain in his chest. His head was throbbing, and he had difficulty seeing more than five feet in front of him. The noise on the street was intolerable. The thought of eating revolted him. His legs began to tingle. For days he had felt this coming, this overwhelming fatigue that was impossible to escape. It was all he could do . . .

He looked at his mother who had a broad, light smile across her face. The tiny lines around her eyes, he thought, looked like angel wings carrying her eyes upward. He had never seen her as happy as she was in Italy. He knew it was because she came here for a miracle and she believed she was going to get one, but Colm knew better.

So Colm thought it best to keep his mouth shut, and he followed the grown-ups down the steps and across St. Peter's Square.

While Brother Rocco was driving around Rome at rapid speed, Colm felt sick to his stomach. He was so grateful when the car stopped and he could get out and walk in the fresh air. They made their way to the Trevi, cutting through the mass of people and tourists and heading toward the sound of rushing water. Cathleen held tightly to Colm's hand, fearful that he would be pulled away by the crowds and lost forever. There were hundreds of people coming from every direction, mostly tourists taking photos, throwing coins, and talking. They could barely get close enough to turn around and throw their coins in. A newly married couple stood and posed for pictures in front of their massive family. It was impossible for Colm to see the full length of the fountain and to take it all in. Even though the fountain was enormous, he could not understand the point of it all. His mother and Brother Rocco went on and on about the carving.

As the four walked away, a boy with no legs pushing himself on a skateboard pulled on Cathleen's pant legs, then extended his hand up to beg. Colm looked at his mother and pleaded with her to give the boy some money, but their guide warned against it.

"If you give him something, he'll only expect more. He'll follow you throughout Rome," Brother Rocco offered rather pragmatically.

Cathleen dropped a euro in the boy's open hand anyway. Her mother's heart could not deny a child. Dr. Basu also dug into his pockets and pulled out several euros to give to the boy.

Colm and Cathleen were several steps ahead by the time Dr.

Basu finished trying to talk to the boy on the skateboard. He was trying to find out if the boy was in need of help, water, or food—and where he lived. But the boy, afraid he was in trouble or that Dr. Basu was a police officer, did not understand and tried to get away from him. When the doctor looked up, frustrated that he could not help the legless, homeless boy, he noticed Colm's gait. The boy was dragging a leg, and Dr. Basu fought through the crowd to catch up to him.

"Colm, what's wrong? Does your leg hurt you?"

"No. It doesn't hurt, Dr. Basu."

"Then why are you walking like that?"

"Because I can't feel it at all."

"What?"

Dr. Basu was about to turn and say something to Cathleen. He was about to tell her that this would be enough of the sightseeing.

But he couldn't finish his thought. He tried to catch the boy as he fell, lunging past Cathleen to get to him. Cathleen let out a shriek, and everyone around the fountain fell silent. Even the boy on the skateboard stopped and turned.

Colm's world went black before he hit the ground. He was gone.

Cathleen began to pray. Dr. Basu worked to revive him—pressing his chest over and over and breathing into his mouth periodically. Someone in the crowd came up to the guide and began to speak something in Italian.

"The ambulance is on its way," Brother Rocco assured Cathleen and Dr. Basu.

The crowd was enormous. They formed a tight circle around

Cathleen and the boy as the doctor kept working. Cathleen could hear the whispers of prayer in Italian and various languages. She heard the familiar cadence and rhythm and knew instinctively that the whole crowd was praying for her son.

The minutes dragged on before Cathleen heard the sirens trying to cut through the dense crowd.

Once they arrived, the Italian medics were aggressive. There was no wasting time. They came quickly to the boy and put him on an orange board and told the mother and doctor to back away. They spoke in furious Italian, shouting at each other, and moving rapidly to rip open the sterile shock paddles. They warned everyone to stay back as they fired away. And for minutes they tried to revive him. They fired again and again and again.

There was nothing. Colm was gone. Cathleen looked at her watch. It had to have been nearly twenty minutes now. *It's over.* She came all this way, all the way to Rome to save her son only to lose him. She nearly collapsed. The guide braced her with his own trembling arms.

The medics looked up at Cathleen and then at the doctor. The doctor nodded, assuring them that they had done enough and that there was nothing left to do. They stood up slowly, looking weary and sad. Cathleen walked toward her lifeless boy to bend down and kiss him. His shirt was torn. His arms spread out away from him as if he were making snow angels on the cobblestone. But she could not do it. Not like this. *Not without his soul inside him,* she thought. She turned back to the doctor and threw her body against his, pounding her arms on his chest, over and over and over and over. The doctor took the blows. He didn't fight back or try to defend himself. He blamed himself, and he wanted so badly to feel someone punish him. He could have done more to help the boy. He wanted her to pummel him into a million pieces, until he dissolved completely into the rushing fountain.

Mothers around them began to weep, but most of the crowd remained silent. Some young people took out their phones to take pictures and video, not fully grasping what was happening around them, not aware yet of a parent's pain. For them it would be another memory for their scrapbooks or blog, a story to tell when they returned home. Cathleen could hear the crashing fountain, the noise of life returning to normal, the crowd breaking up, and people walking slowly away. But still she thought she heard her name, the only name she knew was hers.

Mama.

She turned away from the doctor and looked down at the boy.

"Mama?" Colm whispered again.

Cathleen ran toward him while Dr. Basu stood stunned. The medics stopped and looked at each other and then back at the boy. The remaining crowd burst into huge cheers and exaltation—thanking God in Italian, English, Polish, French, German—and languages Cathleen could not decipher. Mothers and their children hugged and kissed. People everywhere were embracing, crying, clapping, and screaming.

Incredibile!

Meraviglioso!

È un miracolo!

Brilliant!

Colm had risen again. Cathleen pulled him close to her,

squeezing him mightily, kissing him on his forehead, cheeks, and hair. She wanted to consume him, wrap him tightly inside of her, where she could protect him for all time. She was delirious.

Dr. Basu was speechless. He pushed his hands through his hair and cupped his hands to block the sun as he looked at the sky, as if somewhere above him he would find the answers. He closed his eyes and listened again to the shouting and rapid conversation of the people surrounding him, so much louder and more magnified than it had been in Assisi. He squeezed his eyes tighter and listened to the rushing of the fountain, and it felt like it was running through him—like the river that carried his Dhruv and Niranjana. It flowed and surged, its waters breaking at every turn inside his body, rising up through him as if when he opened his mouth, water would pour forth. But instead the power and force of that water rose higher still and brimmed within him. An overwhelming wave crashed through him. He did not care who or what was responsible for it. All he felt was joy. A supreme joy, a joy only known to him once before. And for a brief moment, he did not let his mind do what it was apt to do, which was stop himself from feeling because it knew logically what that joy ultimately wrought when it was taken away—an eventual and inexplicable grief. For a moment, before he could fully comprehend the feeling and stop himself, he walked over and embraced the boy too.

Sean was sitting at the downstairs bar in Eamonn's in Brooklyn, watching the end of the Yankee game.

He was at Eamonn's after every shift lately. It sucked, he thought, to cross the river and head into Brooklyn when there were perfectly acceptable bars right next to his apartment—but none of his crew members would find him here. He could sit and drink alone to his heart's content and no one, especially his sponsor, would recognize him.

He hadn't talked to or seen his sister and nephew in weeks. They were in Italy now—with the faithful, reliable doctor. He was happy Colm had him. At least, he consoled himself, Colm had one solid, good man in his life. At least one guy the boy could count on.

He was about to order up another shot of whiskey when he felt his phone vibrate in his pocket. He pulled it out and looked at the screen. The number was unrecognizable. He thought of ignoring it for a brief second, before he thought, perhaps as impossible as it seemed, it might be his sister calling from Italy.

"Sean?"

"Yes, who is this?"

"Dr. Basu."

"Oh, crap," Sean said, assuming the worst as soon as he heard Dr. Basu's, and not his sister's, voice.

"I will tell you this first. Colm is alive."

"What's going on then?"

"We are, however, at a hospital in Italy."

"You said Colm is fine."

"No, I said he's alive. He collapsed today, but I am afraid he seems to be getting worse. Not better, as your sister had hoped."

"How's my sister taking it?"

"She's tough. She's staying strong. She's relieved he's alive. But I think there are limits to the comfort I can provide for her."

"Don't sell yourself short, Doc. She thinks the world of you."

"Yes, but I think she needs you, too."

"Did she say she 'needs me' specifically?"

Gaspar paused to consider his answer. If he said yes, he knew it would be a lie. But he also knew it would be true. Cathleen would not admit it, but she missed her brother. She felt unmoored and alone. Gaspar knew she wouldn't say such a thing to him, because she didn't want to hurt his feelings.

"She needs you, Sean. She asked me to call you to see if you could help."

"Should I come out there?"

"No. Colm will be released here soon, I am sure of it. He seems to be in good spirits, but his speech is slightly changed. He's acquired a stutter and a slur. A result of being out so long today. You know Colm though, down one minute, up and ready to go the next. We're hoping to take an early flight back tomorrow if all goes well. Cathleen's worried about carrying Colm and the bags and waiting for a cab. Is there a way you can meet us at the airport at eleven? Can I count on you to be . . ." Dr. Basu hesitated again. He didn't feel comfortable talking about Sean's drinking. He felt like he was betraying Cathleen by doing so. She had spoken to him several times about her brother's problems in confidence. But he could tell that Sean sounded like he was in a bar, and it was safe to draw such a conclusion.

"You don't even have to ask. I'll be there—and I'll be sober. I won't take a drop."

Sean slammed a fifty-dollar bill on the bar and staggered toward the door. Under the night sky, he walked until he could feel the ground beneath him. He ended up at the Promenade and looked out over the East River at the transformed New York skyline. He thought of how much it had changed, not just in his own time, but long before it. His own life and Cathleen's were in constant upheaval. Nothing lasted forever—for anyone, anywhere, at anytime.

Staring at the Brooklyn Bridge, he thought of Walt Whitman, his sister's favorite poet, and how she once told him Whitman rode the ferry back and forth between his job in Manhattan and his home in Brooklyn thousands of times before Roebling built the bridge that united the two boroughs. "Imagine," she had said to him, "having had it so difficult for so long, and then somebody comes and builds a bridge and suddenly makes it easy for you and everyone who comes after you to cross over." He thought of how soon after the horrible day in September long ago, after he had changed his mind about the Blue Angels, that she took him to this very spot on the Promenade and made him look at the bridge and the skyline beyond it. She wanted his teenage self to take a good, long, hard look. She wanted to assure him, that though all his plans had changed, some things, like love, didn't change, and that he should *never ever* forget that. She promised she would *never ever* forget what he did for his mother, and the pain he spared them all. But that was before she had her heart broken by Pierce, before Colm came along, before life changed her like the skyline by putting a huge, gaping hole in the middle of her.

As he looked out past the horizon at the small outline of the Statue of Liberty, he remembered their mother reciting *Give me your tired, your poor, your huddled masses yearning to breathe free* whenever she spotted the statue. She always followed up with the story of how she met their da her first day *off the boat* in New York—even though she flew into JFK. He laughed at his mother's unique perception of reality, her ability to tell a big-fish story better than anyone he knew. He remembered her giant, hot temper, the one that still coursed through his and his sister's veins and the accuracy of the name she acquired by marrying their father—*Magee*—the fiery one. He thought how real and human she was, but how unreal and improbable at the same time. Her benevolence, her selflessness, her absolute self-sacrifice for her children made no sense at all to him. *What did she ever get out of it? But d-e-a-d.*

Dead.

As he headed for the bridge that sprang up like a cathedral in the night sky, he decided he would never cross it again—at least to go to Eamonn's. With each step forward, he knew there was no going back to all the "could haves" and "would have beens." There was no time to self-destruct anymore. No time to wallow in his lost dreams. The bridge had been there before him the entire time. Someone before him had made it easy for him to cross. All he had to do was make the trip. His sister and nephew would be on their way home, and he needed to be sober. He needed to be ready. They would need him. They all had a hell of a road ahead of them.

Colm lay motionless on his hospital bed and watched as his mother and Dr. Basu slept upright in the chairs that were pushed up against the wall beside the window that looked out over the busy street below. The day had been long, his mother said; they were supposed to nap and get some rest. He thought she was mad at him and that the nap was his punishment for what he had just told her. Dr. Basu had promised him the day before that she would understand. But Colm wasn't so sure she did. He could tell he had broken her heart, and that there was no going back, no undoing what was already said. His mama was right. Words were something you couldn't put back up on the shelf after playing with them. You couldn't wipe them off the countertop after you let them spill. You couldn't put a Band-Aid on what they cut. The cells wouldn't reconstruct themselves, like Dr. Basu had taught him. No. New cells wouldn't build themselves out of one another after the words had sliced, caused another to bleed. He wanted to cry. He wanted his uncle. He wanted his father. He knew his father would understand and would know what it felt like to have broken his mama's heart. He was sure his father was right there with him, looking at what he was looking at right now . . .

An hour earlier, Dr. Basu had left the room to call his uncle and to make sure he could meet them all at the airport the following day. Without Dr. Basu there, his mother looked worried and frantic. She kept moving between bed and the window, pacing back and forth, while waiting for the doctor to return. Colm was frightened. His mother never showed her signs of worry like this. She never seemed out of control.

"M-m-m-m-m-ammmma, are you m-m-m-m-mad at m-m-me? That the mmmmiracle didn't take? That we came all this way for nothing?" Colm struggled to say each word, but stuttered especially on all the *m* words.

Cathleen winced. This was all new today. His difficulty speaking, his struggle to express himself.

"No, honey, I'm not mad at you," she assured him.

"You look up . . . s-s-set," Colm said.

Cathleen stopped and sat beside Colm and took his hand. Together they looked out the window. "It's a beautiful day, isn't it? Let's just sit here and look at the sky. It's my favorite part of the movie."

"Huh?" Colm asked, confused. "What m-m-m-m-movie?"

"Silly me. That just came out." Cathleen's cheeks flushed as she remembered a secret game from a time that didn't seem to have ever existed.

"What does that m-m-mean?"

Cathleen paused and thought for a second. It hadn't occurred to her how rarely she actually spoke of Colm's father. It wasn't intentional. It was just that it hurt to remember, to say all the things out loud. She thought, however, it would do no harm to tell him just one story—one memory.

"A long time ago, your father and I would pull the kitchen chairs together and face them toward the window at night. We'd get a bowl of popcorn, and just stare out at the sky. Whenever we saw something beautiful like a star or a sunset or heard people laughing down in the alley below, we'd stop and say, 'This is my favorite part of the movie.'" A lump grew in her throat as she said it out loud again. Saying the memory did make it real again.

Colm had never heard his mother speak of his father in this way. She had never even mentioned his name without his asking. Colm couldn't imagine them sitting together in the same room, let alone their kitchen, the very kitchen in which he and his mother ate without him every night.

"That's a nice story, M-m-mama."

"It is. It's one of my favorites."

"Thank you for telling me. For bringing me here. For trying so . . . hard."

"Colm, I'd do anything for you. Anything. I'd go anywhere. Anywhere."

"M-m-mama?"

"Yes?"

"If I tell you something, you promise you won't be m-m-m-m-mad? You promise you'll forgive m-m-m-me?"

"What is it?"

"I don't believe in God. In m-m-miracles. I know now that I am going to die. I am. And God can't stop it from happening. You can't stop it by praying for m-m-miracles or taking me on p-p-p-pilgrimages."

Cathleen felt like a blunt force hit her chest. Her shoulders slouched inward as she pulled her cardigan across her chest. *This is what it feels like when hope leaves,* she thought. *It doesn't slip out the door before you wake, leaving a letter on the mirror. It kicks the goddamn door down.* She exhaled and pushed herself off the bed, then looked out the window and hardened herself. She didn't want him to see her cry.

She inhaled deeply and spoke slowly. Deliberately. "Colm, I am not mad at you. I love you. I do. I am sorry you don't believe in God. But I do. I do." She repeated it over and over and nodded with the rhythm of her speech to convince herself—to grab and drag the hope back in, kicking and screaming. "I have to believe that there is still hope. Some way to fix you. Maybe God sent us Dr. Basu? We tried a miracle, which I haven't completely given up on, and now we will turn back to medicine. Maybe God sent us a man as intelligent and careful as Dr. Basu to save you."

"Mama, Dr. Basu knows it too. He knows there is no God. There's no reason to hope for anything at all."

"Stop this, Colm. Stop. You're going to be fine. Just great. Dr. Basu wouldn't be here if he didn't think so."

"He wouldn't be here if he *did*," Colm said sharply.

"Oh, Colm. Colm. Colm." She had no words left. And so she said his name. To say it as if it were a prayer in and of itself.

"I'm sorry, M-m-m-mama. I'm sorry I said anything."

"Colm, you told the truth. I wouldn't expect you to do anything different," Cathleen said coolly, collecting herself.

"You always told me to tell the truth," Colm reminded her.

"Yes, I suppose I wish you'd just told me the truth sooner . . ."

Cathleen stopped herself from telling the lie. She knew even if she had known Colm didn't believe in God, she would have brought him here; she would have tried anything to save him.

"I know," Colm assured her. "I was afraid to hurt you. I was afraid you would be m-m-mad at me. I could tell that you wanted to b-b-b-believe and I didn't want to change that."

"Colm, you are so, so, so . . ."

The words kept failing Cathleen. She wanted to say *wise*, but it seemed much more than wisdom. Everything Colm said seemed to come straight from his heart. She stopped talking, walked back to the bed, and hugged him.

Colm inhaled the smell of her hair and patted her back. "It's going to be all right, Mama."

Cathleen pulled Colm closer and kissed his forehead again. "I know it will be. I just know it."

"Is everything all right in here?" They heard Dr. Basu's soft voice in the doorway. "Am I disturbing you?"

"No, Dr. Basu. Please come in. I'm glad you're here. Did you reach Sean?"

"Yes, he'll be there tomorrow. He sends his best. He's anxious to see you."

"Thank you. I hope he shows up."

"I am sure he will."

"Colm was just filling me in on some of your heart-to-heart talks, Dr. Basu."

"Is that right?"

"I t-t-told her the truth, Dr. Basu. She knows now."

"I see." Dr. Basu looked at Cathleen and dropped his head and walked toward the chair by the window to sit down.

Cathleen followed him. "Why didn't you tell me this, Dr. Basu," she asked like a petulant teenager.

"Patient-doctor confidentiality."

"I am his mother!" She sat down beside him, then leaned in over him, pleading with him.

"But he asked me not to tell—as his friend. It didn't affect his treatment."

"M-m-mama, don't be m-m-mad at him. He's my friend. He just wanted to help me."

Cathleen looked at Colm and back at Dr. Basu. Both of them loved her. She could see this now. They were trying to protect her. All of this, she realized—the trip, the exhaustion, even the collapse—was her fault. She felt instantly guilty.

"I am so sorry, Dr. Basu. I didn't mean to blame you."

"It's quite all right. You have every right to be upset."

"No, I'm sorry. I'm sorry for pushing all of this on you two. I just wanted so badly to believe. To hope." She dropped her head in her hands and wept.

Dr. Basu bent over her and wrapped his arms around her. "It's quite all right. There is still more we can do."

"Please don't cry. I didn't m-m-m-mean to m-m-make you cry," Colm pleaded.

"Yes. You're right. I'm being silly, Colm. I'm just tired. And yes, I'm grateful he has you, Doctor," Cathleen said, taking Dr. Basu's hand. "Now let's all get some rest. I'm so tired." Cathleen leaned her head on Dr. Basu's shoulder.

Dr. Basu was surprised and let her lean in to him. She seemed heavy, exhausted by the weight of the enormous truth.

Colm looked at Dr. Basu and smiled. He was glad his mother had a friend. Dr. Basu winked back at him in quiet assurance.

"Yes, let's just take a little snooze until they're ready to discharge you. It's just procedure. They can't do so until all the tests come back. You know how it goes . . ."

"I know the drill, Doc," Colm said, sounding like his uncle.

Before Dr. Basu closed his eyes, he smiled and said, "Sweet dreams, son. You need your rest, too."

But Colm didn't sleep. He sat and watched the scene in front of him—his mother leaning on his friend Dr. Basu's shoulder—and he whispered aloud to his father, who he wished with all his broken heart was sitting beside him now, "Dad, this is my favorite part of the movie."

❧ Part IV

It seems only yesterday I used to believe
there was nothing under my skin but light.
If you cut me I could shine.

—Billy Collins, "On Turning Ten"

❧ Chapter 22

CROSSING THE BRIDGE WAS THE EASY PART. STAYING on the other side was a different story. Although Sean vowed he would never drink again and would start attending meetings, he quickly realized it was more than he could handle on his own. On the evening he met his sister, Colm, and Dr. Basu at the airport, he looked like hell. He was sober, Cathleen could tell, but he smelled like the inside of a Starbucks that had caught on fire.

"Geez, Sean," Cathleen said, hugging him. "Kentucky and Colombia called; they want their tobacco and coffee back."

"I know. I went back to the smokes today."

Dr. Basu frowned.

"Don't give me that look, Doc. I picked a new poison is all. This one won't get me fired. And I can drive while doin' it." He winked back. "Let me help you with those bags," said Sean as he grabbed them out of his sister's and the doctor's hands.

"Thank you," Dr. Basu said. Sean knew, though, he wasn't

thanking him for carrying the bags. It was a different thank-you altogether.

"You're welcome," Sean said, smiling.

"Cathleen, it's a step in the right direction." Dr. Basu leaned over and whispered to assure her, even though he was worried too. He saw it many times. Former alcoholics who quit drinking only to pick up another habit that would eventually kill them too in the long run.

"OK, kids. A buddy lent me his big-ass car, so I can drop you all off. Thought that would be easier on Colm than waiting on the sidewalk for a cab," Sean said, leading them toward the parking garage.

"Thanks, Sean," Cathleen said, surprised again by his new transformation.

"I'll drop you two off first, Cathleen, so you can get Colm to bed. Then I'll take Dr. Basu uptown—assuming you live . . ."

"Yes, the Upper West Side. Riverside, but if it's too far out of the way . . ."

"Don't be silly. I'd be happy to."

After Sean and Dr. Basu carried Cathleen's and Colm's bags into her apartment, and got Colm settled in his bed, Cathleen offered to make them a late dinner.

"No, I really must be going," Dr. Basu declined. "You both need your rest."

"I'll take the doc home—maybe out for a beer."

"Sean!"

"Settle down, Sis. The beer's for him. For him. I'll have a coffee."

Cathleen kissed her brother good-bye on the cheek at the door. "Sean, thank you so much. Thank you—for everything. I'm so sorry for the past few months. If you need anything, anything, I'll be here to help."

"Same goes for you, too."

"Stop by tomorrow and we'll talk."

"Gotta work. But I'll take you and Colm out after church on Sunday," Sean said, turning away.

"Wait! No. Could you do me a favor?"

"Say the word."

"I'll fill you in later, but would you mind taking Colm somewhere else on Sunday?"

"Huh? Why? What's up?"

"I can't explain it all now. But I think it would mean a lot to him if he could just pass on the whole church thing for a while. Church is what I want, but it's not what he wants right now . . ."

"Got it. I'll meet you at St. Pat's then—I'll take him out for breakfast."

"Wonderful."

"Sis?"

"Yeah?"

"I'm proud of you. I know this is hard. All of this sucks. I know that. But you're a hell of a person."

"Thanks, Sean. So are you."

"Save it. I know my bag. It's filled with shit right now."

"Sean, please . . ."

"Seriously, Cate. Save that line for when you mean it. When I deserve to hear it. I've been a jerk for a long time . . ."

Cathleen could tell he had already been to a meeting today; he was ticking off his twelve steps in speed-round style, *making amends*.

"All right. Thanks for taking Dr. Basu home then."

"I'll try to get home in one piece."

In the car on the way uptown, Sean wasted no time getting to his point.

"Doc?"

"Sean?"

"You know what we talked about yesterday . . . on the phone?"

"About Colm?"

"Yes. No. Not exactly . . ."

"Your drinking?"

"You got it. I think I'm in a little over my head with this sober stuff. AA meetings aren't cutting it. I feel real sick today. I don't want to worry Cate. She's got enough going on, and I want to be there to help her. I saw Colm today. He looks bad, real bad. To me anyway. I don't think Cathleen can see it. I think she refuses to accept that he's not going to get better. I have to be there for her. For them. I know that. And I know I have to quit drinking. I *know*. To be honest, the guys at work have been riding me pretty hard. Even threatened to suspend me. I didn't want to worry Cate with all that. But I know I gotta do something. Something."

"There are treatment centers, Sean."

"I know. I did my twenty-eight days . . . a long time ago."

"And?"

"Twenty-eight days isn't enough. But I can't just leave Cate and Colm hanging right now. I gotta get help soon . . . and there is this other thing. I think I effed up my esophagus. I've been puking up blood for a while . . . and I think I need a doctor."

"Sean, you certainly do. But I'm not the doctor for you. You probably destroyed your stomach lining. It's probably just gastritis, but you need to go to a specialist to get it looked at in case it's something worse. There are doctors that can help you. There are support groups. There are lots of things you can do. I'll give you a name of a doctor at Good Sam—and a group that meets there. A friend of mine runs it. And whenever you go to the hospital, feel free to stop by and see me, too. Or you can call me anytime . . . as a friend. I'd be happy to help."

"Dr. Basu, you're a good man. Thanks for doing all this—for my sister and my nephew and me. To be honest, I don't even know why you do it. But I don't even care. I'm just glad you're here."

"Thank you, Sean. I am quite fond of Colm and . . ."

"Cate?" Sean asked, smiling and winking.

"Yes, she's a very strong, bright, and beau . . ." Dr. Basu stopped himself.

"Yup." Sean nodded and laughed a bit. "That's Cate in a nutshell."

Dr. Basu blushed.

"It's all right, don't be embarrassed. I am so glad she has you. If you had any idea, any real idea how lonely she's been . . ." Sean shook his head and trailed off. He didn't want to betray his sister or undercut her. "I'm just glad she has somebody like you."

"Thank you, Sean."

"Hey, Dr. Basu?"

"Gaspar. Call me Gaspar."

"Gaspar, what are you doing Sunday?"

"Nothing. As far as work is concerned, I'm technically still in Italy."

"Do you want to join Colm and me for some breakfast and afterward hit the Natural History Museum with him and Cate?"

"Why, yes, that would be nice."

After pulling up outside Dr. Basu's building, Sean leaped out of the car and grabbed the doctor's bags. Handing them to him, he said, "See you outside St. Pat's, across from the Rock, around ten or so."

"All right then. I'll be there."

Though Sean was the one who initiated Dr. Basu's accompanying them on their family outings, it was Colm who asked him to join them whenever the doctor's schedule would allow.

On their first visit to the Natural History Museum, Dr. Basu explained the Earth's elliptical orbit as they all walked through a special exhibit on their way to the planetarium. Dr. Basu explained to Colm how almost every planetary system had a sun. A center. A source. And how every cell in the human body reflected that order. And how all around the world, the entire universe, there was evidence of the same. "Energy begins from a single powerful source, Colm. Even your body is made up of tiny little solar systems. Millions of cosmos. Thousands of invisible stars. Bursts of electricity that keep your heart beating. Your blood pumping. Your brain working. It's one of the great mysteries. The source of life."

Cathleen nodded and smiled and almost opened her mouth to say something about God—and how he made light out of the darkness. But something stopped her. She couldn't say it, especially in front of Colm, who she could tell had found a kindred spirit.

Colm was dazzled by the good doctor. As the doctor spoke, Colm imagined his body built out of stars, all of them glowing from within.

Sean didn't say anything. He just listened and thought of how it all worked the other way around too. He thought of the fires he fought, how a small spark from a frayed wire or a cigarette left unattended had the power to take down an entire building, consume a life—maybe two—an entire family. Or how a spark of religious fervor could explode within two buildings and take three thousand lives. Sean shook it off and he walked, listened, and watched as Dr. Basu taught the boy, his sister, and him about life—living it. Even if there was no known source, no known reason why.

After their first visit to the museum together, Colm told his mother that he couldn't imagine *not* asking the doctor to join them ever again. "He's *amazing,* Mama." Gaspar was part of them now. Part of their little universe. He was trapped in their elliptical orbit, and there was no escaping it.

Cathleen enjoyed being with the doctor just as much as Colm did, but she didn't know how to go back to their moment on the roof under the stars. Still, she kept that moment close to her heart, and she was much more kind to the doctor from that point on. Cathleen never mentioned it to the doctor, and he, ashamed to have taken her from her son that evening, never mentioned it either, so afraid to bring up a sore subject. Instead, he thought of it often, but only privately. Cathleen thought of it every day. She kept the doctor, his son, and his poor dead wife in her prayers every night; and she even lit candles for them at church and remembered them at Grace time. He had become, even when he wasn't around, a part of them. He was, besides her son and brother, the only constant in her life. He was the only one who both believed her son's godless version of the afterlife and at the same time, like her, wanted him to be miraculously healed. He didn't seem to care if religion or medicine was responsible for the cure; he only wanted Colm to be better and for her to finally be at peace. She loved him totally for it.

She didn't need a reason why.

❦ Chapter 23

CATHLEEN SAT IN THE CHAIR IN DR. BASU'S EXAMining room and looked at her son. He was seven now. She wondered where the time had gone; the baby she knew had disappeared before her eyes. She was about to lament it and then remembered how grateful she was that Colm was there at all. She looked at the shirtless boy who sat with his bony legs draped over the edge of the examining table. His shoulders and collarbone jutted out of his emaciated frame, only loosely connected to the tight ropy muscles that stretched over his thin arms. The only thing that bulged out of his body was the silver-dollar-sized disc that sat under the skin below his left shoulder. His long auburn hair just about covered the faint scar at the incision site, and it wouldn't be long until the hair covered it completely. He was still wearing his wool cap. He looked so odd, half naked with a wool hat and gloves on. Even though heat radiated off Colm's chest, he was unable to sweat, and his hands were still always freezing, especially after he ate. If he didn't wear the gloves, his hands turned blue, and he had to be careful to keep a pulse in his hands and feet. Otherwise the pain was unbearable, and he was afraid he would end up losing all feeling. When he didn't steady his hands against the table or stuff them in his pockets, they shook uncontrollably. He had little control over the rest of his body either. Lately, he had been unable to swallow. Cathleen saw him struggling to take his medicine one morning and asked him what was wrong. He said it was nothing, but she knew.

Every day brought with it a new affliction. Ever since they had stepped off the plane from Rome several months earlier, the day they were greeted by a sober Sean, there were parts of her that wondered if she was being selfish by praying for Colm's survival. She knew on a visceral level that if her son were a dog, they would have put him out of his misery already. But she wouldn't let herself think that way for long. At some level she believed there was still a shred of hope. There was a way to heal him. Despite everything her brother, her son, and his doctor believed, she still went to church, she still prayed for another miracle. Because wasn't he a living miracle already?

All she had to do was look at him.

Still, he was going downhill faster and faster. Colm spent most of his days feeling as if he were going to faint. But he always fought through it. He blacked out walking up the stairs to the apartment or just waking up. He had difficulty speaking. No one, not even Dr. Basu, was sure if it was because he had been gone so long during the last collapse, or if it was his central nervous system finally getting the best of him. His symptoms seemed to come and go and made no sense, one way or another.

His schoolmates thought he was faking it, but it was no act. He sometimes mumbled, gasping for air in between words, and had no control over what he was saying. Larger boys who seemed to be maturing physically made fun of him at school, daring him to die and rise again. If his condition were real, they said, he would be able to do it again. One time, when Cathleen picked Colm up from school, she noticed some children mimicking his awkward gait, his rigid limbs, his trembling hands like he was some sort of sideshow circus freak.

However, by Colm's seventh birthday he hadn't had any other near-death experiences after leaving Italy. To Cathleen it was a sign that God was answering some of her prayers. Colm may not have been physically healed, but at least he hadn't died again. Perhaps the worst was behind them. Perhaps the miracle took, she thought.

Colm sat quietly waiting with his mother for the doctor to arrive. Dr. Basu was never on time, even for Colm, his favorite patient. Colm could feel his mother staring at him, and it made him so uncomfortable. He wanted desperately to free her from her constant worrying. If only, he thought, his father were here with them. Over the past six months he had thought constantly of what the friar in Italy had promised him—that he would eventually meet his father. He still hoped it would be soon. He daydreamed about his father all the time. Colm imagined him coming through the door, like the stories of the soldiers who came back from war, the ones his mother talked about after seeing them on the nightly news. Every time he walked down the hall to his apartment, he imagined opening the door to his father there waiting for him, smiling at him. Sometimes at night, while lying in bed, he thought that perhaps while he slept his father would arrive, and he would be sitting at the edge of Colm's bed when he woke. But it never happened, and he only heard his mother's voice from the kitchen yelling to him to get up and get ready for school. He took his heartbreak out on his mother, by being grumpy or ignoring her. She had no way of knowing why he was angry with her, but she always thought it was something she had done or said. She was always feeling his head for signs of a fever and wondering if he was coming down with something, but the only thing Colm was coming down from was the hope that his father would come for him. He had heard the word *forsaken* once, long ago, in church standing next to his mother, and he leaned over and asked her what it meant. She had said *to turn away from* as if she were the *Merriam-Webster's Dictionary* itself. He thought of it every day, all day—why had his own father *forsaken* him?

When Dr. Basu walked in, he did what he always did—greeted Colm first and then reached his hand out and said, "So nice to see you, Cathleen." It was as if they hadn't seen each other in years, even when they had all, in fact, been to the zoo together the week before.

The doctor and his mother always spent a few moments smiling and making small talk. Colm knew it was what adults called flirting. He could tell the doctor was attracted to his mother just by the way he stared and gave her his full attention when she spoke. Colm never knew about Dr. Basu and his mother's night together on the roof in Assisi. But he knew there was a connection—he had seen it in his hospital room in Rome. He was seven, but he wasn't an idiot.

★ ★ ★

"Hello, Dr. Basu," Cathleen said, smiling. She was so happy to see him again, even though the last time they spoke, they had had another disagreement about Colm's treatment, while Sean took Colm to the restroom at the zoo.

"We have to put him on more nutritional supplements; his body isn't able to absorb nutrients, and it may be a sign that eventually, perhaps . . ." Dr. Basu tried to explain what would happen as Colm's body would break down.

Cathleen stopped the doctor midsentence. "Don't say another word. I know where this is going. Don't you dare give up on him. We've come this far, Dr. Basu. You've seen him. You have. You have seen what I have. He has really good days. Great days. You saw how excited he was today. How do we know? How can we say for sure that this is the end?"

"Cathleen, I understand. I really do. I don't want this any more than you do. But we have to be realistic. He's very sick. He doesn't have a lot of . . ."

Cathleen cut him off again, refusing to hear it. "I am the one here being realistic, Dr. Basu. I thought you and I were on the same page." She was trembling now, and the doctor walked over to her and wrapped his arm around her and held her close as she wept.

"I know, Cathleen. I know. I will do whatever it takes. I promise you. I haven't given up on him yet. But I am worried about you, too. I am sorry. But I am having trouble here. I care so deeply for you both . . . and I . . . I . . . perhaps I am not the best doctor for you any longer. Perhaps I care too much for the both of you."

"What?" Cathleen pulled away from him. "Are you dropping us? Are you shoving us off to somebody else? Do I have to start all over?"

"No, no. I am just worried. That is all. I am losing my objectivity here, I am afraid. You see, doctors are not supposed to treat their own family members, because they have a blind side. Sometimes doctors don't want to see what they need to see in the people they love." Dr. Basu couldn't believe he said the word *love* to Cathleen. It slipped out so easily, and it stopped him from saying anything further.

Cathleen wanted to state the obvious, that she and Colm weren't technically his family. But she felt it too. She knew that Dr. Basu had loved and cared about her son like his own. She also knew how deeply he mourned Dhruv, and how all of this was becoming some sort of daily reminder of what he had already lost. Her heart broke for Dr. Basu. She knew it had to be just as painful for him as it was for her. And hadn't they created an odd sort of family over the past two years, meeting regularly in his office, traveling abroad, visiting museums, zoos, and toy stores? Throughout it all, she saw Colm's attachment growing toward the doctor and the doctor growing in affection toward Colm—and she could even feel him growing closer to her.

Cathleen reached out and took Dr. Basu's hand.

"Dr. Basu, please, please, please don't stop being Colm's doctor. Please."

Dr. Basu pulled her close. "I won't give up on you or Colm, Cathleen. You have my word. But, perhaps, we could start taking Colm to a few other specialists, for some more opinions.

I have been doing some research. There are other facilities that might be able to help. I will go with you, if you like."

"If you think it will help."

"I do."

Dr. Basu had so much more to say, but Colm had come out of the restroom and saw them standing close to each other and looked at them curiously.

"What's going on?"

"Nothing, hon. Dr. Basu and I were just talking about how great you're doing."

Colm smiled at her, but he could tell, like he always could, when she was lying to him.

In the office after Colm's checkup in the pacemaker clinic, Dr. Basu looked at Colm, who looked frail and like he had lost some weight since Gaspar saw him just a week ago. He quickly checked his chart to see his latest check-in weight, and it was as he suspected. Colm had lost another two pounds.

"Well, how are things with our Dove today?"

"Same," Colm interjected.

"Nothing new to report?"

"No," Colm said flatly. He was in one of his moods. He woke up hoping again, and his father had not come.

Dr. Basu looked at the boy and then at his mother. He didn't want to do this. He knew it would upset her, but he thought it would be best if he had a moment alone with the boy, so he asked her as politely as he could.

"Cathleen?"

"Yes, Gaspar?"

"Would you mind waiting outside in the sitting room today? We'll come and get you when we're done."

Cathleen was stunned. He was just a boy. She had every right to know exactly what was going on with him, she thought.

Dr. Basu opened the door and stood quietly, waiting for Cathleen to rise and leave.

Cathleen looked back at him, about to have another fight in her head, Dr. Basu and Colm both knew. But the doctor thought he could talk to her later.

When she was gone, Dr. Basu closed the door and jumped up onto the examining table to sit next to Colm. "Now, young man, what is it that you are not telling me?"

"Nothing," Colm said, grumbling under his breath.

"So everything is OK? You've been going to neurotherapy and physical therapy? Doing your exercising, moving your arms and legs every day at home? Drinking your nutrition shakes? Getting plenty of rest?"

"Yes. Everything . . . is . . . f-f-f-fine," Colm said angrily and slowly, beginning to stutter. It was so difficult for him to form words. "I . . . wish . . . everyone would just . . . leave . . . m-m-me . . . alone."

"Are you feeling all right? Let me take your temperature."

"Stop asking me questions . . . and . . . asking m-m-me how I feel. I'm sick of it. I . . . just . . . I . . . just w-w-w-want . . ."

"What? What do you want? I am sorry to have upset you. I was only . . ."

"Trying to help . . . I know. Everyone . . . is . . . always trying to help m-m-m-me. I just want to . . ."

"To what?"

"Live."

"I see. I thought that's what I was trying to do—help you to live."

Colm spoke steadily, trying hard not to slur. "No. You don't get it. I want to live like a normal person. I want to be better. I want Mama to be like she was in Italy—before I got really sick. When she was happy."

For a moment Dr. Basu thought of Cathleen—in her white dress and pink sweater. He thought of how beautiful she was, and how he too could tell she felt free from worry their first two nights in Italy.

"But, Colm, I cannot take you back to Italy. I cannot make your mother *hap* . . ." He stopped. He didn't want to go there with the boy. "Colm, what is it exactly that I can do for you? How can I help you, Dove? Do you want me to talk to your mother?"

"No!" Colm said. "Don't say anything to her . . . I don't want her going off to church to pray for me anymore . . . and she would if she found out."

"Then what? I want to help you."

"I need you to do something for me."

"Oh?"

"I need you to help me find my father."

Dr. Basu looked pained. He knew he could not do this for the boy.

"I know what you're thinking. He's not worth the trouble, like Uncle Sean says. But I have been thinking about this a lot lately. I bet he wonders about me. I bet he cares. He just has to.

The only reason he hasn't come for me is—Mama never told him that I was his. Right? I mean he must not even know I exist or that I am his. This has to be it. Otherwise, he would be looking for me, or he would know where to find me. He must not know that I am his son. Otherwise, he would have come. He just wouldn't leave me—*abandon* me."

"I am sure you are right." Dr. Basu was not prepared for this. Although he had come to love the boy as his own, he did not know how much until he heard the boy say he wanted to find his *real* father. But more than his own pain, Dr. Basu felt Colm's. *What a burden to place on a child. What a terrible fate for Colm, a child who loved a father who could not love him back.*

"I know if you were my son, and I knew you were out there, I would come for you. Colm, you must know that. You must know that this has nothing to do with you. Have you spoken to your mother about this? Does she know you want to talk to your father? Find him, as you say?"

"I wouldn't even mention it to her or my uncle Sean. I've heard some things he's said, and I don't think so."

"You mean—when he called him a *deadbeat*."

"Uncle Sean doesn't like my father. The couple times that I asked my mama about him, she seemed kind of weird about it. You're the only hope I have."

"What you're asking me is a very a big deal. I will need to discuss it with your mother . . ."

"Please, Dr. Basu. She won't understand."

"I think you underestimate your mother. I think if you did speak to her, she would be happy to take you to Los Angeles to find him."

"He lives in Los Angeles? How do you know that?" Colm jerked his body away from the doctor's and looked at him in disbelief.

Dr. Basu paused. Did he remember incorrectly? Did he say the wrong thing? Had Cathleen told him that the boy didn't know where his father was? That it was a secret? It had been months now since they last spoke of the boy's father. He had no idea. He stopped and looked at the boy and opened his mouth to apologize, but Colm cut him off.

"You mean *you* know. You know where my father is? *You and my mother* have known all this time?" Colm grabbed his shirt and began to dress.

"Now, Dove. Settle down. I can explain. I . . ."

"You and my mother have been lying to me this entire time! You've known about my dad the entire time!" Colm screamed. He had never felt so much rage. "You claim to be my friend—you and my mom. You say you love me. My mom says she knows what is best for me. She tells me to just tell the truth. And you . . . you guys just lie to me!"

Colm opened the door and ran through the waiting room, stumbling a bit but making it past his mother. She tried to get up and chase him, but the doctor stopped her.

"Cathleen, we have a problem."

"What?" She quickly turned, trying to keep Colm in her view as he headed out the door of Dr. Basu's office.

"Cathleen, I have made a terrible mistake. Colm just told me that he needed my help to find his father."

Cathleen was stunned and speechless, moving toward the door and hallway to chase after Colm.

Dr. Basu followed her, explaining to her as she exited his lobby and stepped out to the center of the hall, "I accidentally let it slip that his father was in L.A. Remember how you told me how you thought he was there—you told me when we were in Italy?"

"I have to go, Dr. Basu. You shouldn't have said anything. Oh my God. Oh my God. He'll never forgive me." As Cathleen ran after the boy, Dr. Basu yelled after her, "I am so sorry, Cathleen. I didn't mean to upset him . . . to cause you . . ."

"No, no. It's not your fault. It wasn't fair of me to blame you. It's mine. It's all my fault. I have to go get him." Cathleen chased him, but Colm slipped in between the closing elevator doors before Cathleen could get to him. Before she could yell out his name, he was gone.

❧ Chapter 24

ATHLEEN HIT ALL THE DOWN BUTTONS IN FRONT OF each bay of doors and began to pace, shaking her head and contemplating taking the stairs, but she feared it might take too long to run down seven flights. After several long minutes, an elevator finally arrived. While she rode the elevator down to the lobby she called work and said she would not be making it in for the rest of the day because something had come up with Colm. Her supervisor hung up before she even finished her explanation. Everyone was tired of her excuses. If her son had some known, popular disease, she sometimes thought, maybe she would have garnered some sympathy, but she knew people tended to grow weary of other people's pain. She couldn't blame her boss for being angry with her.

As soon as the elevator doors opened on the first floor, Cathleen burst through them. She checked the lobby and then the gift shop where Colm liked to look at the toys. She ran to the bus stop, and as the bus pulled away, she saw Colm glaring at her from the backseat. She looked for a cab to hail. *Where the hell was a cab when you needed one in this city?*

She comforted herself with the knowledge that he had his bus card with him, along with the twenty-dollar bill she had sewn into his coat in case of emergencies. Maybe he would just go home. She waited for the next bus, transferred to the subway, and after arriving at her stop, ran to her apartment, hoping to find him there. She opened the door, calling his name and looking for him in every room.

For ten minutes, she paced back and forth in the living room, berating herself for letting him go. She tried to reassure herself: he was more than capable of taking the bus and subway home. He had done it for years. But then she panicked, thinking of that day on the subway platform. *What if he collapsed and he was all alone? What if he went down again and this time fell onto the tracks? What if he fell while crossing the street or was hit by a car?* She didn't want to do it, but she called Sean and got no answer. He had given Colm a copy of his shift schedule to keep posted on his bulletin board, and when she checked, she saw Sean was on duty and headed back to his engine company in Midtown.

When she arrived at the station, all the engines were gone. She panicked and buzzed to get inside. "It's Cathleen Magee!" she screamed into the intercom.

The first-year probie who was forced to stay behind didn't know who she was. It shocked her for a second. She thought everyone on Sean's crew knew her, especially the older guys, but then she remembered the younger, newer ones would not have recognized her name. There were so many other widow's children to remember now.

"I need to get ahold of my brother, Sean Magee," Cathleen shouted again.

The probie couldn't make out what she was saying, so he went downstairs and opened the engine garage doors. She was in the truck bay before the doors were fully open.

"I have to find my brother, Sean Magee. Do you know where he is?"

"He's at a call."

"I need him."

"I can call his lieutenant and see if he can get ahold of him if it's a family emergency."

"It is. Can you do that?"

"Absolutely."

Cathleen thought of all the times she was pulled out of work by his crew. *Have you seen him? He was supposed to be here twenty minutes ago. He's gonna be put on probation if he doesn't show today.* The older guys, who had known their dad, were always looking out for him and covering for him—never wanting to see him fail. They were *brothers*, they said, and they went to the wall time and time again for each other. She'd have to leave work, vowing to help them find *their* brother. Ripping her heels off while running down the street, she'd scream into her phone: *"So help you God, Sean! I will kick your ass myself if you're not in the shower by the time I get to your apartment."*

And if she found him sober, albeit hungover, she would drag him down the street to the door of the fire station. She thought of the time he was off duty and a bartender, who said he was wearing Sean's vomit all over his shirt, called her at two in the afternoon screaming obscenities at her and telling her to get her *sorry-ass excuse of a husband.* She corrected the bartender, who said he didn't care if Cathleen was his wife, sister, or undertaker, he just wanted Sean out of his bar. She asked him how he knew to call her if Sean was passed out, and he explained that he got Cathleen's number off Sean's phone. It was, he said, the only number he ever seemed to call on it.

"I checked the call log. I figured by the number of times he called you and you called him you were his old lady," the bartender said.

The only one, Cathleen thought. *The only freakin' one. Really?*

Cathleen wanted to feel badly for interrupting Sean at work, but she knew he owed her big-time. She waited impatiently, and finally the probie gave her the phone to talk to Sean.

"This better be good, Sis."

"Are you at a real fire?"

"False alarm, but having a probie call my lieutenant is not cool. Not cool. We're on our way back to the station."

"Colm took off."

"He's seven. Where could he possibly go?"

Cathleen tried to explain everything, knowing every minute counted. She knew New York City was not Assisi and that there was little likelihood of Colm holding court with friars.

"I have no idea, Sean. Dr. Basu told him Pierce was in L.A.—I don't have time to go into it. He took off from the doctor's office. I checked the apartment. I checked everywhere. Should we get an Amber Alert? Should I call the police? Sean, what the hell should I do?"

"Give me an hour. You go back to the apartment, in case he turns up. I think I have an idea where he is. I'll see if I can take off early."

When Sean told his lieutenant about his sister's call—and that there was an emergency with his nephew again—the lieutenant didn't think twice about it. "We're family, Sean. We take care of family. You go take care of *yours*."

Sean couldn't believe what he heard at first. His first inclination was to correct his lieutenant. *The kid's not mine. It's just my sister's kid.* Then he stopped himself. *Colm is . . . Yes, Colm is . . . He is my own.* Sean peeled off his gear and leaped out the door at the stoplight, heading toward the subway.

As Sean descended the fire truck's steps, his lieutenant shouted, "Hang in there, Magee. I'm sure the kid's gonna be OK."

Sean jumped on the B train. He hadn't taken him there in weeks, but he knew Colm loved the Natural History Museum. When he arrived, he bought a ticket for the Planets and Stars show and ran toward the planetarium.

When he got there, the show was about to end. Sean stood by door and scanned the theater looking for Colm's hat and long hair. The large-domed room seemed to turn, and the giant planets spun over his head. Surprised by the realism, Sean held his arm over his face as if to shield himself from the planets that were crashing toward him. Embarrassed by his own confusion and his startle reflex, he stood upright and looked around to see if anyone noticed. He knew he shouldn't have reacted that way. He and Colm had seen the show countless times, but every time the room began to spin and the universe revealed itself in all its infinite parts, Sean's entire body shuddered, and he seemed to forget for a moment where he was.

When the lights came on, Sean spotted the tip of Colm's hat. Colm wasn't getting up, wasn't planning on moving. Sean guessed he was going to try to catch the last show—he had probably been there all afternoon. *Like mother like son,* Sean thought. He had found his sister in almost the exact same spot a little over seven years ago. She had stayed there all day, too, watching the star shows, holding her swollen belly. She had no idea what she was going to do, she told him. When Sean sat down next to her, she handed him a note that she had found earlier that day. "The dumbass," he had said aloud to her, "left a note. That's rich." The note from Pierce said how much he loved her and how he knew her better than she knew herself or saw her more clearly than she saw herself or some other bullshit nonsense, he thought. Sean couldn't care less what Pierce had written or thought. All he knew was the guy was a bastard who took off and left his big sister all alone. He crumpled the note and threw it on the floor, but Cathleen picked it up and stashed it in her coat pocket. *The bastard left her crying with a broken heart and a baby to take care of all on her own and she's holding on to his goddamn note,* Sean thought. Then he sat down and put his arm around Cathleen, and for the first time in his life, he saw his sister crumble in his arms and sob.

As Sean looked at Colm, he remembered something Dr. Basu had once said to him in one of their long chats on Sunday afternoons while Cathleen made them dinner—*Grief never ceases to transform*. Cathleen had never stopped wondering, never stopped worrying, never stopped loving Pierce. Neither had Colm. And for the first time, he could see it all so clearly. Sean got angry even thinking of Pierce, *the bastard who left her,* and the boy, *Cathleen's very own bastard* who looked just like his father. The very same boy who was breaking her heart all over again by choosing his deadbeat father over her. Sean couldn't believe it. He tried not to be upset, but he wasn't Colm's uncle today, he decided. He was his sister's little brother.

"What's up, Bud? You too cool for school now?"

Colm stared straight ahead. "Did you know about my father?"

"Come on. Let's get out of here. Let's go have a bite."

"I'm not going anywhere—not with you, not with Mama. You're both liars! You're all liars!" Colm screamed.

Sean could barely contain his rage. He knew the boy was only seven, but somehow he didn't care. His anger seeped up slowly through the veins in his neck, moving up through his cheeks and settling in the protruding veins in his forehead. "You gonna call me a liar to my face?"

"You gotta problem with that?" Colm said, like he was born to fight. Like he was cut from the same cloth as Sean himself. Sean had never been so proud—and so mad at the same time.

"As a matter of fact I do." Sean walked toward the boy. He grabbed Colm by the neck, pulling his hair along with the folds of his jacket and dragging him out of the chair.

"You're hurting me. Let me go, Uncle Sean. Let m-m-m-me go!"

"Come on, tough guy. Let's go put your money where your

mouth is. You think you can take me? You think you got what it takes to take on your old uncle? Call me a liar. Go ahead, I dare ya!" Sean was holding Colm up by his shirt, and Colm's legs were dangling as he tried with all his might to wrestle free.

"Let go of m-m-m-me! You've lost it, Uncle Sean!"

Not intending to harm the boy, Sean dropped him to the ground. But Colm stumbled as he tried to balance himself, and he fell hard. From the ground, he looked up at his uncle, who looked like a giant.

Sean stood over him and tried to help him up, but Colm recoiled.

"Get away from me! P-p-please! Just leave m-m-me alone."

"Do you have any idea what you're doing to your mother? Do you? She's given up her whole goddamn life for you. Anything you want, you get. Any medicine you need, she's on it. Any goddamn video game, book, sneaker, stupid hat, you got it. She spent the last six months praying to God for you while all you do is shoot your mouth off about there being no God to her because you said you needed to tell the truth. Well, let me tell you somethin' about the truth. It's over goddamn rated. The truth hurts people. And all the while you've been telling your truth—she's been praying to God to save you. And you have the nerve to be pissed at her. Pissed 'cause she spent her life trying to protect you—trying to protect that sorry-ass father of yours. Trying to protect you from the sad, horrible truth. So the TRUTH is, yeah, I knew where he was. She did too.

"He walked away from you, Colm. Is that what you want to hear? Because I know your mother never wanted you to know. She wanted to protect you—and she never thought she was lying to you. She loves you, goddammit. And I don't think I can say the same thing about your father—because he's not the one worried sick about you right now. Your mother is. I am. Dr. Basu is. All the people who love and care for you are right here in front of you, tough guy. Open your goddamn eyes!"

Colm finally scrambled to his feet and said nothing. His uncle terrified him. He had never seen Sean so angry and had never heard such ugly things come out of his mouth—from anyone's. Colm's legs were rigid, and he could barely put one in front of the other. His stance was wide and ungainly. He looked pathetic, broken. Colm stumbled and fell, tried to walk several times, but kept stumbling. By the third time he fell, Sean lunged for him. He could not see Colm in any more pain. Watching Colm about to fall, Sean snapped out of it. He remembered again who he had been yelling at. It was not Pierce. It was not Cathleen. It was Colm. His *own* Colm, he thought.

"Oh God," Sean moaned. "I am so sorry, Colm. I am so sorry." Sean felt an overwhelming need to vomit. He had said things he could not take back, that Colm, no matter how long he lived, would *never ever* forget. He disgusted himself. He tasted the bile in his mouth, the bitter anger on his tongue. He was ashamed.

"P-p-p-please, let go of m-m-me, Uncle Sean," Colm whispered softly, ashamed of himself and his failing body. Sean tried to help Colm to his feet. "I c-c-c-can do it, Uncle Sean." Colm struggled to stand on his own.

Sean's eyes smarted. He felt awful. Colm, he could tell, was crying. He was shaking. Sean saw the darkening streaks run down Colm's pants as he wet himself. Sean had broken his heart and had told him the things his mother had spent his entire life trying to prevent him from ever knowing, to spare him from just this one pain in life that was too much for a child to bear.

"Please, Colm. I'm sorry. Let me carry you home. Your mother is going to be so angry with me if she finds out how much I hurt you—if you get sick because of me. Let me carry you. Do me this one favor?"

Colm was silent. He didn't want Uncle Sean to be in trouble with his mother. He didn't want another terrible fight between them because of him. He didn't want to get sick and cause his mother to worry.

Colm put up his arms, and Sean melted. His stomach gave way, thinking of Colm as a baby and how he came to him with open arms. He had ruined it all. He had done what he vowed he would never do—he had crushed someone else's dream. He took away the one thing a child has that is totally his own, *hope*.

Sean hoisted him up on his hip. Colm slumped over, resting his head on his uncle's shoulder, and whispered in his ear, "Why doesn't he love me? Does he know? Does he know how much I love him—want to know him?" Colm began to cry softly, and Sean felt the boy's tears mix with his own as they ran down his neck.

Sean squeezed the boy mightily. He held him because he knew better than anyone what it was like to grow up wondering about the father, the invisible father who overshadowed everything he tried to do and tried to be, who was as mysterious as he was wonderful and frightening. He thought how much harder it was for Colm, because his father chose to leave him, while his own was taken, consumed by fire.

"I am sorry, Colm. I don't know why I said those terrible things. I didn't have any right. I was just so angry. Not at you, but at the situation. Nothing in this life makes much sense."

"It's OK, Uncle Sean. I forgive you," Colm said, lifting his head up and looking into his uncle's eyes.

"You don't have to . . . forgive me, Colm. I don't deserve it."

"But, I do . . . because I love you."

❧ Chapter 25

CATHLEEN HAD BUSIED HERSELF WITH DINNER AFTER she hung up the phone. Sean had found Colm and was bringing him home. "Everything's fine. Don't worry," he told her.

Cathleen was overjoyed. She made Colm his favorite—shepherd's pie with extra whipped potatoes. She set the table for three, even putting out placemats and fabric napkins and lighting a candle. When she heard the buzzer, she pressed the button to unlock the door. She assumed it was Sean and Colm coming up.

When she heard the knock at the door, she was pulling the pie out of the oven.

"Just come in, Sean and Colm. The door should be open."

She heard the knock again, and a single set of footsteps came down the hall. She put the pie on a cooling rack and stepped out of the tiny galley kitchen

"JesusMaryandJoseph!" Cathleen gasped.

"Oh, I am so sorry. I didn't mean to startle you. I-I tried to knock, but you insisted that I let myself in."

"Oh, yes. Of course. Why . . . , Gaspar. Why are you here?"

"I was worried. I felt awful about this morning. I wanted to check on you and Colm. I wanted to apologize in person. It was not my place. I should not have said anything."

"Yes. It did cause quite the stir."

"Is he here? Is he OK?"

"I never made it to the elevator to stop him. He took off for the day. I sent Sean after him. They just called about a half hour ago. They were on their way home—should be home any minute, I guess. Would you like to join us? It's no Sunday feast. But it will do."

"Oh, I don't know. I don't want to intrude," Dr. Basu said, scanning her tidy, small apartment, with its stacks of books along the floor, and the numerous pictures of Colm and his artwork all over the walls.

"Nonsense. I have plenty. I made enough to feed an army. Please, you know you're always welcome. Here, let me take your coat," she said, reaching for it before he could even get it off.

Dr. Basu looked at the table, which was set for three and had candles, and felt like he would be an unwelcome guest today. He hadn't been invited this time, and she was only expecting Colm and her brother.

"I should leave. You, Sean, and Colm have a lot to talk about tonight," he said as he stepped toward the door.

"Don't be silly. Colm would be so angry if he knew you were here and I sent you packing."

"I know, but today . . . his running away. It was my fault."

"Come on. How did you know that he didn't know? How could you have possibly remembered every word I said months ago in Italy. Besides, what is there to say now? He knows as much as I do. His father lives in L.A. It's not like his dad has been beating down my door to come and get him. I never brought it up because I thought it would hurt him to know . . . the truth, and guess what? News flash: it did."

Dr. Basu smiled at her. She was trying, he could tell, to hide how hurt she was.

"Please, just stay, Gaspar . . . *for me.*"

They heard Sean and Colm come through the door. Colm ran in and went directly down the hall to his room to change. He didn't want his mother to see what he had done or to have to explain it.

"What's going on, Sean?"

"He just had an accident. He needs to change."

"Oh . . . He's been doing that a lot lately. Should I go and help him?"

"No, he'll be fine. Leave him alone for a few minutes."

After Colm changed, he came out and ran to his mother and hugged her. He had missed her so much. The universe was no place for him without his mother.

"I . . . am . . . sorry . . . Ma . . . ma," he stuttered. "I m-m-m-miss you s-s-so much."

"I'm just glad you're safe, but don't ever do that again. We'll talk about this later. Let's just get some food into you." Cathleen hugged him again and turned to Sean, to whom she was so grateful for finding her son. "I would have never known where to look, Sean! Thank you so much for bringing him home safe and sound."

Sean winced. He had done a terrible job. "No problem, Sis." Sean looked at Colm, and Colm looked at Sean—they each knew neither would tell Cathleen what had happened.

Sean didn't want his sister asking any more questions, so he tried to pretend everything was normal. "So, Basu my man, what's up?" Sean slapped the doctor roughly on his back and winked.

"I just came to check on Colm and Cathleen and to apologize, especially to you, Colm. I didn't mean to upset you," Dr. Basu said.

"It's not a big deal," Colm said quietly, but everyone noticed something different about the boy. He could barely keep his head up, and he looked as if he was about to cry.

"Colm, Dr. Basu is going to stay for dinner. Go wash up and grab another place setting. Then we can all eat."

"Yes, M-m-mama." Colm limped away toward the kitchen.

"Thank you," she said as she watched him. She hated making him do things, but she knew if he was going to grow up, he would have to know how to do things like set the table.

"Sean—do you want a Coke? Gaspar, I have some wine." Sean's ears perked up when he heard his sister use the doctor's first name. He saw them and he knew. And he smiled a big grin at Cathleen.

She blushed with embarrassment, and so did Dr. Basu.

"Yes, Cathleen, a glass of wine would be fine," Dr. Basu said sheepishly.

When Colm was finished setting the table, the four gathered round it. Cathleen asked everyone to join hands. "Please, guys, let's say Grace."

Sean saw Colm smiling at his mother, but his eyes had lost their sparkle. He wasn't smiling a real smile. Sean knew he had taken something from his nephew that no one had the right to take away. He wished he could take it all back. But Colm looked at him and nodded, trying to pretend that he would be just fine.

They all laughed and passed the food back and forth. Colm and Sean told jokes, performing for Cathleen and their guest. Gaspar sat back and watched. He was so happy, so content to just be able to share a meal. There was truly no better way to spend the night than among friends.

Just as everyone seemed to forget the day's events, Colm asked to say something.

"Go on, Colm, we're all ears," his mother urged him.

"I shouldn't have run off like that. I shouldn't have said what I said to you, Dr. Basu, or to you, Uncle Sean, and I shouldn't have made you worry, Mama. I'm sorry," Colm said flatly without stuttering.

"Come on, Colm. It's no big deal. You were right; I should have said something to you awhile ago, when you first asked me about him," Cathleen said.

"No, Mama. You were right. You were just trying to protect me. I understand that now," Colm said, looking across the table at Sean.

"Oh, Colm. I love you. We all love you, and we all want what is best for you. Just because your father, for whatever reason, couldn't handle being a dad doesn't mean something is wrong with you, that you're less worthy of being loved. You need to know that."

"I know, Mama. I know. But . . ."

Colm looked around. He hadn't quite expected his doctor, his only friend in the world, to be there when he made his announcement to his mother. He didn't think his uncle Sean would be there either. But Colm knew he had to go through with it, and he had to go through with it today. Colm had thought long and hard all day in the planetarium, and he had made up his mind before his uncle Sean had shown up. He was going to go home on his own anyway. He wasn't going to let his mother worry. But he was going to go home and ask her to help him find his father. He had to know, he thought. As much as it would hurt all of them, and as much as he didn't want to hurt them, he knew he had to do it.

"Mama?" Colm said quietly.

"Yes."

"I need you . . . to hear . . . me . . . out. I . . . need you all . . . to hear . . . me out for a second," Colm said slowly, deliberately.

"Sure, hon, whatever it is, just shoot."

"Mama, I'd like to find him."

Cathleen felt the blood rush to her feet, her head suddenly lighten, the room begin to spin.

Sean braced himself against the table. After everything he had just told him, everything that had just happened, Colm was actually doing this. Sean was about to open his mouth, but Cathleen put up her hand to tell him to stop. "Don't say a word, Sean. Not one word."

Cathleen inhaled and closed her eyes. She had known this day would come. If Colm lived long enough, she knew it was inevitable. It was the other edge of the sword. She had bartered with God—had promised over and over—if he let Colm live, then she would do whatever the boy wanted. If he ever wanted to leave her, go live with his father, do anything to break her heart, she would let him do it. She promised God, over and over, she would do anything to let Colm live. If the miracle took, this was the price she had to pay.

She took Colm's hand and squeezed it and shook her head. She didn't think she could do it. Sean opened his mouth again to try to speak, but Cathleen shot a cold stare at him. Dr. Basu sat quietly, not knowing his place, fearful of saying anything to upset anyone else.

"I am sorry, Uncle Sean. I really am. I just. I just have to go. I have something else to say . . ."

Everyone stopped and looked at Colm, and no one was prepared to hear what he was about to announce.

"I think this is it. I know you don't want to hear this, Mama. But I think Dr. Basu already knows."

"What are you talking about, Colm?"

"Mama, I don't have much time. I need you to understand this. I do. Please. The miracle didn't take. I know it didn't. And I am going to die, and I need to do this one thing. Just this one thing before I go. I need to see him. To know him. Please, Mama."

Cathleen gasped and pushed herself away from the table and walked into the kitchen. Sean threw his napkin on the table and went after her.

Colm looked across the table at Dr. Basu, and they both sat quietly as they listened to Cathleen crying in the kitchen, and Sean trying to get her to stop.

Sean spoke softly, so Colm wouldn't hear. "Sis, he's just a kid. He doesn't know what he wants or what he's talking about. Come on, Sis. Don't buy this bullshit guilt trip. This is taken from Mom's playbook. Christ, it must be in the DNA. He knows how to get to you. He's not dying, and you don't have to go taking him to Los Angeles to prove to him how much you love him or any of that other bullshit drama. You got it?"

Cathleen whispered quietly, "Look at him, Sean. Look at him. Maybe he knows? Maybe he's right. Dr. Basu tried to tell me the same thing last week—he tried to, but I wouldn't listen."

Sean whispered back, "Cate, he's sick. I know that. But no one, and I mean no one, knows when they're gonna kick it. Not even Colm. Yes, he's sick. I am all for being prepared and being honest. I am. Trust me. But I think he's just trying to get you to do this. And, Sis, you don't have to do it."

Just then, Dr. Basu stepped into the kitchen with Colm trailing close behind.

"I will take him," Dr. Basu said with a calm, quiet voice, shocking all of them.

Cathleen and Sean turned and looked at him. He looked at Colm. In turn, Colm looked up at him with quiet gratitude.

"What?" Cathleen and Sean said together.

"I'll take him. If you think it will be too painful, Cathleen and Sean, I will take him. Besides, I have been doing a lot of research. There is a doctor at the Children's Hospital in Los Angeles who has been working on an experimental treatment with severe neurological disorders, and he's on the cutting edge of science, and perhaps we could get Colm into the study. And since Colm is in no condition to get on a plane, and no commercial airline will take him, I will drive him myself. We're going to need to be able to make stops. We'll need to be close to hospitals should anything happen or if he collapses again."

"How come I have never heard of this doctor before? Or this treatment?" Cathleen asked.

"You have, sort of. He is one of the doctors I mentioned to you last week, one of the experts I told you I would be consulting going forward."

"And you think this doctor has the answers?"

"I am not sure, but we could see what he has to say. He knows more about degenerative diseases that affect the heart and brain than I do. And he might be the objective mind we're looking for—he might have alternatives and offer us some hope."

Cathleen heard the word *hope* and she smiled. Yes, that's exactly what she needed.

"Well, I have to think about all of this," Cathleen said, looking at Colm.

"Mama, please. I want so badly to go. Please," Colm begged.

"Colm, you need to understand, if and only if, I decide to go, we're not just going to find your father, we're going to see another doctor and a new hospital. And I don't want to hear any more of this dying business. Do you hear me? We're going to get you better. We are."

Colm nodded. He was willing to agree to anything if it meant he would get closer to seeing his father.

Sean, annoyed that there was still even talk of Pierce and Colm looking for the man, wanted to push the envelope with Cathleen. "So where is this guy? Why haven't we heard anything from Mr. Wonderful in seven years?"

Cathleen shot a dirty look at Sean. "Not in front of Colm, Sean. Not now."

"Come on, Sis. Colm wants to know. I'd like to know."

"Colm, ignore Uncle Sean. It's getting late; why don't you go get in your pajamas and brush your teeth and I'll be in to tuck you into bed in a minute and we'll talk . . . alone," Cathleen said, staring at her brother.

"I want Dr. Basu to tuck me in."

Cathleen looked at Colm, surprised, and Dr. Basu smiled back at the boy.

"I'd be happy to, Colm. Run along and I will be in to say good night when you're ready."

After Cathleen thought Colm had left and was out of earshot, she looked at both Sean and Dr. Basu, who she could tell wanted to know more.

"Well, Sis, where is the Father of the Year?"

"I honestly have no idea. I really thought he was in Los Angeles. I know that's where his family was from. I also know while we were living together he was struggling to make it in New York and thought he would go back to Los Angeles to try music out there. I had a feeling back then he was just going back home though—to get away from me and the baby—and avoid responsibility. Who knows? A few years ago, I tried to find him again and I even contacted his parents, who live just outside L.A., but I think they were worried I was after their money or something. They hung up on me as soon as I introduced myself. But maybe I was mistaken. Maybe it was Pierce they didn't want anything to do with. How should I know? It was so long ago, but I vaguely remember Pierce telling me his father was kind of a jerk who didn't understand him. I think they may have even been estranged while we were together in New York. I never pushed him to talk about it. Although, after I got pregnant, Pierce accused me of planning the whole thing to get at his family's money. It was, I recall, one of his less stellar performances," Cathleen said, remembering all the things Pierce said to her and how foolish she had been.

Colm, who was hiding in the hall as he listened to his mother talk about his father, shook his head. *No, no, no. It couldn't be.* He was ashamed of his father. He couldn't believe the man he had imagined all this time would have ever said such things to *his* mother.

"I've sent packages to Pierce and his parents, too, at times—with letters, artwork, pictures, everything for years, hoping either Pierce would get them or his parents would pass them on to him," Cathleen assured them all. "They just get returned to me unopened."

Colm was shocked by all of his mother's efforts and embarrassed for saying all those ugly things to her earlier. He thought of how hard it must be for her, too, waiting for him to come and knowing what she did about him.

Cathleen grew quiet—trying hard not to move, not to let the men know that she was terrified. *What if he chooses him over me?* All this time she had been so worried about losing Colm to death that it never occurred to her she would lose him to a better life, possibly a better parent, a better future with someone else. *What if Pierce had married—had a wife and children of his own?* She had to stop herself from thinking of all the possible scenarios. And even the impossible ones.

Colm stood quietly in the hallway waiting to overhear the

adults make their final decision. *Who would take him and when?* Even though he knew what he knew now—his father didn't want him and was sending pieces of him back one envelope at a time—he still wanted to see him. He still wanted an explanation. He still believed that if his father saw him—just once—he would regret it all and come back to him.

"Cathleen, do you think there is any chance he is still out there? We don't want to take him all the way to L.A. with the hopes that he will find his father only to disappoint him," Sean asked now, seriously considering Colm's heartbreak.

"I'm not sure. I guess I have to look into it. But, honestly, the only thing I care about right now is getting him better. What if this friend of Dr. Basu's can help?" Cathleen looked at the doctor.

"We won't know if we don't try. But I am willing to, if you are, Cathleen. I'll work on the arrangements on my end. I will have to reschedule some elective surgeries and get some other doctors to cover my appointments and emergencies. It may take some time to arrange. I can't promise I can leave immediately, although I have several weeks of unused time. Excluding our trip last year, in all the years in my practice, I haven't gone anywhere."

"I have plenty of time saved up, too, Cathleen. And I'll go only if this trip isn't just about finding Pierce. I can help you with Colm and with the drive," Sean agreed.

Cathleen looked at both of them. "So we're going to do this? We're going to take him to L.A.?"

Sean and Dr. Basu nodded.

"Well, I'll need to get some money together, rent a car, check out hotel rates, get some maps . . . I need to get some books from the library on how to take a trip across the United States. I need to plan this stuff out. Maybe we can find a private investigator or something like that to help track Pierce down." Cathleen started to do her thinking outside her head.

"Cate, don't worry about this Pierce bullshit. I mean it. Stay focused on Colm and this new doctor and hospital—and real medicine, real results this time around. Finally, a trip worth taking," Sean added, making a final dig at his sister and her ill-fated quest for a miracle.

Cathleen shot back a look. "I told you, Sean, I was just trying everything. That's all. And I am willing to give new doctors and hospitals a chance too. But, Sean, you know as well as I do, Colm will be so disappointed if we drive all that way and put him through all of the pain of traveling, and he doesn't get to find his father."

"Well, there is no guarantee with this guy, is there? I mean, say you do find out where he lives—then what? What do you think is going to happen? We show up and what? He's going to come running out to Colm with open arms? Come on, Sis. Be realistic. You're setting him up for a heartbreak. You're setting yourself up for one."

"I know. I know, I hear you, Sean. I get it. I just feel awful. I am his mama. I am supposed to help him."

Colm knew Dr. Basu would be coming to tuck him in soon, so he tiptoed back to his room, slipped off his clothes, put on his pajamas, jumped into bed, and yelled out down the hall, "Dr. Basu, I'm ready!"

"I will go talk to Colm," Dr. Basu said, taking his leave from Cathleen and Sean.

"Thank you, Dr. Basu," Cathleen said.

Dr. Basu nodded in acknowledgment and walked down the hall.

Dr. Basu stepped into the dimly lit room toward Colm and sat next to him on the bed.

"Good night, Dr. Basu."

"Sweet dreams, son."

"Thank you for telling my mom that lie about the doctor in Los Angeles."

"It wasn't a lie." Dr. Basu looked at Colm in surprise.

"But it was. I know when people are lying. You know as well as I do that this is it."

"What do you mean?"

"We've had this talk before, Dr. Basu. And I am telling you, it's time."

"Do you feel especially ill? What hurts you most? If there is something serious, you must tell me. I can help you."

"You can't. Once a body is set on dying, it's going to die. There isn't a doctor in the world who has ever been able to keep someone alive forever. When it's a person's time, he has to go. It's science, Dr. Basu. You know that. That's what you always say."

"But you're just a little boy—you just turned seven. You have plenty of life to live. Don't you want to live? Don't you want to see your mother and uncle grow old? Don't you want to finish school? There are so many beautiful places to see in the world. So many wonderful things to do. How can a little boy like you want to give up so soon?"

"I'm not giving up, Dr. Basu. I've fought so hard for so long to stay with Mama as long as I could to make sure she'd be OK without me. And she's ready. I'm ready."

"Now I've told you, it's not your job to worry about your mother. You have to worry about living. Don't you see there is so much to live for—right here on Earth?"

"I know. That's why I need you take me across it. I want to see it all before I go."

Dr. Basu squeezed Colm's hand. *How could the boy know?*

"Like Uncle Sean, I want to see the mountains, the plains, and even the Pacific Ocean. And, most of all, more than anything or anybody, I want to see my father before I go."

"But there is no guarantee you will see him. Your mother doesn't know where he lives."

"We'll find him. I know it. The friar told me so."

"What? What friar?"

"When I was lost in Italy, a friar told me I would see my father. He was sure of it. He promised me."

Dr. Basu closed his eyes, thinking the friar was probably speaking of Colm's *heavenly father*—making Colm another false promise, one that the friar had no right to give. But Dr. Basu didn't want to crush the boy, not now, so he went with it. "Oh, I see. Did he tell you where or when you would see your father?"

"No. But I know. I just know this is it. And you'll help me find him."

"I do hope I can help you, Colm."

"You already have, Dr. Basu."

"Oh? How have I helped you? I haven't been able to make you

better. I haven't been able to cure you. You said yourself you're dying."

"But because of you, Dr. Basu, I have lived. I really have. And soon when we go to Los Angeles, you're going to help me live my dream. That's all a person can hope to do before he dies. Just have one dream come true. One wish. That's what heaven is. It's not where God is. It's not up there or out someplace after we die. It's right here. We make it heaven. You can make it for me. I see that now. When I first met you, and you told me your name was Gaspar, I thought you would save my life. But now I see—there's more than one way to save a life or to give life. And that's what the first Gaspar did. He gave a *gift,* like you have given me."

"Oh? How is that? What gift have I given you?"

"You gave me *you.* You're the best friend I ever had. And now you are Mama's and Uncle Sean's, too. And I don't have to worry about them anymore. They have *you.*"

Dr. Basu bent over and softly kissed the boy on his cheek.

"You are some sort of special child, Colm Francis Magee," Dr. Basu whispered softly, his voice cracking.

"I know. The friar told me that, too."

"Well, he was right about that."

"And he's right about my father."

"I hope so. With all my heart, I hope so. Now good night, Colm."

"Night, Dr. Basu."

❧ Chapter 26

A COUPLE OF WEEKS LATER, ON A COOL SPRING SUNDAY morning, they all met at Cathleen's apartment. Dr. Basu pulled up in his large Mercedes sedan and sat in it to keep it running so that it would be comfortable for Colm. Sean arrived first with only a backpack, taking the notion of a road trip to heart.

When Sean saw his sister and nephew at the top of the stairs, he ran up and grabbed their bags, and Dr. Basu hopped out of the car to help Sean load the trunk. When they were through loading, Dr. Basu ran around the side of the car to open the passenger-side door for Cathleen. Sean helped Colm into the car and slid in alongside him.

It was so odd, Sean thought, sitting in the backseat. Finally, the trip out West he always dreamed about as a boy. They were headed off to see the world together, to see new and wonderful things.

His sister turned around and flashed a warm bright smile at her two boys in the backseat.

"Now, behave back there you two," she warned jokingly.

"Yes," Dr. Basu added. "Don't make me pull over!" And he flashed a wink in the rearview mirror.

Sean leaned forward, grabbed the doctor's shoulders, and shook him gently.

"Buckle up!" Dr. Basu announced as he pulled away from the apartment. Cathleen looked up at her apartment building and wondered for a brief moment if she would return alone. Colm looked through the back window, too, at the apartment, the sidewalk, the neighborhood—all he had ever known. He knew he should have been sad to leave it all behind, but he couldn't lie to himself. He had never felt more hopeful or more alive.

Sean and Dr. Basu were already at war over the radio. "What's this crap you got on, Doc?"

"It's NPR."

"N-P-who gives a shit. Let's put the FAN on or get some music, old man."

As they drove out of the Lincoln Tunnel and headed into Jersey, Colm, Sean, and Cathleen turned their heads to look behind them. Dr. Basu looked in the rearview mirror. They saw the sun rising behind them over the sparkling city. The morning sky was crisp and blue. Not a cloud was in the sky.

They were on their way.

They had to stop more than they originally figured they would. Colm had to go to the bathroom every hour. He could not get comfortable. His jerking and constant movement and trembling was starting to drive Sean nuts. In between Colm's nervous fits, they spent a lot of time getting to know each other, in a way only a long car ride permits, by teasing one another incessantly. For two days they drove, without much to see but rolling hills with the first signs of spring—pale green and pink deciduous buds that speckled the highway and beyond. Colm was restless, worried about their route. Cathleen assured him they would try their best to get to L.A. by Sunday, but she reminded him that their appointment at the hospital in L.A. wasn't until Tuesday, so they had time. But Colm was adamant. He wanted to get to L.A. by Sunday; he couldn't care less about the doctor's appointment. He knew that was Dr. Basu's way of getting his mother to make the trip. Cathleen reminded Colm that it might take a little longer than expected, because after they reached St. Louis, where they would pass the Arch, they would then drive north, to see the Nebraska plains and the northern Colorado ridge of Rocky Mountain National Park. Colm winced, thinking it might take too long, but agreed. Even though he wanted to see the mountains, he knew his uncle Sean wanted to see them more than anyone.

On Monday morning when they left Cincinnati, the car was filled with the smell of hotel soap and shampoo. They drove for several uninterrupted hours. Colm seemed to be getting more comfortable, and by midafternoon he even managed to fall into a deep sleep, slumped over Dr. Basu, who was taking a break from driving and sitting in the backseat next to him. At the wheel, Sean was the first to see the large, silver catenary curve of the Arch rise in front of them.

"Hey, Doc? Get him up, will ya?" Sean said.

Dr. Basu gently touched the boy's shoulder and shook him awake.

"Colm, Colm, wake up. Look!" Dr. Basu said, pointing out the window.

As they crossed the Mississippi and looked to their right, they saw the giant Arch sweep up to the heavens. "It was," Cathleen explained, "an architectural and engineering stroke of genius." Colm stared as they passed by it and gave the *Wow-Cool* that had been shouted countless times by children from all over, who with their parents on a journey over the Mississippi passed by it not expecting its height, its grandeur, and its mystery. *How does it stand up without tipping over?* Colm asked innumerable questions, waiting for all the adults to answer, but they all sat silently, unable to explain how certain things worked in the world. Even Dr. Basu, who seemed to know everything, sat quietly, saying nothing. Some things, he thought, yes, perhaps, remained best a mystery.

They had been on the road three days when they crossed the Iowa-Nebraska border and saw the Welcome sign, glossy and green with white reflective lettering, shimmering in the sparkle of the high afternoon sun. Colm smiled, believing the message had been written for him alone. Life, a good one, it promised him, lay just beyond the endless barrage of billboard signs.

The road continued to roll under the Mercedes's tires, and they moved forward—out of Iowa, out of the East, out of all they had ever known and into Nebraska, home of the good life, sandhill cranes, steers, and corn. Safely buckled in the doctor's car, they all thought the stars seemed to align, the planets moved into position, the angels took their rightful posts, cars parted and let them pass. Free and first, they were well on their way.

Cathleen talked incessantly about how harsh the country still was, how raw and new it all seemed compared to the concrete jungle they had just come from. But she acknowledged it was still a different experience to take a road to Nebraska from the East Coast today than it was a hundred or two hundred years prior when it must have been a long, hard road. She remembered an English class she had taken in high school, and her teacher who loved Willa Cather, the great Nebraskan novelist. Cathleen recalled what Cather had said: *It is not the destination but the road—the road is all.*

"Can you imagine it, Colm?" Cathleen asked. "What it would have been like?"

Cathleen was trying to picture it herself. She found it almost impossible to imagine, while soaring down the interstate at a cool eighty miles per hour, how arduous the trip must have been for those first few brave souls to travel through the roadless mountains and valleys of Pennsylvania and Ohio and the hot, drab, and grassy plains of Indiana, Missouri, and Iowa.

"Colm, imagine traveling all that way only to find even more grass just beyond the Iowa bluffs in this endless state of Nebraska? I think I would have cried. I would have absolutely died. To think you traveled all that way, hoping for something amazing and you were met with this?"

Cathleen pointed out the window to the vast, empty plains. "Nothing."

She looked out the window and felt so small, so hopeless—erased, just as Cather said she felt—staring down a gargantuan red sky that swallowed her whole as she moved toward its large, hot yellow mouth.

"I don't know, Mama. I think it's pretty cool. Pretty amazing," Colm said, looking out the window.

Sean looked out the window, too, and put his hand on his heart and began to sing in a deep baritone, "Oh beautiful for spacious skies, for amber waves of grain . . ."

"All right, cut it out, wise guy," Cathleen said.

"What? I'm serious. It's beautiful, Sis."

"You're making fun of me, Sean. You're always making fun of me."

"I'm not. I think you're right. It's really hard to wrap your brain around it—the majesty of it all. It kinda makes you think."

"It makes me wonder about so much," Cathleen said as she quietly stared out over the dashboard to the long road in front of her.

"What, Mama? What does it make you think of?"

Colm thought he knew what she meant. He thought she was trying to prepare him. What if he traveled all the way to California and his dad wasn't special? *Wasn't anything to write home about,* he thought.

But Dr. Basu and Sean knew what Cathleen really meant. She was having another existential crisis. What if all that praying, all that wishing and hoping for a place like heaven, a final reward for her hard road here on Earth, was just a big, fat, Nebraska-size letdown? What if it all amounted to *nothing*?

"Maybe Nebraska was proof. Proof that there was nothing beyond. Maybe it's a cosmic metaphor," Cathleen finally said aloud.

"Proof of what, Mama?" Colm asked, totally confused.

"Proof that there is no heaven. That you're right, Colm. That it's all about the road. That we shouldn't be putting these big expectations on life—on people, the afterlife. Maybe it's a sign."

"Come on, Sis. Leave that crap alone for twenty minutes and enjoy yourself. It's just a big old lot of land where corn grows. Don't read too much into it. Maybe it's not proof there is no heaven, maybe it's proof of *hell*."

Dr. Basu spit out the coffee he was drinking. Sean always made him laugh.

Cathleen laughed too, knowing that she was bringing everyone down. "I know, I know, Sean, you're right. I need to relax. It's just sometimes I start thinking . . ."

"Never bodes well for you, Sis. Never."

"Thanks a lot, jackass."

"Come on, Cate. I'm kidding."

"So am I," she said, punching Sean in the shoulder.

"So, Mama, does this m-mean that you don't believe?"

She laughed. "No. It just means that even belief has its limits. Even those who believe wonder. You can never, ever know for sure."

"I know, Mama. I know."

Cathleen said nothing else until they were just outside of Grand Island, where they pulled off and stayed in a weather-beaten motel. It was dark when they arrived, and all agreed to go to bed early so they could get up at dawn to make it to Denver by afternoon.

When they made it out to the car the next morning, they saw what looked like a swarm of giant birds, tens of thousands of them flying overhead in the early amber and purple sky.

"What in God's name are they?" Cathleen said, looking up.

"They're the sandhills," Dr. Basu said. He had already been outside looking intently up at the sky. "They're huge cranes and they migrate here every year, like they and their ancestors have for millions of years, long before us. In the spring, they fly north for the summer. It's here, on the plains of Nebraska, where they land and dance. They do the ritual dance for each other, and they find their mates for life. When they return next time, those who found mates will have a baby with them. Thousands of people from all over the world come here just to see it."

"Let's go see them!" Colm said eagerly. "I want to see them dance for each other!"

"I think we just need to find an open field somewhere, where they land and feed," Dr. Basu said.

They drove along the road until they found signs that led to a nature preserve. When they arrived, there were rows of cars, vans, and buses parked, and all around the fields were people with binoculars wrapped around their necks. There were even observation decks built to look out over the fields where the birds landed.

There were thousands of cranes, more than the eye could see. They were dancing for each other, lifting their giant wings back and forth, then one leg, then another, showing their mates they had what it takes to be there for them for the rest of their lives.

Colm, Sean, Dr. Basu, and Cathleen stood looking out beyond the birds at the rising sun. They stood speechless. There was no explanation for it—for the order, the precision, the devotion. How amazing was the world and how all of its infinite parts fit and worked together, Dr. Basu thought.

"Amazing," Dr. Basu gasped. "I heard about the birds on NPR's *Earth & Sky,* but I never imagined it was so—so *heavenly.*" He was dancing for Cathleen now, saying things he knew she wanted to hear.

"It is, Gaspar. It is. It's breathtaking," Cathleen said.

"You crazy nerds ready to get back on the road or what?" Sean broke in. "If we're smart about it, we're in Denver tonight, and we can be on top of Mt. Evans by tomorrow morning."

"We're ready," Dr. Basu said, forgetting for a moment he was not in Italy and grabbing Cathleen's hand to walk toward the car. Cathleen did not resist, and together they came down the stairs. Sean, shocked by this outward sign of affection, followed them, curious to see where this was going. They had already reached the car, and Dr. Basu was opening the door for Cathleen to get in when they all noticed Colm hadn't followed them.

"Colm?" Cathleen yelled.

"Colm?" Sean and Dr. Basu yelled.

"Where the hell is he now?" Sean said, acting angry, but secretly fearing the worst.

Sean ran toward the deck and then up the stairs. Colm was still there. He was leaning over the guardrail and looking out at the birds.

"Colm, what's going on? Why aren't you coming? We gotta get on the road. We're keeping your schedule, remember?"

"Uncle Sean?"

"Yeah, Bud."

"Why don't you think Mama and my father mated for life? Why do birds—these birds—even know how to stay, and how to take care of their family? How come my father didn't?"

"I don't know, Colm. Maybe that's something you can ask him when you see him. I'm kind of curious about that myself, to be honest with you," Sean said while leaning over the rail now, too, and looking out toward the birds.

"Yeah. I mean Mama is pretty great . . . and so . . ."

Sean knew what he was about to say and cut him off. "Yes, so are you. You're awesome, too. There is nothing wrong with you or your ma, if that's what you're worried about."

"You mean something was wrong with my dad?"

"I don't know, kid. What the hell do I know? I just know someone had to be pretty messed up to leave you or leave your mother. I know that for a fact."

"Do you think he'll be happy to see me?"

"He'd be a fool not to. Now let's go. You worried your mother . . . again."

"I always worry her."

"She's a mom. That's what they do."

"Well, I worry about her—and you. I just need to know she has you and you have her. You need each other."

"Come on, now. She already has you. She doesn't need anyone else."

"I just need to know you'll always take care of her. You won't take off on her—ever. Like that night in the hospital. No matter what she says."

"I won't. I promise."

"I am glad she has you, Uncle Sean."

"Looks like she has another someone too," Sean said, nodding toward the direction of the car.

"You mean, Dr. Basu?"

"Yeah. I think he likes her."

"I think so too," Colm agreed.

"OK. So nothing more to worry about, right? Ready to see the Rockies?"

"Yup."

Colm wobbled beside his uncle, who wrapped his arm around the boy's waist to support him as he walked down the steps. Sean was dancing for Colm too, letting him know he wasn't going anywhere. For life.

They drove all day through Nebraska, down through Sterling headed toward Denver. By late afternoon they all saw what looked like a purple cloud formation off in the distance.

"I've never seen clouds like that," Colm said.

"Those aren't clouds, Colm," Dr. Basu said.

"Those are the Rocky Mountains," Sean added.

"You've got to be kidding me," Colm said. "They're beautiful!"

"I know. I have always, always wanted to see them myself," Sean said. "In the morning, we'll be right in the middle of them."

The white caps of the mountain peaks took on the color of pink and lavender in the morning sun. As much as Colm wanted to just get on the road, he knew his uncle was right. He didn't want to miss climbing Mt. Evans for anything in the world. Mt. Evans was one of the few fourteeners in the United States accessible by car—so people like Colm, who couldn't otherwise ever climb or reach the summit from its base camp, could. It was also on their way west. But when they got to Echo Lake to turn onto Mount Evans Highway, they found the road closed.

"I guess there's still too much snow up on the mountain. It looks like it opens up in summer after Memorial Day," Cathleen said after reading the sign and getting out her guidebook.

"Shit," Sean said.

"We can always come back someday," Cathleen assured Sean.

"Yeah. I guess."

"Let's look for an observation pull-off somewhere, Sean. We're almost eleven thousand feet up—that's still two miles higher than New York City. Come on, don't get upset," Cathleen said as she tried to assuage him.

Colm felt bad for his uncle. He knew he really wanted to reach the summit of a mountain. He seemed to be trying to reach the mountaintop his entire life, only to find a roadblock at every turn.

As Sean threw the car in reverse to turn around, he barked, "Story of my damn life."

Colm heard him, touched his shoulder gently, and said nothing. He understood his uncle's disappointment all too well. When Sean felt Colm's hand on his shoulder, he thought of the boy—and the boy's own disappointments—and he couldn't help but stop feeling sorry for himself.

"Sorry about that, guys. It's really no big deal. We'll come back someday together, Colm, when you're older and we can climb the whole damn thing. Sound like a plan?"

"That sounds awesome, Uncle Sean. Maybe even my dad can come too!"

Sean closed his eyes and bit back what he wanted so badly to say. He had learned his lesson, so many lessons, from Colm.

"That would be great, Colm. Just great."

Colm smiled and looked out over all the mountain peaks that jutted into the sky like tyrannosaurus teeth. Deep down he knew he would never make it back with his uncle, but it brought him joy to think that someday even without him there, his mother, his father, Dr. Basu, and his uncle would climb them. And as he thought of this he smiled. Because in just a few days he would finally see him, his father. His very own mountaintop. *He. Couldn't. Wait.*

❧ Chapter 27

FOR THE NEXT TWO DAYS, THEY DROVE THROUGH barren desert toward the dry, hot West. It seemed to Colm like they had left the planet Earth. He had never seen topography like this. As they drove through Nevada, Colm pretended to be on Mars.

"Mission Control, Mission Control. I see Martians. Yes, Martians. I need backup. Lasers and all your forces," Colm said in a deep voice, as he tried to create static sound effects by forcing the back of his tongue up against the roof of his mouth, "*Khhkhhhkhhhh,* I am losing you, Mission Control. I am losing contact!"

"Mission Control, here. We're sending in the Giant Robotron-Superhero-Special Forces," Sean said. "Be ready for battle. Man your weapons!"

"The Martians—they have attacked. We have been defeated! Our forces are destroyed! Mission Control: We are Martians now!" Colm shouted.

When Colm didn't want to be an astronaut anymore, but a Martian, Sean fashioned foil antennas out of the leftover wrappers from their burritos. They sat in the backseat with their Martian headgear and busied themselves for hours in Colm's imaginary world and watched as the world flew by them in streaks of red, orange, and brown. Occasionally, Colm would leave his uncle on Mars and cross his eyes, while staring out the window. He liked to watch the colors swirl and the world shift and change before him.

When Colm and Sean weren't on the United States of Mars, Cathleen and Sean were at each other's throats, yelling about when to stop, where to eat, and how long to stay. Dr. Basu and Colm often looked at each other, rolling their eyes, exasperated by them both.

"Would you two just stop it?" Colm shouted.

"Why can't you two just get along? Don't you see how stupid it is to fight? Try to have a little fun, Mama. Uncle Sean, try to be nice."

Dr. Basu smiled and winked at the boy every time he came to their rescue and saved them from each other time and time again.

By the evening of their fifth day on the road, Dr. Basu pulled into a roadside motel that he could tell had a pool. "I think we could all use a break. Maybe a swim, no?" Dr. Basu asked.

"Yes!" Colm shouted out. "I'd love to go swimming!"

"Yes, it's awfully hot. A dip in a pool would be nice," Cathleen agreed. "Are you sure you feel up to it, Colm?"

"Yes!" Colm shouted. He couldn't wait to get out of the car.

Cathleen smiled and thought quietly, *It's a sign. He's getting better.*

Dr. Basu checked them all in and gave them their keys and told them to go and change. "OK. We'll see who can get changed and get in the pool first," Dr. Basu said, laughing.

"I'll race you, Dr. Basu," Colm said. Colm and his mother ran to their room. "Come on, Mama! Hurry, hurry. I don't want Dr. Basu and Sean to win."

"OK, OK." Cathleen stepped into the bathroom. "I'll be out in a second. Your suit is in my bag. I packed a new pair of trunks for you I bought for this trip," she yelled through the door.

Colm looked in his mother's bag and found a pair of navy blue trunks with white stars all over them. "Aw, Mama. I love them. They're sooo cool."

"I'm glad. I knew you would like them, hon. Don't worry. I'll be right out."

Colm pulled on his new trunks, threw on his T-shirt, and began bouncing outside his mother's door. "Let's go, let's go." Colm always felt like he was waiting for his mother to just move on and go already.

Chapter 28

WHEN CATHLEEN AND COLM EMERGED FROM their room and made it to the pool, Sean and Dr. Basu were already swimming. Colm was annoyed and looked at his mother.

"They beat us here 'cause it took so long for you to get ready," Colm said petulantly.

"Come on in, Cate, the water is great!" Sean said, splashing the water up at her.

"Sean, so help me God. If you splash me, I'm leaving."

"Come on, Sis. Have a little fun, will ya?"

Dr. Basu couldn't take his eyes off her. She had let her hair down, and he remembered the last time he had seen it down, on their night in Italy. They all looked on as Cathleen took off her cover-up. Colm thought her body had turned blue, but Sean and Dr. Basu knew it was only taking on the color of the pool below her. To Colm, though, she seemed to be glowing. The tiny sparkles on her white bathing suit caught the light from overhead and made her entire middle shimmer. Colm loved to see her shiny black hair loose and flowing down around her bare white shoulders. She was, as she had always been, the most beautiful woman he had ever seen. Dr. Basu, if he could have heard Colm's thoughts, would have agreed.

"Beautiful," Dr. Basu said quietly, not realizing he said the word aloud. But Sean heard him and splashed him hard, startling him.

"Simmer down there, Pops. That's my sister you're looking at."

Dr. Basu, embarrassed, dropped down through the water. When he came up, several inches from Sean, he looked up again at the pool deck and saw Cathleen and Colm.

"I'll race you to the pool," Cathleen said playfully to Colm as he pulled off his T-shirt.

Cathleen almost gasped. Under the harsh light, Colm's ribs appeared as though they were protruding, and his stomach was bulging. Dr. Basu and Sean looked at each other. They were both horrified. Colm looked transparent, as if they could see through him, or he would, at any moment, disappear before their eyes.

"Colm, are you up for this?" She looked concerned.

"You all right, Bud?" Sean asked, concerned now too.

"You bet," he said, taking off and running awkwardly for the pool.

Cathleen, always surprised by his energy and playfulness no matter how ill, chased him.

Colm ran toward the edge of the pool. He launched himself into the air wildly and with the complete abandon only a child could have. His arms made large circles as he tried to keep his momentum going in the air while his legs moved quickly below him. From behind, he seemed to be walking on water.

Suddenly, his body disappeared into the pool. Cathleen stopped at the edge, afraid to jump in as quickly as Colm. As much as she wanted to be that kind of person, the type to just let go and jump, she could not do it. She could not go in without testing the water first. As she dipped her foot in and looked down at Colm swimming up toward the surface, his hair spread out around him like a golden halo, he seemed to her, despite his ghostly appearance, more alive than ever before. And just for a moment, she stopped worrying and thought that perhaps the miracle had worked. *Yes, the miracle took.* It would be impossible for her to lose him now. That knowledge made her feel light and ready to break free. She bounced slightly on the balls of her feet and dove in over Colm's body, hardly making a splash or sound, slipping into the silence of the water.

When she rose to the surface, Colm was waiting for her, making a ring with his arms to catch her and hold on to her so he could ride along her back. She pulled him, swimming slowly and softly with the gentle force of her undulating body. Like a mama dolphin and baby move through the ocean, Cathleen and Colm moved as one. When Cathleen finally submerged her face in the water and dove downward, Colm held on tight, following her under. Once they were deep under the water's surface, he let her go. From far below her, he looked as she swam away from him toward Sean and Dr. Basu, eventually heading for the surface before making her final breakthrough. Below, Colm moved his arms to tread, feeling weightless and free, no longer dependent on his failing legs, and looked up at his mother and the two men splashing and playing together in the distance. And Colm knew.

She's going to be just fine.

While Cathleen, Sean, and Dr. Basu, exhausted from the long day and the swim, slept, Colm sat on the balcony of the motel. He could not rest. He was in agony. If he had been able to, he would have driven himself right then and there to Los Angeles. He could barely contain his excitement. He stood all night looking up at the night sky and out to the west—out toward L.A. Tomorrow he would be there. He would finally meet his father. He felt if his body could, it would burst. And when it did—he would shine.

❧ Part V

You will hardly know who I am or what I mean,
But I shall be good health to you nevertheless,
And filter and fibre your blood.

Failing to fetch me at first keep encouraged,
Missing me one place search another,
I stop somewhere waiting for you.

—Walt Whitman,
"Song of Myself," *Leaves of Grass*

Chapter 29

"MAMA, DO YOU HAVE IT? DO YOU HAVE THE LETTER with the address?" Colm shouted from the backseat as the Los Angeles skyline came into view.

"Yes, Colm, I have it. I have it right here. When we get to the hotel, we'll put it in Dr. Basu's GPS."

"Can't we just go? Why don't we just go there first?"

"No! Colm! We talked about this. We all need to rest, shower, and clean up. I am not going to pull up to the doorstep of your father's house, my ex's, dressed like this . . . looking like this. I haven't seen him in years."

"So? Who cares?"

"I care, Colm. I care. That's enough," Cathleen said.

"Hey, Colm, just drop it, OK," Sean added. "Leave your poor mother alone. She came all this way for you. Your mom wants to look nice and get herself together. Let's just enjoy the evening, OK? Speaking of which, what's on the agenda, Gaspar?"

"No agenda. I booked us rooms on the beach in Santa

Monica. I thought we could see the ocean and spend the evening relaxing."

"Santa Monica? Isn't that St. Augustine's mother?" Sean asked Cathleen.

"Yes. She prayed for her son's conversion," Cathleen answered flatly.

Colm did not understand what his mother meant.

"Where is Santa Monica, Dr. Basu?" Colm asked anxiously. "Is it far from L.A.? Will it take forever to get there?"

"No, Dove. We'll be there soon. We made it across the United States in six days, we can get to the Loews at Santa Monica soon enough."

When they finally arrived in front of the hotel, Cathleen looked at the entrance and swore. "You have got to be kidding me, Gaspar?"

"Excuse me?" Gaspar asked.

"Look at this place! What are you thinking? We can't afford this," Cathleen said, shaking her head back and forth.

"I wanted to do something special. It's my gift to you. You deserve it, Cathleen."

Sean shook his head. Dr. Basu was trying so hard to impress her, and all he had to do was show up. This was his sister, Cathleen, Dr. Basu was dealing with. She hadn't been on a date in more than seven years, let alone received a child support check, and she still carried a torch for the deadbeat, he thought. Dr. Basu looked like a goddamn hero in comparison. He didn't need to do any of this, he thought.

"Gaspar, you're doing way too much," Sean said. "Take it easy. You don't have to impress her anymore; she's crazy about you."

"It's okay, Sean. I'm happy to do it—for all of you."

Cathleen could not believe her eyes. It was one of the most beautiful hotels she had ever seen. Dr. Basu took her bag and let her walk through the giant glass atrium lined with palm trees that reached up to the sky like giant cathedral arches framing the view of the Pacific. Cathleen walked through them with her head held high—the way Dr. Basu remembered her in Italy. Together they went through the atrium doors and walked out toward the beach. The palm trees spread out over the sand, and the Pacific Ocean crashed loudly along the shore. Colm looked down the beach and could see the Santa Monica Pier—the Ferris wheel, the bright lights twinkling in the distance.

Sean looked at Dr. Basu and nodded in appreciation. "Ya done real good, Doc."

Cathleen stood speechless. She felt the warm breeze against her cheeks, the wind in her hair. She could not help but think of it, even though she was here with Gaspar and she had come to love him, she could not help but remember the night with Pierce at the shore, the night they had walked together along the beach. She closed her eyes, trying to remember it all—his auburn boy-cut hair, his deep blue eyes, and fair skin that was burnt red by the summer sun.

"Pierce?"

"Yes, babe."

"I have something to tell you."

"What?"

"I am going to have a baby."

She could not see his face. He was walking in front of her, and he didn't stop. She should have known then. She was never able to do it—just let go and be. She wished she had had the strength then to turn around, to forget him right then and there—to have been the one to leave him first. But she chased after him, pulling on his arm.

"Well, what do you think, Pierce?"

"I guess what I think doesn't matter a whole lot now, does it?" He pulled his arm from hers and walked quickly away.

Cathleen felt her heart plummet, diving and lodging itself deep within her womb, her broken heart taking up residence in her growing son. She would forever feel guilty. Forever blame herself.

"You'll make a wonderful father," Cathleen called out. "You can teach him how to play the guitar and sing. You would be so wonderful! I just know it!" She chased after him.

"I'll be home later. Don't wait up for me."

"You're leaving me here? Alone? Pierce, come back!"

"Here's a few dollars for the train." He threw money at her feet.

"Are you kidding me? That's it? A few dollars for the train? You bastard. You bastard!"

"Oh, stop with the melodrama, Cate. I'm going for a drink. Go home, and I'll meet you later. We'll figure this out."

"So *we'll* figure it out. That means you're not going to leave? You're in this for the long haul?"

"I'll see you at home, Cate." Pierce looked at her flushed face with tears rolling down her cheeks, and he walked away, leaving her alone on the beach staring out into the blank and lonely sky.

"Mama? Mama? Mama? Is everything OK? Why are you

crying? Mama?" Colm called out to Cathleen and brought her back to reality.

"Yes, Colm, what is it?" she said, walking toward him.

"Is everything all right? Aren't you happy?"

"This place is just so beautiful. The ocean, everything, all that we saw on our way out here. It's just overwhelming. All the beauty around us. That's all."

"Mama?"

"Yes, Bud."

"You look beautiful. I just thought you should know. No matter what you wear, Dad is going to love you. He's going to know how beautiful you are. I just thought you should know that."

"Oh, Colm. Thank you. Come here."

Colm came to her, and she held him. She took his face and looked him deep in the eyes. "I am so proud of you. You've never been afraid. Most children could not have done what you've done and be so brave. I need you to know that you can't break my heart. That it won't hurt me, if you need to go . . . be somewhere else, with someone else."

"Mama, I'll always be with you. I just need to know . . . find out who my father is. I've always wanted to know him. I've just been missing him so much."

"I know, babe. I know. I missed my father when I was a little girl, too."

Colm looked at her and remembered his mother had had no father either. He had never made the connection that perhaps she had missed her father too, just as he did.

"What was it like for you, Mama?"

"I missed him. I imagined he was everywhere, looking at me and talking to me. He was a good friend to me when I was little. But sometimes I was angry with him because he wasn't there for me. Sometimes I was angry at God for taking him from me."

"Mama, I feel the same way. Except for the God part. God doesn't have anything to do with it for me. But I'm like you, sometimes I pretend he's right here with us, but then sometimes I get mad 'cause he's not. He should be taking care of us."

"Oh, baby. I know it's so hard. I wish I could make it better."

"So you never got to see him again? You never got to see your father again? Didn't that make you sad?"

"I guess it always helped me to know that someday I'd see him again. Someday, maybe up in heaven, we would be together. I still believe that. I believe that when I die I'll get to see my mama and my father. It comforts me."

"I'm glad you think that, Mama. I want you to be able to meet your father too, like I'm going to meet mine tomorrow."

Cathleen closed her eyes and wished for her son to get his wish. She prayed deeply with her entire body: *Please God, please let Colm have this one wish. This one miracle.*

"I know, honey. I know. It is very exciting. I'm sure he'll be thrilled to see you. You know you look just like him?"

"I do, Mama?"

"Exactly. Every time I look at you . . . I see him. I see your father."

"Wow. Do you have a picture of him?"

"No, not with me. I'm sorry. When we go back to New York, I'll look for one."

"But I won't need one, Mama. I'll see him tomorrow and we can take a new picture together—of all of us."

"Won't that be nice?" Cathleen said, hoping that they would be able to.

"Mama, everything is going to be OK."

"It will be. And whatever happens tomorrow, I need you not to worry about me. I know you do, and I want you to know that I have your crazy uncle and Gaspar. I don't want you thinking you have to take care of me anymore."

"I know, Mama," Colm said, surprised that his mother knew. Colm hugged his mother. He held her close, wrapping his arms around her waist. "I love you, Mama."

"I love you, Colm Francis Magee."

The two took off their shoes, and, holding hands, walked to the shore and let the water cover their feet, washing away all of the steps they took that led them to this place.

Dr. Basu and Sean stood back and watched mother and son admire the sunset, with their feet firmly planted in ground that was slowly ebbing away from them.

Chapter 30

LATER BACK IN HER ROOM, WHILE SEAN AND DR. BASU took Colm to the pier, Cathleen sat at the desk gazing at the scribbled address on a faded piece of notebook paper. It was her only evidence of Pierce's earthly existence besides her son. She could imagine him in his apartment writing down his new address and sending it to her. He sent her a letter just a few months after Colm was born. It was the last time she ever heard from him. He wrote to tell her he was settled in L.A., that he was doing what he set out to do, write and create music, and that he was happy, and hoped the same for her. He never asked about the baby—never asked about her. At first she was too proud. She never wanted to admit that she needed him, that she needed him more than anything in the world. She would never have admitted it. And certainly not in a letter. Instead, as Colm got older and went to school, she sent only brief update letters along with photos and homework and special drawings. All of it was sent back unopened.

What if he wasn't even here? What if he had moved on? For all she knew he was still busking on the streets of New York. *He could be anywhere,* she thought. *How stupid could I have been?* All this time she had been so worried about herself, so worried about her own heart being broken by her son, that she hadn't spent enough time thinking that it was Colm's heart she should have been worried about. If Pierce was still at the address, he would get the surprise of his life, she thought. And if he wasn't, she didn't know what she would do with Colm. He would never forgive her for taking him all this way without knowing if his father existed at all.

Meanwhile at the pier, Colm and Dr. Basu stepped onto the Ferris wheel while Sean ran to get them all hot dogs and sodas.

"Are you OK, Dr. Basu?" Colm asked. Dr. Basu looked afraid to be on the ride.

"Yes, nothing frightens me, son," Dr. Basu said as they were pulled back to circle the wheel.

As they moved higher, Colm asked one of the things he always wanted to know. "Dr. Basu, why do you call me son?"

"Oh, I don't even think about it. In India, older folks call all children their sons or daughters; and all children call the adults aunt or uncle."

"Why?"

"Because, I suppose, they think of everyone as family."

"Are you my family, Dr. Basu?"

"Would you like me to be?"

"Yes."

"Well, then, yes, I am your family."

"My mother loves you, Dr. Basu."

"She does? How do you know such a thing?" Dr. Basu looked at him, surprised.

"Because sons know what their mamas love. They know it better than anyone."

The wheel turned faster, sending them soaring over the crest and down again and again as the wind whipped through Colm's wild hair, making him feel light and free. He lifted his arms from the bar and closed his eyes. Instinctively, Dr. Basu grabbed him out of fear that his small body would slip and fall out of the seat. An overwhelming sense of terror swelled within Dr. Basu, and for the first time on the ride, he realized there would be nothing left for him without Colm. He had not realized how much he had grown to love the boy. How great the love truly was. He could not, he thought, remember a time that Dhruv did not exist, even if he thought he was only a star in the sky now. *Hadn't he been there the entire time?* He could not conceive of a moment when Colm would not exist—and the pain that rose up in him when he realized the time was coming soon when he would be alone again without either boy was almost too much to bear. Fear consumed him entirely, and he held tighter still to the boy, as if squeezing him would somehow prevent him from slipping away. He could not lose this son too, he thought. *What would the universe do with one more star? Didn't it have enough?* He knew his reasoning sounded foolish and illogical, but while the boy whooped and hollered, enjoying the thrill of the ride, Dr. Basu silently, and at first without his own recognition, began to pray a mantra he had not heard since he'd left India. There he had heard it often, the most common of all his own Niranjana's mantras, and like Cathleen's Hail Marys that came to her without thinking, before even fully waking, he said it aloud as he had said it long, long ago.

Asato maa sadgamaya
Tamaso maa jyotirgamaya
Mṛiyor maa amṛitan gamaya
Om shaanti shaanti shaanti

From the unreal,
lead us to the Real;
from darkness,
lead us unto Light;
from death, lead us to Immortality.
Om peace, peace, peace

Colm, Colm, Colm, please do not take my Colm.

From the ground, Sean, coming back with an armload of food from the concession stand, looked up and saw Dr. Basu gripping the boy with his eyes closed. Sean laughed, thinking Dr. Basu must have been afraid, after all, of something—*he must be terrified.* What Sean didn't know, couldn't know was that Dr. Basu's terror and grief were transforming him. With each revolution of the spinning wheel, the steel trap secured tightly around his heart unsnapped. For the first time in a long time, instead of his brain sending messages to his heart, Dr. Basu felt a strange and powerful reverse force as if his heart were beating furiously, rapidly, sending message after message to his brain— messages that had been locked in time, trapped somewhere deep within. At last there was interconnectivity. His heart and brain were functioning together, no longer moving and circulating as separate entities. All this time he had been explaining it to his patients, to Cathleen, to Sean, to Colm: *The heart and brain are interdependent. They cannot exist without each other.* Suddenly he remembered something he believed his brain had not let his heart believe since that awful day. *Someone, far away, someone high above him loved him. Loved him enough to send him a son like Dhruv and another like Colm. Someone loved him enough to recognize this love and give him this mantra, this prayer that would sustain him.* And he said it rapidly, as quickly as he could again and again, until he felt the wheel slowing and could hear Sean's voice. "Hang in there, Dr. Basu, It's almost over!"

Then Sean spotted Colm. He looked to him like he was at home at the edge of the earth, just ready to take flight, while Dr. Basu was clinging to him for dear life.

"Poor bastard," Sean said as he laughed. "Hang on! Just hang on, my man! You've made it, buddy! You did it! Good for you!" Sean encouraged as the ride came to a halt.

❧ Chapter 31

Before breakfast, Cathleen stood in front of the hotel mirror for a long time, changing her part from left to right. She couldn't remember how she wore it and how Pierce would remember her. She examined the fine lines around her eyes, and the ones between her brows from constant furrowing. She stood back taking all of herself in—and admiring the white sundress she had bought for her trip to Italy. She slipped on the pink sweater, turned to the side, then all the way around, taking in a view of her backside and smoothing out the skirt. She did not feel beautiful. She did not feel as she had in Italy. For some reason, everything felt more real here. Every line appeared larger, every curve more pronounced.

"It's hopeless," she said and turned away from the mirror.

Just then Colm stepped out of the bathroom. He had bathed all on his own, and his hair was still wet and shiny. He had parted it carefully with a comb. She imagined he had taken great pains to do such a fine job with his usually long, mangled mess.

He wasn't wearing his hat. He had put on his good slacks that she'd packed for him and the button-down shirt that she hadn't even been able to get him to wear to church. He had dressed to impress. *Like mother, like son,* she thought. She wanted to run to him and make a fuss. She wanted to tell him how handsome she thought he looked, but she knew it would only embarrass and upset him.

"Let's go get the guys."

"Are you excited, Mama?"

"Yes, honey, I am. I'm excited *for you.*"

"I have been waiting for this moment my entire life!" Colm shouted.

Cathleen felt the pang rise inside her. She'd had no idea. *I should have known better.*

At breakfast, Colm could barely eat, he was so excited. He tapped his foot and fidgeted in his chair. When Cathleen ordered her second cup of coffee, he lost it.

"Really? Can't we just hurry up and go already?"

Sean, Dr. Basu, and Cathleen looked at Colm. He was at the edge of his seat.

"OK. I'll get the check and we can go," Dr. Basu said. "No use making the boy suffer any longer."

"Thank you, Dr. Basu. Thank you! At least someone understands," Colm said, crossing his arms. He didn't want to throw a tantrum, but he couldn't help it. He was so anxious. He couldn't control what he was feeling.

❧ Chapter 32

D R. BASU BROUGHT THE CAR AROUND TO PICK UP Cathleen, Sean, and Colm. Cathleen handed Dr. Basu the address from the faded paper, and he typed it into the GPS.

2000 E. Observatory

"We're all set," Dr. Basu said to Colm.

Dr. Basu listened to the directions and turned accordingly. Despite his mother's protests, Colm unbuckled his seatbelt prematurely and leaned over the front seat, listening with bated breath and watching the red line of the car on the map. They ascended a tall hill, which had signs along the way for Griffith Observatory, and he could tell they were getting close—the road on the map was about to disappear.

"It looks like we're almost there," Colm said in disbelief. His heart was racing. His palms, oddly, began to sweat. He couldn't remember ever sweating, ever.

"Maybe it's wrong, hon. Maybe there are roads that shoot off by the observatory—maybe he lives up in these hills. Now sit back and put your seatbelt back on. The car's still running," Cathleen said.

"This isn't right. This can't be it," Colm said. "Mama? Did you write down the right address?"

"I didn't write anything down. This is the letter your father sent me." Cathleen imagined a number of scenarios. *Maybe he works here?*

As they crested the hill and could see the observatory in the distance, the GPS announced their arrival.

Dr. Basu pulled out his phone and handed it to Sean to double-check the address.

"Says here that the actual observatory address is *2800 E.* There is no known person living at *2000 E.* in reverse lookup," Sean announced, shaking his head.

"There must be some mistake," Colm said. "This can't be it. This can't be it. LIAR! Liar!" Colm screamed out again. "He's a big, fat, phony liar!"

"Colm, I am so sorry. You're right. It's just the wrong address. He probably wrote it down wrong."

"No, he didn't, Mama. You're holding his letter. The one he wrote. He knew his address. He lied to us. *He lied to me.*"

Sean sat stunned himself. He couldn't believe Pierce had been even more of a jerk than he was already. "None of this makes any sense."

"Maybe he worked here. How should I know?" Cathleen said again.

"At the observatory? I thought he played the guitar?" Colm said back.

"Maybe he couldn't get a job as a musician, and he got a job as a janitor or in one of the exhibits," said Dr. Basu, offering his own rationalization.

As Cathleen went through the scenarios again, Colm began to shake and stutter from all the excitement and agitation. "This can't be it. We c-c-c-came all this way. All this way, and he, he, he . . . he . . . he is not . . . even . . . here."

As they continued driving slowly, the Griffith Observatory loomed atop the hill that overlooked the entirety of L.A. As Cathleen studied the maps on her lap, looking for some logical explanation for it all, Colm jumped out of the car while it was still moving. He fell at first, but got up, steadied himself, and tried to run. Cathleen jumped out too and ran after him.

Colm began to shout, running awkwardly up toward the observatory, his arms windmilling as he had done trying to gain air to jump into the pool. He was screaming loudly, "NO! NO! NO!" It was a low moan punctuated by sobbing.

"Where is he, Mama? Where is my father? I don't understand any of it, Mama. Why?" He continued to run away from her.

Cathleen chased after him, trying to assuage him, but nothing came out of her mouth. The pain in her heart, watching her son's suffering, seemed more than she could bear. If she could have taken it all away, she would have. So much in this life defied explanation, she thought.

"I don't know, baby. I don't know if we'll ever know. I'm so sorry. It's all my fault," she said, still chasing after him as he moved closer to the edge of the hill. Behind her Dr. Basu and Sean were also running up the hill, trying to get to them both.

Colm tried to think of all the reasons *why*—he thought at first it was because of him. Then he thought of his mother but dismissed those thoughts. *There is nothing wrong with us,* he finally concluded. He tried to remember a time when he hadn't dreamed about his father, the father who must love him and that he was so sure was waiting for him. "This was not what the friar said would happen," he said aloud. Nothing was happening as he had hoped. He tried to think of all the things Dr. Basu and Sean and his mother had told him. *You're special, Colm. I love you, Colm. I'm so proud of you, Colm. I'll be right here waiting.* He covered his ears and continued to shake his head back and forth, hearing all of it—all the things he had refused from the people who did love him, hoping instead to hear them from his father. They were right in front of him, waiting for him, loving him. He felt his body might rip open, and when it did, he was sure millions of pointed, hot, electric stars would explode and spill out all over the mountainside. The thought of all of that love split the universe in two, tore open the sky, and he finally realized what he had known deep inside the entire time: *We're doing fine without him.* There before him was his uncle Sean. He had been there before he was even born, already loving him and his mother, and already accepting him as his own. There was Dr. Basu who had come into his life so quickly. He hardly even knew Colm, but he had come to love him so easily. *I didn't have to prove a thing,*

Colm thought. He just had to be him, Colm—the only Colm he knew how to be. Dr. Basu had loved him and protected him from the moment he met him. And he had protected his mama, too. No, Colm didn't need a father to protect his mama anymore, he thought. There they both were—two of the strongest, bravest men he had ever met, ready to catch her and hold her up. He loved them all so much. He wished he could tell them. He wished he could speak the words, but no words would come.

A small crowd had gathered around the spectacle playing out before them. Then everyone stopped talking and all anyone could hear were the sobs of a small child, and all anyone was looking at was the heaving of his body with each inhalation.

Until suddenly everything stopped.

Cathleen reached out to touch him, but before she could, he stopped moving. He looked back at Dr. Basu and Sean, who were now both standing beside his mother. He smiled at them when he saw them, knowing she would be well cared for, knowing she would be theirs for all time. They looked at Colm, not knowing what he would do next. But Colm nodded at them. He looked at all the people standing in front of the observatory, staring at him, looking for a show, hoping for a miracle. He wished he could give them all one, especially his mother.

But he knew.

He could feel the blood being pulled toward his feet, and he knew his broken heart wouldn't be able to continue beating much longer. It would only be a matter of seconds before it was all over, and this time, he somehow thought, *this must be it*. But he wanted to take a final look. Behind them was the City of

Angels—and he laughed at the thought of it—all his mother ever did was talk of angels. *She had finally made it.* A small smile spread across his face as his body began to fall.

Images of beautiful cathedral windows bursting with light flashed before his eyes. Glorious works of art, fountains, stars, and planets floated in between the massive Arch, the Brooklyn Bridge, and the shiny, shimmering skyscrapers, while flocks of giant birds swooped in and spread out over the purple Rockies before landing on the shore of the crashing blue ocean where he stood atop the spinning, twinkling Ferris wheel. From above, Colm could see his uncle dancing his mother across the sky on a cloud and he could see Dr. Basu carrying a small boy the same way he had carried him up the streets of Assisi. Wanting to go to them, to be with them all one last time, Colm dove from the top of the Ferris wheel and splashed through the water. Below the mighty waves, he found his mother again wearing her white dress and pink sweater, swimming toward him, coming for him. Her mouth was open and she was screaming his name. She was telling him to come back. But he turned and began to swim forcefully away from her. A powerful tide pulled him away, and he could not resist its force and might. He emerged atop the surface of the water and appeared before a sparkling, magnificent white light.

That's when he caught her eyes with his own as he fell. She reached for him, catching him midfall, and he landed across her lap as she tumbled to the ground. She held his head against her breast. She knew there was nothing left to say. No word, no gesture, would stop it all from unfolding, but she called out his name anyway, and it echoed through the entire valley below before a serene calm washed over her. For the first time, she saw what it was Colm so long proclaimed life after death would be like. It was, for her, the end of everything; a deep, dark, cold abyss, staring back at her. Her son, her only son, was gone.

Dr. Basu and Sean went to her and tried to take the boy from her arms and begin resuscitating him. Cathleen put her hand up and stopped them. She shook her head as each realization came to her. No. She had finally learned to let go, to let him be. No. She would not let him suffer anymore. No. She would not bring him back again so she, *she* could have her miracle. And though she never thought she could do it, she did. She chose her pain, her suffering over his. She closed her eyes and kissed him good-bye. At the moment her lips touched his forehead, it occurred to her like an explosion—a sudden spark that ignited everything. Her entire being warmed. She felt electric— radiating, she was sure, heat and light, and from that light she could see the permanent, heavy truth. Yes, the truth. All this time she spent searching, traveling the world in search of a miracle or an answer, and here he was, her miracle, her answer right in front of her. All she had to do was look.

He had loved her. She had loved him.

It was enough.

❧ Chapter 33

JUST BEFORE HIS EYES CLOSED, COLM SAW SOMETHING else too. He saw what it was that his mother had spoken of for so long. At the moment of Colm Francis Magee's final mysterious death, he saw arms reaching for him, enveloping him in an unconditional loving embrace. He felt the warmth of her touch, and he knew it would be all the love he ever needed. And he too smiled as he thought of it: she had been there the whole time.

Heaven was right there in front of him.

Yet, suddenly, before him appeared his Irish nana, Maureen Magee, so young and beautiful, and she was holding the hand of his enormous grandfather, Michael. He was as huge and strong as his mother always promised he would be. And he saw two people who he did not know, who he had only heard his mother speak of. Niranjana, with sparkling green eyes like his own mother's and wearing her white sari, held her son, Dhruv's, hand. Colm wanted so badly to go to them. But something stopped him.

He had someone else to meet, someone who he had never met either, but who he would recognize without anyone having to say a word. Colm saw him instantly—he had his guitar strapped across his back and he had short, auburn-colored hair, and his face, his face was unmistakable.

Pierce looked just like him—and Colm knew—it had been his own face, the face he stared at in the mirror his entire life.

"Dad!" Colm ran screaming his name. His legs worked better than he imagined they could. They were strong, stronger than they had ever been, and with them he launched himself into his father's open arms.

"Oh, son. My son. I am so sorry. Please forgive me. I wanted to go back to tell you, to tell your mom how sorry I was. I made such a horrible mistake. So many. Please forgive me."

"I do. Daddy, I forgive you. You're here. You're really here," Colm said, wrapping his small arms around his father's neck and squeezing him as tightly as he could.

"I would have come sooner, but I had other plans . . ."

"It's OK. I understand. You would've if you could."

"You have to go now, Colm."

Colm looked at Pierce, Maureen, Michael, Niranjana, and Dhruv, who were all suddenly standing on what looked like water to him. They were all slowly fading, dissolving before him.

"It's not time for you."

"But I don't want to go. I want to stay," Colm cried.

"We'll all be here waiting," Pierce said, kissing the boy on the cheek. You can tell your mama she's always on my mind and I see her clearly—I always have—and she's beautiful. Can you re-member that? And don't ever forget that I'll be right there beside you when you wake up, when you're at school, when you're playing. You can count on it. I'll be there like I've always been," Pierce said just before he disappeared completely before Colm's eyes.

"Daddy, no! I don't want you to go!"

As each one disappeared below the water's surface, Colm shouted for them to come back.

"Please, come back! Come back! Please don't leave me again, Daddy! I love you!" Colm's sobs echoed around him, and he covered his ears and shook his head. As tears rolled down his cheeks, he shouted, "Daddy, why? Why can't you just stay? Just love me?"

Though he could no longer see him, Colm heard his father say, "Whatever pain you feel, like the pain you are beginning to feel now as you leave me, you must understand it will all disappear someday, and no matter what—you will endure. Because you will never be alone. You have so many people who love you. *You'll see. You'll see.*" Colm nodded and tried to smile, the same angelic smile he had flashed the night he was born, the night his mother believed the angels stood beside him in their lonely hospital room.

Colm did not understand what was happening. He looked around everywhere for his father. "Don't leave me here alone!" He could not tell if it was all real or if it was a terribly frightening dream, one in which he could not believe or wake up from. Everything around him was turning black. He didn't know what to believe. What to think. Or whether thinking and believing were two altogether different notions. He heard voices shouting at him from every direction: Dr. Basu's, "It's like a dream, a trick of the brain. You're really not dead." He heard his uncle's voice. "It's a chemical reaction." He heard his mother's voice. "You have to believe. To hope. To know that there is always a chance, a way to fix you." Then he heard her say, "*You're my miracle, Colm.*" Her voice seemed the most clear. The finest tuned. He heard her singing now and recognized the familiar song. He went toward the sound, and he cried out for her, "Mama! Mama? Are you there? I can't see you. Mama! Mama, I need you!"

Then Colm thought he could see them, his family—Dr. Basu, Sean, and his mother—all wrapped tightly around a small boy. And though they could not hear him or see him, Colm saw them and he knew . . .

He walked toward the trio and reached out and touched his mother's shoulder. At that moment Cathleen's heart filled, and the deep, hollow hole that had grown inside her sealed itself. She grabbed the boy she held in her arms and held him to her breast, while rocking and singing, *mo chuisle, mo chuisle.*

Colm let her love him, falling further into her body, loving her as he had never loved her before. She had found heaven before him, and she made it easier for him to find. All he had to do was make the trip. And it was all so beautiful. It was all proof. All the proof he ever needed.

Proof of heaven.

Then, like a sudden spark that arrives from a singular, unknown source, Colm opened his eyes and he saw.

He saw it all so clearly.

🌿 Acknowledgments

THE BOOK YOU HAVE IN YOUR HANDS IN ITS PRESENT form was made possible by all of the talents of many capable editors and readers who helped me revise, refine, and in many cases, rewrite my crude first draft. I'd like to give my most heartfelt gratitude to my spectacular literary agent, Marly Rusoff, for not only being my first reader, editor, and tireless champion, but for having faith in me, even when the evidence "was not yet seen." I'd also like to thank my editor at the Marly Rusoff Agency, Julie Mosow, whose patience, kindness, compassion, and understanding, not to mention her impeccable attention to detail, helped me write a better novel and become a better writer. Thank you to Allison Dickens, my freelance editor, for her insights, encouragement, and capable content editing. I'd like to express my utmost gratitude to my accomplished and brilliant editor extraordinaire, Lucia Macro, for her wit, speed, and intelligence, not to mention her ability to see my "potential potential" and help me get closer to it with her excellent edits and insights. I found a kindred spirit in her, and my writing is all the better because of her. I would also like to thank my precise and accomplished copy editor, Laurie McGee; Esi Sogah, Lucia's assistant; and all the people at HarperCollins who read, commented, copyedited, proofread, designed, promoted, and even filed, packaged, and shelved my book, especially Tavia Kowalchuk, Mary Schuck, Danielle Bartlett, Shawn Nicholls, and Megan Traynor. I appreciate it all. Thanks to my first readers who gave me the courage to submit my manuscript for publication: especially my husband, Greg Hackett Jr., and his father, Greg Hackett Sr., and my coworkers and dear friends, Mark Sullivan and Sandy Digman, as well as my family, Sean Curran (who took my frantic phone calls about this book, received drafts at midnight and commented on them by seven A.M., and who is the reason there is a book in the first place. I believe his words were: "Screw it, kid. Do what you love. Write your own damn books." I would also like to add that he is *not* a firefighter or a falling-down drunk, but like Sean Magee he is a font of wisdom; and he is a giant, bigger than life itself, with a heart of gold, a quick, dry wit, and a salty, salty Brooklyn mouth. He's also one hell of a dancer and all-around good time); his lovely wife, Tara Curran; and my little sister Eileen Curran (who also moonlit as my website designer, personal assistant, stylist, fan site administrator, and comic relief during some hellish late nights).

The *story* you have just read though would not be possible without the following people who inspired me, put up with me, and even saved me—from myself—more times than I can count, and a few who actually saved my life on more than a few occasions. As far as I am concerned the following people are all the proof I ever need: my tireless, selfless, faithful, and loving teacher, storyteller, and mother, Maggie Curran; my mysterious, tough-as-nails (though lovable), gregarious, constant, hardworking father (and world's best firefighter), Phil Curran; my siblings, Dr. Val Curran, Coleen Gillotti, Sean Curran, Maureen Gilmartin, Eileen Curran, Margie Heron, Suzy Fitzpatrick, and their spouses, Dawn Curran, Patrick Gillotti, Tara Curran, Kevin Gilmartin, Patrick Heron, and Ed Fitzpatrick; and finally my nieces and nephews, Molly, Kevin, Kiely, Abby, Elise, Macy, Liam, Rowan, and Declan (and all other expected and unexpected Curran progeny born during or after the printing of this book). And all the family members who do not share our last name, but who are no less a part of us, especially Jay and Skyler Driscoll, Dave Lorye, Ella Peddie, and our DFD family, especially the Morris, Melody, and Tomaino families.

Most especially, I want to thank my husband, Greg, who sat up with me and listened to me read each page and gave me his thumbs-down when I needed to see it. Most important, he encouraged me to never give up, especially on my two day jobs (not to mention the laundry, the cooking, or the housework), but mostly on myself, while writing this book. He cuts me no slack, but I am a better person—and writer—for it. He's not a man of many words, but he's my Gaspar, my Wiseman who saved me and my daughter, who "he loved in no time at all." From behind his guitar, *Discover* magazine, and architecture books, he always makes me wonder with his many questions—*What if? Why not? Let's just see. Where to next? How 'bout we knock off work and laugh for a bit* . . . For all that and so much more, I thank you. I love you so much.

And last but not least, my children, ultimately the reason for this book, the reason for it all. You are my angels with dirty fingernails and scratched-up knees. Brigid, my strength, my rock, my brain, you are the toughest, brightest, most beautiful girl I know. Someday I hope to grow up to be just like you. You're more than I ever dreamed or hoped you would be. And more than I deserve. I am so lucky to be your mom. Colm, my joy, my peace, my heart, you keep me running and my heart beating strong. I would go to the moon and back again for you—especially on your rocket "bachine." Anytime. I'm there. I love you both more than all the words in the world could express. But I hope someday, when you are old and gray and I am long gone, you will read the words in this book and you will know, and perhaps you might remember this: your mama loved you. *And it was proof. All the proof you ever needed.*

✣ Other Thoughts

T HIS BOOK IS ALSO WRITTEN IN LOVING MEMORY OF Martin "Butch" Melody, Local 801, Danbury, CT; Joseph Halas, Local 801, Danbury, CT; Daniel Pujdak, Ladder 146, Brooklyn, NY; and all the heroes of 9/11, New York, NY, as well as in loving memory of all the other sons and daughters of heartbroken mothers and fathers everywhere whose miracles came in a different form, especially, family friends and family members: James "Jimmy" O'Keefe, Greg and Patricia Ann Livolsi, Benjamin Bisbano, Christopher Hardy, Jonathan Brandis, Brian Simon, Michael and Daniel Fitzpatrick, and Brendan McQuade. To all others who have passed and whose *Book of Life* I have read and by doing so I have healed my broken heart: Valentine (Boppy) Marfiak, Eileen (Grandma) Marfiak, Paul Marfiak, Joseph Marfiak, Anne Marfiak McGuinness, Grace Marfiak, Patricia Marfiak, William (Papa) Curran, William Curran Jr., Kay Curran, Dorothy Curran, Catherine May Curran, Ronald Espitee, Theodore Cooke, Joseph Smith, Thomas Morris, Mary Beth McGowan, and Mary Eileen Hackett.

And for children, young and old, longing and loving their mysterious fathers and mothers. You are loved and you are wanted. Somewhere there is a family for you too.

And for all my readers everywhere: never stop looking for proof. It's right in front of you. *You'll see.*

A+
AUTHOR
INSIGHTS,
EXTRAS, &
MORE...

FROM

**MARY
CURRAN
HACKETT**

AND

WM

WILLIAM MORROW

Story Behind the Story

This story began to unfold nearly thirty years ago. I was sitting at the kitchen table with my mother and my siblings, when my father, covered in soot from a fire he had fought the night before, walked into our kitchen and threw himself onto my mother. Her body almost collapsed under his weight, but somehow she mustered the strength to hold up all two hundred fifty pounds of him. His body convulsed as he told her that my uncle, Butch Melody, and my father's friend, Joey Halas, had been crushed when a floor of a burning warehouse collapsed on top of them. They died instantly.

I ran and hid in my parents' closet, clutching my father's church loafers and inhaling the faint scent of his pipe smoke and Vitalis. That morning, I prayed to God over and over: *Please don't take my dad.* From that moment on I realized two things: (1) In an instant, everything I knew could be gone, and (2) I was powerless to do anything about it. My parents were devout Catholics, who raised us with the belief that if you prayed to God, he would listen and that when we died, we would all go to heaven, where we would be together as a family and where God, the angels, and the communion of saints would be waiting for us.

My family life was bookended by these two realities: fire and God. On one end, we were held up by the Fire Department and the unique sort of family that came with it, and on the other, we had our church. We were Secular Franciscans, the type of family who said rosaries when we got in the car. We said Grace before meals, and prayers and novenas before bed. We stopped wherever we were when the sirens sounded and prayed for God's and St. Florian's protection for my father. We went to the stations of the cross together on Fridays during Lent, and to all of the High

Mass services. My brothers were altar servers, and we girls sang in the choir. My mother taught our parish's first religious education classes from our kitchen table. For years, children streamed into our home, where my mom would tell detailed stories of Jesus's love and sacrifice for us. She dressed us in costumes, and we acted out the Nativity or the Crucifixion on the hearth in front of our fireplace. I believed my mother was the greatest storyteller who had ever lived, and I attribute my love for a good story to her and the Bible as much as I do to Laura Ingalls Wilder, Mark Twain, Harper Lee, Charles Dickens, and Louisa May Alcott.

We children were extreme in our devotion, too, but we were far more disgruntled. We hated that my parents always invited wayward guests, lost souls, lonely widows or widowers, introverted bachelors, and even priests to our house for dinner on Sundays and even precious holidays. My parents' idea of family literally included everyone they met. The kettle and the pot of coffee were always on, and my mother and father could be found holding court at any time of the day or night. (And to this day, in the evening, a bonfire burns at the end of our street, and around it you will find my parents and countless friends and family members circled round it, laughing, drinking, loving, and living the only way they know how.)

But throughout my childhood I had a secret and it was hard to keep. I wasn't so sure I believed it all. Throughout my childhood, I had never actually seen or experienced God in spite of all my piety. Like the character Colm in my story, I collapsed on a regular basis as a child (and never experienced the visions I had often heard people with near-death experiences had). I was what my family called "delicate" or "a fainter." I was frequently short of breath, listless, weak, in incredible amounts of pain, and prone to unconsciousness. I missed school often, and at one point in the sixth grade, I was absent for more than a month while the rest of the family went on with work and school. As a teenager, I pushed myself by playing sports and even training for marathons because I didn't want anything or anyone to slow me down. But since my first collapse, which occurred more than twenty-five years ago, I have probably hit the floor nearly a hundred times. I have gone down on busy Metro platforms with subways ripping by within inches of my head, in museums surrounded by crowds of strangers, on sidewalks, and always it seemed, at the most inopportune moments.

One night in 2003, when I was twenty-six, my heart stopped beating while driving my daughter home from preschool, nearly killing us both. I remember the world going very quiet and still while looking at her for a brief second in the rearview mirror, and I knew there was nothing I could do before it all went black.

My father, who happened to be outside on that cold January day chopping wood, stepped out into the road because he heard a speeding car. As it came closer he saw my body slumped over the wheel, and the car accelerating as it barreled toward him. He leaped out of the way as my car crashed through a large, icy snowbank and came to a stop within a couple of feet of my parents' living room window. He ran immediately to my daughter and pulled her out of the vehicle. She was safe, thanks in part to the snowsuit that packed her so snugly into the car seat. I don't have any memory of any of the accident, but in the ambulance I remember my friend Nibby, an EMT fireman who knew my father, yelling at me to come back, screaming at me to stay with them.

I was met at the hospital by a police officer who had come to take away my license. As sick and confused as I was, I was more upset about losing my license than the accident. Without the ability to drive, I couldn't get to my job. I was a single mom at the time and had mountains of debt. I received no child support from my daughter's father, and I was living in my parents' basement while juggling a demanding career and side work. Losing my license was equivalent to financial suicide.

Shortly after, I moved to Cincinnati to be close to my boyfriend (now husband) and where I would have access to reliable public transportation and good hospitals. It was in one of those hospitals during a routine doctor's appointment that I flatlined again. When I woke up, there was a cluster of doctors and nurses standing over me—others rushed at me with needles and paddles and screamed at me to wake up. (I woke up spontaneously after almost two minutes of being asystole.) Later on, through the chaos, I found the calm, smiling face of an Indian doctor, who said, "There you are, my good girl." Within days I had a pacemaker installed and a treatment plan for the rest of my life. I was eventually diagnosed with several related disorders all linked to a form of dysautonomia, which was explained to me as a condition in which the brain was at war with the heart and other parts of my body. It summed up my life perfectly in more ways than one. My brain and heart often wanted entirely different things.

I have since been diagnosed with malignant neurocardiogenic syncope disorder, postural orthostatic tachycardia syndrome (POTS), and left atrial reentrant tachycardia. However, my conditions are well managed (I can even drive now), but I've been told they are incurable, so I do my best to take care of myself and my children.

This particular novel, however, first took root in me in 2006, when while bathing my son, I watched as he stopped breathing and began to die in my arms. He was sitting up one minute in the water and then suddenly he collapsed. He would have slammed his head on the tub had I not caught him in my arms. Within seconds, his face went ashy, his lips turned blue, and he stopped breathing and moving. It transformed me. I had never been on the other side of watching someone lose consciousness. To deal with my fear of losing my son to what I thought was my own condition, I began to write *Proof of Heaven* after I returned home from the hospital. (Colm's collapse was thought to be a possible epileptic attack or severe asthma attack. It was most likely the latter, since he has since suffered from several subsequent asthma attacks.)

That night a million thoughts raced through my head, but in the end all I could think was: What would I do? What would I do if I lost my son? How does any mother go on? Later that same night when I couldn't sleep, I sat staring at him and I had a vision (the closest I have ever come to a religious experience) that I knew I had to get on paper. The first chapter flowed out of me, but I left the file on my computer untouched. Meanwhile, I taught English literature, acquired and edited several books for others, and continued to write all sorts of other stories and articles. One day while cleaning my computer, I accidentally found a file named PROOF, and as I was about to press Delete, for some reason, I started to read it. Cate, Dr. Basu, Sean, and Colm started to live and breathe inside my head; and they literally wouldn't let me sleep until I finished putting their story on paper. In writing this novel, I was able to see things clearly for the first time.

For me this story is really not about proving whether there is or isn't a heaven, or a God. I leave those questions for my readers to decide. What interests me are the questions we face in life and how we mere mortals deal with them. My wish is to understand the limitless capacity our hearts and minds have to embrace and understand love. It's about what makes a family a family, because many of us, like the characters in my book, craft our own version of a family. *Proof of Heaven* is also about sacrifice—we all make sacrifices every day for the people we love. And, ultimately, this story is a love story between a parent and a child—the unique sort of love that knows no bounds. It travels the world. It's bigger and shinier than the largest, most ornate cathedrals, both the ones built by man and the ones found in nature. It blossoms from the soul and expands and grows and eventually explodes—with an energy only equaled to the electricity and energy of the stars—and the human heart.

Q & A with Mary Curran Hackett

How long did it take you to write *Proof of Heaven*?

There are three answers to this question: I could say, "It took me two weeks." But then I would have to amend and say, "Well, if you included edits, it took two years." And then upon thinking further, I would have to say "Actually, it took me about thirty-five years—because in some way, everything in my life was leading up to this moment." All would be the right answer, but I'll start with the first answer.

Most writers will not believe me when I say that I wrote the first draft in two weeks—all four hundred original pages of it in October 2009 (with the exception of the first chapter and last chapter, which I wrote one night after an agonizing night in the hospital with my sick son in 2006). The rest I wrote between October 16 and October 31 to be exact. On October 16, 2009, while cleaning out a flash drive I came across a file that simply said PROOF. I almost pressed Delete, but miraculously I didn't. Instead I opened the file to see what it was. As soon as I began reading, I felt an overwhelming rush—like an electric charge—go through my entire body. I just knew I had something here. I could hardly believe I had forgotten about it or left the file alone for so long. I suppose at the time I first wrote it, I simply thought of the story as a cathartic exercise—a way to purge the fear and anxiety I felt after almost losing my son.

Going against all the rules of the publishing world, I threw a query letter together quickly, attached it to the chapter, and e-mailed it to an agent I came across on a writers' blog that I subscribed to. I said I had "a novel" I thought she might like to consider. When I awoke the next day, the agent in NYC had responded and said she wanted to see the entire manuscript. Of course, I didn't have an entire manuscript. I had a first chapter. I wrote back and asked for "a couple of weeks" to tidy up the manuscript. (OK, I don't suggest lying to people, but something told me I could write this baby if I put my mind to it.) So I went to my husband and laid it out for him. Between teaching two classes at the University of Cincinnati, carrying a full editing load at my day job, and caring for two kids, something would have to give—most likely sleep and the weekends. I would need all day Saturday and Sunday for a couple weeks to work straight through, and I would need his help to keep the kids busy at night. That meant bath time, homework help, and story time were all on him, so I could work. And work I did. After my day jobs, I came home, threw on my writing sweater—a dingy, Irish wool housecoat—and went to work.

I have to admit, as exciting as it is to say "I wrote a book," what I am most proud of is, not just writing it, but how I did it. In those two weeks, I got the kids up and ready for school, dropped them off, picked them up, made it to class every day, handed in my manuscripts for my day job on time, made every dinner (they were not my best), moved every load of wash (my husband folded), and still made it to the fall festival—hayride and all.

I was no prima donna writer—there was no whisking myself off to a silent room or a quaint coffee shop to write in peace. I wrote while sitting on the couch while my husband watched *Family Guy* and crunched potato chips. I wrote lying on my son's bed while he crashed trains into tractors and made explosion sounds. I wrote in my daughter's room while she practiced her recorder and sang Taylor Swift songs at the top of her lungs. For two weeks I subsisted on coffee and M&Ms. I laid off my meds (I don't recommend this either) so I could rely on my natural propensity for my heart to beat 200 beats per minute—just to keep awake. A couple days before I sent out the manuscript

I read the entire thing aloud to my husband, and meanwhile I had my father-in-law, brother, sister, and a couple of friends read it as well, and they all encouraged me to send it on. So on October 31, 2009, just before dressing the kids in their Halloween costumes—I clicked on Send and put the story of my life in the hands of someone else.

Of course, between then and the publication of the book, two years passed. And in that time the real work happened. I did a lot of rewriting and editing. I think I changed the ending no less than six times. To make a very long story short, with the help of my wonderful agent, Marly Rusoff (who, as it turns out, was not the original agent who was interested in the novel in October 2009) and my editor, Lucia Macro, we have the *Proof of Heaven* you hold in your hands today.

Are your characters based on anyone you know?

Yes. There are four main characters in this story—Cathleen, Sean, Dr. Basu, and Colm. Each one is near and dear to me. While these characters are based on people I know in real life, the experiences and their stories are all complete works of fiction. They speak, act, and do things as their character and the story dictate. But for a little more background on each character—here you go:

CATHLEEN

Cathleen is by and large based on some of my own experiences. My middle name is Cathleen. I grew up being called Mary Cathleen. And like Cathleen, I have to take faith day by day. I have had fits and starts with my devoutness too. When I was at Catholic University, I went to Mass every morning with a boy. I was absolutely head over heels for him. There was nothing real about my devoutness though. I think a lot of the reason I got up and went to church each morning was so I could sit next to him!

It was really a show. I don't think I ever felt close to God then. I had no idea how to really pray. I had so many doubts. I was reading a lot of the existentialists then, and I had more doubt than true faith—for sure. I was so confused by it all. The "boy" and I would stay up all night and talk, and he would tell me about this "flame" inside him or this dripping faucet that was about to overflow—and how he "heard" God "calling" him. I was at once jealous—because I didn't have any experience like that, and because he loved God *more than me.* How could I compete with God? A blonde, maybe. Now I could take that on. But God? No competition. But there have been times in my life when I think the act of getting up and praying has gotten me through the day. When I was a single mom, I took my infant daughter to Mass every morning. I didn't do it because I *believed,* or because of some sort of devoutness, or even out of fear or guilt. I did it because it got me out of the house early and it framed my day. I also felt great comfort in hearing the words of Jesus, "Blessed are those who are persecuted" and seeing him suffer on the cross. It was truly the loneliest and hardest time of my life. I had so many people saying things about me and judging me, and in many cases, just being cruel. Just knowing there was someone out there—dead or alive—who had felt and known that pain of being misunderstood helped me get through every day.

Also, like Cathleen, I fell in love with a gorgeous boy who was a musician—although unlike the character Pierce, who played the guitar, my daughter's father played the banjo. I don't think I ever prayed, bartered, or begged more with any man or God, to have him stay with me and my daughter. But, in the end, my love wasn't enough. Nothing I could do or say would change what his heart felt. And in the end, it was all as it was meant to be. It took a very long time for my heart to accept what the body and mind already knew. I am grateful now for his honesty and his truth. Because without it, I would still be pining. He made it possible for me to build the life I have now with my daughter, my husband, and our son. I forgive him, love him no less, though in a very different way, and wish him all the best. I truly believe if it weren't for that experience, I wouldn't be the person I am today, and I actually thank God every day for it—the pain and all— because without it, I wouldn't have Brigid, I would never have met Greg, and I wouldn't have our wonderful son, Colm.

SEAN

Sean is an amalgamation of men in my life—especially my two brothers, my father, and my husband. No men in my life have meant more to me or shaped me more than these guys. My father was a firefighter—but before that, he was in the seminary. He wanted to be a priest as a young man. He and my mother are probably the most devout people I have ever met. (With the exception of Mother Teresa, who I met while I was at Catholic U. She kind of holds the record in my book.) I can honestly say, though, that everything my parents do, they do for God. Even having us kids was—in a way—for God. My father felt the call to be a priest as a young man, but something in him, like Sean, changed. A few years after that change of heart, he married my mom. Also, my father's mother died when he was a toddler, and he grew up not knowing her. My husband's mother also died when he was a boy, and it fundamentally changed him, too. So that aspect of Sean is definitely pulled from real experiences. But Sean's attitude, temperament, and motivations are all my brothers', especially my brother Sean. He's a giant, and he too spoke of being a priest when he was younger. He's wild—the life of every party, a phenomenal dancer, and has such a quick wit and easy way about him. He's also very loyal. He'd pretty much walk through fire to help out anyone he loves. He's also lost many people in his life he has loved—especially some of his closest friends—and like the character Sean, he has had to reach inside himself to find the strength to go on without those people by his side. He likes his "sauce" as he says, but he's not a falling-down drunk (although he knows plenty of them). The darker side of the character Sean—his volatile temper and passion—I have to say belongs to my brother Val, who, like the character Sean, had aspirations to be a fighter pilot. Val did end up joining the navy and flew in some superfast planes. As children, we did go to the *Intrepid* and spent hours watching Blue Angels shows as kids. But Val has been known to fly off the handle at times in his life. He's one of the most driven, passionate, fiery people I know. But I know his intensity is just an expression of his love—combined with fear. I have been on the receiving end of his temper, and looking back, I know it was coming from a place of helplessness and frustration. He just wanted the best for me and loved me so much. I think it was—at times—even physically difficult on him to watch me seemingly self-destruct. He definitely lost it on me a few times in my day. And like the character Sean who recognizes this and is ultimately forgiven, so too is my brother. I love him.

I love them all.

DR. BASU

Dr. Basu was originally named Dr. Gandhi. I had editors say that was a little clichéd, and it made them picture Ben Kingsley as Gandhi! But I had a different vision of who Dr. Gandhi was. When I flatlined in 2004, the doctor who stepped in and took action and put a pacemaker in and diagnosed me—finally—was my own Dr. Guarang Gandhi. He was a young man—from India—and he had a wonderful bedside manner. He took his time with me, spent time talking to my daughter, and had a warm, kind smile. In fact, he walked into the office much the same way Dr. Basu does in this book. He immediately started talking to my daughter (Colm hadn't been born yet). He bent right down and started asking her questions about her name and how old she was, and he told her a little story. He seemed very calm and so different from all the other physicians I had ever had. But two years later, he left the practice and I was assigned a different doctor. And that is where the similarities end.

Dr. Basu in this story is really much more like my own husband, Greg. Greg is an architect. I often imagine his brain to look like a drafting board with a blueprint on it—or sometimes I picture him with drawings/plans floating above his head. He is very pensive. He doesn't say very much, but when he does, I can't help but listen. He's always deconstructing things and asking questions. We spend a lot of time together watching scientific documentaries and listening to NPR. And like Dr. Basu and Cathleen, Greg and I had an interesting start. He too met me when I was a single mom. Like Dr. Basu, Greg fell in love with Brigid in no time at all, and he was so wonderful with her. It was like they were destined to be together. They have a very special bond. Sometimes I feel like an outsider looking in, but it's great to bear witness to it. They are great friends. It was wonderful to become a family the way we did. I couldn't imagine it any other way now. Greg is a wonderful father. The best there is. My children are incredibly lucky.

COLM

Colm is a hybrid of both of my children. I chose the name Colm for two reasons—one, it is my favorite name in the world (hence, why I named my son Colm) because of its beautiful meaning and significance; and, two, because it would literally drive me insane to say my son's name to people and they would say it right back to me, as if correcting me, and say, "You mean Coal-m." "No, I mean Col-um." How hard is it really to say, Colm? You'd be amazed. I hope to popularize the name a bit, but also share with people the story of a truly incredible boy—Colm Magee.

My own son, Colm, collapsed in a bathtub and stopped breathing several years ago. It is a moment I will never, ever forget. Mostly because the moment felt (looking back) like hours. It was truly only moments. But he was blue, gone, lifeless. All I remember was screaming his name. I felt the world literally spinning around me. I will never, ever forget how his body looked lying on my bed, wet and blue. It terrifies me even to write about it—as if doing so will make it all happen again. Writing about it helps, though. And that's exactly why I write about it. It takes the edge off. It makes it all less frightening, because when I write about it, I have some control over the outcome!

While Colm's medical condition in the book is an extremely rare condition, I do suffer from a form of malignant neurocardiogenic syncope caused by dysautonomia. It wasn't a stretch for me to talk about all the medical tests, the office visits, or what it feels like to collapse, because I've been there and done that—over a hundred times—and counting.

Finally, the allegorical—and physical—search for the father is not foreign in the least to me. My daughter has grown up the majority of her life without having seen or knowing her biological father. He consented to the termination of his legal rights to her when she was an infant, and about a year later, we ceased contact for a number of reasons. Brigid has not seen him since she was two years old, but surprisingly she has memories of her brief visits with him as a toddler. However, unlike the character Colm, who was kept largely in the dark about his father, my daughter knows everything, and if she's old enough to ask a question, I figure she's old enough to hear the answer. We've always been open, and she feels comfortable about sharing her feelings. She does receive letters and packages from her biological father quite regularly, and over time she has developed a relationship with his mother and sisters. Over the years, however, she has asked me hundreds of questions, not unlike Colm Magee's many questions, about her own father. In fact, many of the questions young Colm Magee asks have come right out of my own daughter's mouth— word for word. She has ached, longed, and wondered, not unlike other children who have always felt a part of themselves missing. I would say one of the most painful parts of being a mother to a child whose father has chosen not to be around is to convince the child that it's not her fault he left. But I know no matter how much I love her and care for her, a part of her is always a little sad, a little broken—and always wondering and longing for that mysterious father.

But Colm's quest for the father is not just a physical one either. It's emblematic of all our quests. For those of us who believe, want to believe, or just don't know if there is a God, we all have to wonder, what type of parent is he/she? We just want to know him/her.

Why do your characters go on a pilgrimage and a road trip?

It's totally clichéd, but faith is a journey. It's a road, a quest, an adventure. Some of us travel the world over looking for meaning, beauty, truth—a piece of heaven on earth, and often we discover it's not so far away after all. It was important for me to juxtapose the journey to Italy, which represented a spiritual healing, against the road trip across the United States, which on the surface was for a scientific (medical) healing but ended up being a healing of souls through friendship and love. I traveled throughout the United States during college and afterward, and it was on the road that the world and all its beauty revealed itself to me. I often found that my most "spiritual" moments weren't actually in a church, but on the precipice of a mountain cliff, near a crashing surf, in a field of cranes with miles between me and the rest of the world. And often, I found my moments of truth and beauty took place—more often than not— when I was sharing it with another person whom I loved.

In 2008, I did have the opportunity through my day job (for the Province of St. John the Baptist) to go on a pilgrimage to Assisi and Rome. I met some of the most amazing people I have ever known while on that trip. I never intended to make friends or be transformed by friendship, but that is exactly what happened for me. It was at night—on the roof overlooking Assisi— that my spiritual healing began. I realized through talking to a mother whose son had died a year earlier that love and faith and truth reside in the heart, and through her eyes, I came to understand we are all nothing more than broken hearts wondering and hoping for healing and belonging.

While I went through the healing rituals on the pilgrimage, I was reluctant, to say the least. The inner skeptic emerged at every turn, and I was looking for a scientific or practical reason for every miracle I learned about or every legend or story I heard. But I will admit something overwhelming happened to me in one church. In a small chapel outside of Assisi in a place where Francis tended to lepers, I knelt down and, I guess, I attempted to "not pray." I wanted to do what our pilgrimage leader had kept advising us to do—just listen. While I was kneeling there and thinking about the history of the building and all the pilgrims from all over the world who had sat where I was sitting, a rush came over me. And I could have sworn I heard a voice say, "Write about me." But I know it was my brain telling me, *Someday I will have to put pen to paper and write about this experience.* I doubt it was St. Frank talking to me in the leper colony, but a part of me still wonders . . . Who knows, maybe all of this—this book, this story—is because of that trip? I have no idea. A writer doesn't question her inspiration—she just hopes to get it!

So which is it? Faith or reason?

The juxtaposition of faith and reason in the book is no accident. Each character has a different way to believe, to understand his or her world. Each, regardless of his or her religion, or lack thereof, has to wrestle with the big questions: Why are we here? Where do we go? How come all of this is so hard? I don't think there is a person out there who hasn't wondered these things. The push and pull between faith and reason, the heart and the brain if you will, is the ultimate quandary. I have always been torn between the two myself—my heart and brain often want entirely different things—physically and metaphysically. And one always seems to win out. It's the rare times in life when the heart and brain are in sync—that we feel like "we have it figured out" (if only for two seconds!). I do believe there is a place for both—the rational and the irrational, or rather the unknowable. My favorite quote of all time is by Socrates. It loosely translates to "I know that I do not know." Yes, knowing that one doesn't know opens an entire universe of figuring out, hoping, believing, dreaming, and perhaps, ultimately truly "knowing." So my answer is really a question too: *So what do you think/feel?*

What's with malaria? Can people really die from a mosquito bite?

I have had more than one reader say to me, "Can a person really die of malaria—even a doctor's child?" The answer is—sadly—absolutely. In fact, half of the world is at risk for malaria, 250 million people get it every year, and out of that—1 million die (World Health Organization). Those in developing countries are at the highest risk, and often the poor suffer most. The disease is treatable with medication, but many communities simply don't have access to the medication. Prevention is another issue—something as simple as mosquito nets can help reduce the risk of malaria. Malaria just doesn't kill people, it affects a nation's birth weight/infant mortality rates, general population growth, and health of the global economy. It's essentially everyone's problem. I wanted to illustrate with Dr. Basu that the loss of one child is not just felt by a parent, it's felt by an entire community; and when more people are made aware, it can be felt by the world. And I also wanted to illustrate that the loss of any one particular child is no less significant than another. A middle-class mother from New York City grieves no more than an impoverished mother across the globe. The loss of a child is a universal loss. The pain and memories imbed themselves and never leave. In a world where we see images of suffering people daily, we can become immune to the sufferings of others, or lose the sense of urgency to help others. When we make stories personal, suddenly they do become more urgent.

I also had a reader tell me she thought Dr. Basu's backstory was contrived and forced—that death to malaria simply doesn't happen anymore and that the story wasn't even necessary. But, I thought, who would Dr. Basu be if he didn't have that story? I couldn't imagine. To me so much of his vision of the world links back to the initial suffering. How like us is he? How many of us can point to a moment in our life when we felt the rug pulled out from underneath us, a moment when everything we ever thought we knew to be true, simply wasn't? Dr. Basu was a rational man, a happy and content one, but the loss of his son transformed him. I don't think he would have met and bonded with Cathleen or her son if he hadn't been transformed, and I don't think he would have fallen in love with them if he hadn't been transformed again.

Reading Group Guide

Introduction

Proof of Heaven is as much a story of a mother and child, and their quest for healing and love, as it is a story that resembles all of our quests to understand life's Big Questions: Why are we here? Where do we go when we die? And why is all of this so hard? Each main character—Dr. Basu, Sean, Cathleen, and Colm—and even minor characters, like the Monsignor and Pierce, all participate in this quest, but each character begins at a different starting point and each comes to his or her own realization of what indeed is proof of heaven.

Questions for Discussion

1. *Proof of Heaven* opens with several quotations, one of them by Blaise Pascal: "The Heart has reasons that Reason does not know." Why do you think the author picked this quotation? What do you think the quotation means? How does this quotation relate to the story, the theme of the book, and each character's particular journey? Can you relate to these words? Has there ever been a time in your life that you felt your heart and mind wanted different things? Do you find yourself torn between the two? Are you more apt to follow your heart or your mind?

2. Each character has a different way of approaching his or her faith in God and of thinking about what happens when we die. What does Cathleen believe? What does Colm? Dr.

Basu? Sean? The Monsignor? Do you identify with any of these characters' approaches to his or her belief? Does anyone's belief system particularly bother or upset you? Why? Do you see yourself or any of your loved ones in any of the characters? What are your beliefs? Do you feel they fit into any particular religion? Why or why not?

3. How do you think Cathleen and Sean's religion informs (or doesn't inform) their beliefs? They are both Catholic, but they have very different perspectives on their religion and their faith. Whether you are Catholic or not, can you identify with the characters' struggles to make sense of the religion they have been raised to believe in but come to feel differently about as they have grown up and experienced it?

4. Dr. Basu was raised a Hindu but becomes an agnostic. What changed his belief? Does he transform again?

5. Colm doesn't believe in anything at first. What do you think he comes to believe in the end? And do you believe in a higher power or God?

6. Do you think Sean's call to become a priest was real? Do you believe people can be called by God to a vocation? Why or why not? What changed in him?

7. Do you think religion offers a reasonable framework to discover God? Do you feel that a religion is necessary to experience the divine? Why or why not?

8. Compare and contrast the relationships that Cathleen has with her son, her brother, Monsignor, and Dr. Basu. How does she interact with them differently? Similarly? Why do you think so?

9. Each character has the opportunity to interact individually with another character at least once in the story. For example, Colm has several one-on-one conversations with his mother, Dr. Basu, and Sean. Sean gets to talk to his sister, Dr. Basu, and Colm one-on-one as well. And Dr. Basu forms unique bonds with Colm, Cathleen, and Sean through several intimate conversations. While all of the characters ultimately end up on the journey together as a group, which individual friendship struck you most? Dr. Basu and Sean? Dr. Basu and Colm? Cathleen and Dr. Basu? Cathleen and Colm? Which relationship did you respond to most positively? Why?

10. When the story begins, Cathleen and Colm are very much alone. Colm's father is gone and Cathleen's parents are gone. Cathleen is the center of Colm's universe, and Colm is the center of hers. How does their "universe" expand over the course of the story? Who becomes part of it? Who do you think becomes the "center of gravity" by the end of the story? Or is any single person the center? Why do you think that?

11. Throughout the story, the universe—its expansion, form, and matter—is alluded to in connection with characters, the plot, and even the human heart. Did you ever think of the heart as an "electric" organ, or did you ever conceive of the electricity and energy of the stars being compared to that of the human heart and brain? How does each character embody this connection? Which scenes do you find illustrate this relationship best?

12. In this story, the author intended to juxtapose the earth and sky, or earthly and heavenly pursuits, in the story's characters and settings. She designed each character to represent the elements of earth, wind, fire, and water. Cathleen embodies the concept of mutability and water. What about

her is mutable or changing? Does she strike you as someone who transforms or changes often in situations? Does she ever appear with or by water? What do you think the significance is in each of these water scenes? Dr. Basu is very much grounded to the earth. He's a pragmatic man who looks for his answers in the world that's at his fingertips, through science and empirical data. Which scenes strike you and show you that he is rooted to the earth? Does he ever seem to change and take on other elements as he grows and opens his heart to the other characters? Sean embodies all that is explosive—his attitude, early calling (and later his addictions), anger, passion, and even his profession are linked to fire. Which scenes stand out for you when Sean exhibits this element? Colm embodies the wind, or the spirit. His name even means "dove" or "peace." What part of the story strikes you as Colm most embodying "the spirit"? Do any of the characters transform at all or take on other elements throughout the story? Where? How?

13. The author also modeled the characters in another way—after familiar characters in Judeo-Christian tradition. Cathleen, whose Gaelic name means "pure one," represents Mary, the mother of Jesus; and Sean represents at various times both Joseph, the foster father entrusted with the earthly care of Jesus, and later the trusted disciple John, whom Jesus charges with caring for Mary at Jesus's death. (In Gaelic, Sean means "John.") Dr. Basu, or Gaspar, represents the wise man from the East (most probably from the country that is now India), and he embodies the gifts, wisdom, and protection offered to the child Jesus. Did you see the connections in the story? Does Colm strike you as Christlike? What about him reminds you of the story of Jesus? What doesn't? Which parts of the story sound familiar—something you may have heard in the Gospels or seen in familiar Christian stories?

14. Throughout the story, the author juxtaposes heavenly and earthly settings. Where does each character find he or she is closest to the divine? Which character finds solace in church? In nature? In the presence of other people? In his or her own mind? Where do you feel closest to the divine? In a church? By the shore? Under a night sky? Amid nature's phenomena? In the arms of a loved one? In the eyes of a child?

15. Cathleen, Dr. Basu, and Colm travel to Italy to try a healing ritual at a place where many miracles have been alleged to happen. Do you think it was responsible of Cathleen to put Colm through such an ordeal? Do you believe in miracles? Have you ever prayed for a miracle or experienced one? Do you think Colm's "miracle" was realized? In Italy? Or on his road trip? What do you think makes a miracle a miracle?

16. Colm's quest to find his father resembles the larger quest of all of humanity's attempt to understand where we come from and where we are headed. Most of us have feelings about whether we believe or don't believe in God. Colm doesn't believe in heaven but he hasn't given up hope in finding his father. Do you think we are all a little like Colm: reluctant believers who deep down want to know or believe that someone is out there, loving us from afar and keeping us within their benevolent arms? Does Colm find what he is looking for? What do you think? Have you found what you're looking for?

17. Do you think the characters in this story find proof of heaven? Where and when does Cathleen? At what point do you see her character make a dramatic turn? When does Sean become transformed? Do you think he overcomes his physical and spiritual proverbial demons with alcohol addiction? Does Dr. Basu become transformed? Where and when? What is significant about this moment? Where is he and who is he

with? How does this relate to Dr. Basu's oscillation between the earth and sky, the mind and heart? What about Colm? Do you think he goes to heaven? Or do you think it is just a dream, a chemical reaction in his dying brain? Do you think he believes in God? Do you think he finds his father?

18. The final quotation in the book is by Walt Whitman. He writes, "Failing to fetch me at first keep encouraged, / Missing me one place search another, / I stop somewhere waiting for you." Why do you think the author chose this quotation? Do you feel a kinship to those whom you have lost in your life? Do you find your lost loved ones in unexpected places?

19. Do you think the characters find what they were looking for? Where does Dr. Basu find his lost son? Where does Cathleen find Pierce, her mother, and her father? Where does Colm find his father? Where does Sean find his mother?

20. Where do you look for, and have you found, proof of heaven?

Joseph Moss

MARY CURRAN HACKETT is the mother of two children, Brigid Claire and Colm Francis, and is married to Greg Hackett. She received an M.A. in English literature from the University of Nebraska and a B.A. from the University Honors Program at Catholic University in Washington, D.C. Born and raised in Danbury, Connecticut, she has traveled extensively and lived in various places throughout the United States, but her favorite place in the world is home with her kids, her husband, and her stacks of books. Like her character Colm Magee, Mary suffers various heart and brain ailments, but thanks in part to her brother, a physician, as well as her own doctors, she now has a pacemaker and a heart that beats on its own—at least most of the time. This is her first novel.

Mary Curran Hackett